Lucas

OF BLOOD AND DREAMS - BOOK FIVE

KIM ALLRED

STORM COAST PUBLISHING, LLC

LUCAS
Of Blood and Dreams, Book 5
KIM ALLRED

Published by Storm Coast Publishing, LLC

Copyright © 2024 by Kim Allred
Cover Art by Dark City Designs

Print edition March 2024
ISBN 978-1-953832-31-3

The journey of a thousand miles begins with one step."
Lao Tzu

Chapter One

I STARED at the front door of the hotel from the plush lobby chair, watching for anyone who might have followed us. This was the sixth—no, the seventh hotel Lucas and I had stayed in since leaving Santiga Bay a little over a week ago. I turned around to get a look at the vamp at the front desk, who was registering for two nights under an anonymous name.

I smiled. We'd started a game at the third hotel where Lucas made me guess the name he used to sign us in. The game included an interesting form of strip charades and a bottle of tequila, ending with laughter and hot sex.

It eased the tension of our days as we attempted the impossible task Devon Trelane, Lucas's boss and leader of the House Trelane, had given him. The House Trelane didn't have the largest Family in the vamp world, but the House was sizeable enough with over seventy extremely well-trained vamps. Even the children learned martial arts at young ages. Well, for the number of children there were.

Vamp fertility rates had dropped drastically over the last couple of centuries, and no one knew why. But I digress. Cressa, my best friend in the whole world, would say I have too much to say, so it just comes tripping out of my mouth. I'm still deciding if that was a compliment or not.

I've always had a hard time focusing. I don't know if I was born that way or whether I simply got bored easily. But that was also a story for another day.

"Ginger. Hey, are you daydreaming again?"

I glanced up, not realizing I'd been doing exactly that. Lucas's eyes were the color of a summer sky, and his hair was a sandy blond that looked streaked from the sun. He had the face and physique of a beach boy, who spent his days on his board waiting for the next big wave. A shiver shimmied through me at his knowing smile.

"I'm not sure I want to admit to that."

He laughed. "Come on. Dinner first, then some fun. But there's not a chance you'll figure out the name I used this time."

I stood on tiptoes to whisper in his ear. "I guess that means I won't end up wearing much clothing."

He lowered his head, and his warm breath tickled my ear. "If I play it right, you won't be wearing any at all."

I pushed him toward the elevators, both of us laughing. "Do we have to do dinner first?"

We kissed on the ride up to the thirteenth floor. Our arms were locked around each other's waists as we stepped out, an overnight bag hanging over each of our shoulders. I stared into his eyes, wondering what it would be like for him to mesmerize me. Was it possible for me to be more attracted to him than I already was?

The whir of a blade sliced past the back of Lucas's head. I jumped back, slamming into the elevator wall. Lucas pulled me to him as we turned to see two vamps racing toward us. The one on the right held a blade in his hand, so it must have been the other one who'd thrown his.

The vamp on the right drew back his arm, ready to throw his dagger when a throwing star hit him in the base of his throat. I didn't have to look to know Lucas had thrown it. He was masterful with shurikens—or, what most call ninja stars—and he constantly practiced new routines.

Unfortunately for us, he'd demonstrated that skill several times over during the last ten days. Somehow, vamps found us again as if someone had given them our exact route as soon as we planned it. We assumed we were being tracked since leaving California, but after several thorough searches, then dumping and buying new supplies, they were still one step ahead of us.

Satisfied the second vamp was incapacitated enough for me to keep him occupied, Lucas turned his attention to the first one, who'd already drawn another knife. But now, we were close enough for Lucas to launch himself as he kicked out, landing a solid blow to the vamp's chest as he fell back. Lucas landed, ready to swing a leg out, but the vamp was prepared and was able to block Lucas's kick, forcing him off balance.

From there it was vamp on vamp. Lucas had drawn a dagger, and the two fell into fighting stances as they prepared to dance.

I glanced down at the other vamp, who'd removed the blade from his throat. He was still on all fours but was beginning to rise. My first kick hit its mark in the vamp's midsection, which knocked the air out of him. The next one hit his lower chin with enough force that I might have heard his teeth rattle. I grinned with a manic glee when blood dripped from his mouth.

I took a moment to check on Lucas, who was wearing his opponent down. The vamp had been cut in multiple places. Talk about death by a thousand cuts. I didn't think Lucas had planned on taking that much time.

My vamp got a second wind. His neck had healed, and he was rising to his feet. I couldn't waste any more time. If I let him stand with his speed and agility, the fight would end up in his favor. I flung a throwing star that sliced into the side of his face. He howled.

The vamp had to know I was human, which might have been

why he leaned back and howled again, this time in apparent frustration. A bad move on his part to leave his neck exposed.

The slice across his jugular startled me, though it shouldn't have. It wasn't the first time Lucas made the injury as grievous as possible, if he didn't outright kill them. Whatever it took to make a quick escape without pursuit.

The other vamp had the same problem. The slice to his neck was so deep it would take some time for it to heal.

Lucas retrieved my silver star, which he wiped clean. "Your aim is becoming quite consistent."

"Well, you know what they say—practice, practice, practice. Though, I have to admit, as much as I hate Sergi's training sessions, they do seem to be paying for themselves." I checked the hallway, but no one else was around.

I used the bottom of Lucas's shirt, which had pulled out of his pants, to wipe the blood off his face. "You got us a room on the thirteenth floor? I mean, I didn't think hotels had a thirteenth floor."

"When did you become so superstitious?"

"After the surprise attack at the third hotel."

He picked up the overnight bags and handed me mine. "From now on, no more hotels with a thirteenth floor." With a last look at the two vamps, who would be strong enough to crawl away in the next thirty minutes, assuming hotel security didn't come calling, Lucas kissed my temple.

"We'll have our evening. Just not here." He swung an arm over my shoulder as we hurried toward the exit sign that would open to the stairs.

Next stop—hotel number eight.

Chapter Two

I ROLLED over and stretched like a well-fed cat. Sun peeked through the blinds. A simple sign that I was going to love this day. There was nothing more beautiful than a morning after an evening rain. The city washed clean, leaving behind a particular sharpness to the landscape as if a thin veil had been lifted.

I reached for Lucas, but his spot was empty. The sheets were still warm, and his heady scent made me gooey inside.

Then I remembered. This was day four.

After the insane but successful mission the team had pulled off in rescuing Hamilton and, most assuredly, pissing off Devon's greatest enemy, Lorenzo Venizi, Devon had given the Family a three-day rest period. No work. No training. A true mini vacation. We just couldn't leave the estate. We were, in effect, on a lockdown that would last until Devon's war with Lorenzo was over.

I groaned as I sat up and rubbed my face. Back to training for me. For as much as I griped about it, the exhaustive sessions seemed to be working. I hadn't needed my new martial arts skills or my growing array of fighting techniques for what I called the Hamilton heist, but it came in handy when Lucas and I ran into vamps at the Renaud Library in San Francisco. And with whatever was coming, maybe I should consider doubling down on the training as my normal routine.

A delicate white jasmine blossom rested on the bathroom counter next to a hand-scribbled note. I picked up the flower and gave the spicy scent a deep sniff as I read the message.

Devon called a staff meeting that will fill the entire morning. Cressa told me to let you sleep. Get a decent breakfast. She'll meet you in the training room at eleven. How about a late picnic by the lake?

I sighed and took another whiff of the jasmine before sticking it in a glass of water and setting it on the writing desk near the window. That vamp knew how to push all the right buttons. I shook my head. Who would have thought I'd fall for a vamp? The thought sobered me. An ill-fated relationship to be sure, but I tucked the thought away. I wasn't the type to dwell on those things, preferring to live in the moment.

Once I freshened up and dressed, I wandered down to the kitchen, jonesing for a cup of Lucia's fabulous coffee. One thing about Devon, he didn't skimp on his chefs. I dearly loved Cook, who owned his kitchen at the coastal manor, but Lucia gave him a run for his money where coffee was concerned. She was a dazzling chef in her own right, and like Cook, proudly displayed her certificate from an internationally famous culinary school.

The kitchen was less frantic than during the three-day hiatus when a continuous buffet had been set up in the dining room. Since no one was on a time schedule except for the security patrols, Devon made sure food was available throughout the day. Just like on a cruise—or so I'd heard, never having been on one. Now, we were back to our regularly scheduled programming.

Lucia greeted me with a cup of coffee that she shoved in my hands. "Good morning, Ginger. Do you mind taking your breakfast in the dining room this morning?" She lowered her voice.

"Anna is in there by herself. She's been out of sorts since she arrived with Lyra before the island raid and doesn't seem to know what to do with herself."

Inside, I cringed. It wasn't that I didn't like Anna. She was a nice enough person, and a human, but she was so rigid and serious, she reminded me of an old English butler. Not that I knew what an old English butler was like other than in movies. On the outside, I smiled and patted Lucia's arm. "Of course, we girls have to stick together."

The relief on her face was enough to encourage me to make the best of my morning with Anna. When I considered my role in the Family, I didn't have many duties. In fact, I only had one—training in the gym. Anna drove Cressa crazy with all the etiquette and history lessons. After the last mission and the previous threat of Council sanctions against House Trelane, maybe it was time I took living in the household more seriously. I wasn't a fan of etiquette. My spirit was too rebellious for that, but it was important to know how to fit in among vamps. And though I wouldn't admit it to most, I was fascinated by history. Maybe an hour or two with Anna wouldn't be such a hardship.

Anna was halfway through a meal of eggs and fruit when I strolled into the dining room and plopped into a chair across from her.

"Good morning, Anna."

She'd been so focused on her plate that she jumped at my greeting and choked on her food. Fortunately for her, I knew the Heimlich maneuver, but it wasn't needed as she cleared her throat and sipped water.

"I didn't hear you come in." She appeared more dazed than pleased to see me, but she was like that with everyone. Devon saw something in her, so I would find that spark that was buried deep inside. My own personal mission.

I smiled. "I didn't mean to startle you, but you were definitely interested in those eggs. Lucia does something different with them than Cook."

She calmed and nodded. "It's the cream."

"Cream?"

She nodded. "Lucia adds a touch of cream, which makes the eggs, well, creamier. Cook prefers water to make them fluffier. Then, of course, they both use different herbs."

"Wow, I hadn't thought of it before. I've always just whipped the eggs together and was grateful not to burn them." It was a bit of a lie. I enjoyed cooking and did a pretty good job of it, but I never had the money to try new things. Not until Devon put me up in a condo. It was actually Cressa's condo, but she rarely stayed there. She preferred being with Devon, which made sense since their relationship had grown intimate. Either way, having the condo and a constant supply of fresh ingredients gave me the opportunity to cook and try new recipes. Those days were gone for a while, at least until the lockdown was over.

My breakfast of oatmeal and a scrambled egg was served by one of the kitchen staff along with a small carafe of coffee. Anna preferred tea, and she received a fresh teapot.

Then silence descended.

Anna seemed a bit skittish and would probably finish her breakfast and leave without another word. The poor thing. The question was, did she not like me? Did she find me too... I don't know, me? Or was she just shy unless the topic of history and vamp etiquette came up?

I decided on the casual approach. "Did you enjoy your three days of holiday?"

"A bit. The library here is in such disarray, I'll need weeks to straighten it out. I'm surprised Simone allowed it to get so out of order."

Of course, she worked through her holiday. There were a few humans on staff at Oasis, but how well did Anna know them?

"Well, from what I've heard, no one has your experience with the books, so can you really blame her?"

Anna's head tilted, and a bit of a smile appeared along with a slight blush. "All it requires is a bit of training."

Another thought hit me. "How are you doing with this lockdown? You've lived in Devon's household for some time, right? You must be used to this sort of thing."

She shook her head and leaned in, her voice low. "To be honest, I'm a bit terrified. I mean, war is a dangerous game. There hasn't been an officially declared war in a century. I'm not even sure what that would be like in today's times."

"I didn't think it had been officially declared yet."

She shook her head. "No. Not yet. Devon will want his allies aligned. And while he doesn't need Council approval to declare war, he'll want to have a clear declaration of his intent and grievances. Then he'll officially put it on paper."

That did sound pretty serious. Lucas and I hadn't discussed it, preferring to keep Family business out of our three days together.

I scraped the last bite of oatmeal from the bowl. "Do you have any defensive training? I mean, Devon's security is pretty tight, but do you know how to defend yourself?" I wasn't sure why the thought hadn't crossed my mind before, but what did the other humans do in the middle of a vampire attack?

"There's a panic room here and at the coast manor. All the humans go there at the time of an attack."

"What happens if someone gets cut off from getting to the panic room."

Anna shivered. "Then it's up to the attacking vampires and their leniency with humans."

I gulped. "No wonder you're terrified. Do you have any defensive training?"

"It was some time ago, and it was up to us whether we wanted to continue. I've always been more of a book nerd."

I laughed. "And from what I remember, that saved the House from sanctions when Devon was framed for Boretsky's murder."

Her blush appeared again. "That was Cressa's idea to have Lyra take leadership."

"And how did Cressa know to suggest it?"

Anna's gaze lifted to mine, and she sat a little straighter. "It was her classwork."

I pointed my fork at her. "Exactly."

She perked up and poured another cup of tea while I jammed scrambled eggs in my mouth in between swallows of coffee.

When I pushed my plate away, I said, "I have to admit. I've learned a lot from Lucas and Cressa about vampires, but, I don't know, it seems like I could learn more. You've probably noticed I'm not big on etiquette."

She snorted but didn't say anything.

I laughed. "Right? But I'm learning a lot about defensive training."

She shrugged. "That's a specialty of the cadre as well as all the vampires in the Family."

"But it sounds like Devon doesn't mind if the humans learn it as well."

She moved her plate an inch to the right and set her fork and knife across the top of it. Even with empty plates, there seemed to be a proper way to place the utensils.

I leaned toward her. "I have an idea. Just listen to the whole thing and then tell me what you think."

Her expression became guarded, and her brows knit together with suspicion. "Alright."

She was a tough nut, but I was far from intimidated.

"I'm not an expert by a long shot, but I've got some pretty impressive defensive skills I didn't have a month ago. And it appears my training in that area is going to be continuing. What I don't have is education on vamp society, the history of the House, the squabbles with House Venizi, and what all this war stuff is about. I can't even imagine what form it would take. And all this business with the shifters and their place in vampire history. This is stuff you know in your sleep."

Her brows relaxed, but she still appeared dubious. "Go on."

She was hooked. She might not know it yet, but I was pretty good at baiting a line. All those years living on the edge of the Hollows taught a woman something.

"I was thinking of a trade of sorts. You spend an hour with me in the training room every day. It gives me extra practice. And you get me up to speed on the subjects you know the best." I held up my hand when her eyes began to twinkle. "This has to be like a speed-reading education. I'm not saying it doesn't have to be deep, but it has to be spot on for what the House will be facing over the next who knows how long."

"What about your training with Cressa and the cadre?"

"That will continue. I don't have a choice in that, but that doesn't mean I can't do my own training. We might have to rearrange our schedule to accommodate the cadre, but I think we can make it work. What do you say?"

Anna leaned back and sipped her tea as she studied me. Judging my ability? Sizing me up? Wondering if there was some hidden agenda? She set her teacup down. "We start this afternoon."

Wow. I should have known once she committed, she'd be all in.

"I have a late lunch planned with Lucas. How about meeting at three for the education session, then we'll finish up in the gym? I can check with Cressa for a more specific schedule."

She brightened. "Agreed. I'll find us a suitable classroom."

I cringed at the term, but this had been my idea. Suddenly, I was excited. I stuck my arm out for a fist bump, and Anna just stared at it.

"Okay, this isn't a defensive move, but it will be important when we end a session. Fist bumps are critical."

Her brows wrinkled again with a dubious look.

"You have to trust me on this. Once your endorphins kick in from the exercise, it's a way to release them. Here, just try it." I repeated the gesture, and she stretched across the table to bump her fist against mine. It was weak, but it was a start.

"Don't worry. You won't be able to help yourself after the first session."

"I'll take your word for it." She stood and brushed off her linen pants. Before she reached the door, she turned back. "Oh, and one more thing. In exchange for the fist bump, you'll have fifteen minutes of etiquette training with each session." Then she all but raced from the room.

She was a sly one. But I couldn't help grinning as I poured another cup of coffee.

Chapter Three

LUCAS STARED at the display screens on the wall of the conference room. They'd been through the security updates, shift changes, and convoy procedures several times over. He should stay focused on it, but the minor tweaks Sergi and Simone continued to review weren't of interest. They could spend hours on the finer details, as was their job, and while he retained the pertinent information, he let his mind wander.

Only two things held his attention that morning—Ginger and the book. He smiled. He supposed the book should be his priority, but as important as the *De første dage* was to their success over Lorenzo, and he believed that with his entire being, Ginger had somehow become an integral part of his life.

At first, it had been an instant attraction to the fiery human, who daringly lived life by her own rules and had an insatiable curiosity. From the first day he'd seen her, huddled in her closet, holding a stuffed teddy bear as tears streamed down her face, leaving black smears from her mascara, he'd thought her brave. The apartment that she and Cressa shared had been ransacked, and she'd been interrogated by men who turned out to be thugs working for Underwood, Cressa's estranged stepfather. When

Cressa pulled her out of the closet, he expected Ginger to have a cup of tea and curl up in bed for a day or two.

She did have a cup of tea. Then she wanted to go out and hit the bars. And once her gaze caught his, her demeanor changed, getting that look he'd come to recognize as curiosity. More than that. She wanted to push boundaries, and discovering he was vampire hadn't fazed her.

In those early days, she might have run from danger, but not before ensuring Cressa or anyone around her got to safety as well. It was one of her stubborn streaks. Once she began defensive training, she blossomed into a fighter. He should have expected it, considering where she and Cressa had lived. The Hollows was one of the poorest and roughest sections of Santiga Bay. Druglords and other hoodlums ran their neighborhood, and for as rough and tough as those men were, they all had a soft spot for Ginger and Cressa. As it turned out, so did most of Devon's Family.

Lucas worried about Ginger with the coming war. They hadn't discussed what it meant to the House or vampire society at large. He wasn't sure himself. Most of it depended on how many allies Devon could bring to his side. The shifters were a huge boon to their efforts. A relationship that had begun with Devon's father, Guildford, and was cemented with Devon's friendship with The Wolf, the current alpha of all wolves. But Devon required alliances from strong Houses. Seen from a battlefield perspective, House Trelane had to build an army so large, Lorenzo's best option was surrender. And that would be a challenging task.

The strategizing required to accomplish something that massive piqued Lucas's interest. More than that, he wanted to understand what motivated a person to make one choice over another. He chuckled to himself. It would take many decades in Devon's cadre to learn from a master. And perhaps one day it would make his own decisions easier to make.

His thoughts shifted to the picnic lunch he'd promised Ginger. He'd asked Lucia to pack several of Ginger's favorite items along with Lucia's famous raspberry iced tea. He'd gotten up early to prepare their spot by the lake, complete with blankets, a fresh bouquet of jasmine—her favorite, and a cup of duck food. She loved to feed the wildlife.

"Lucas."

He snapped his head around to find Simone frowning at him. "Sorry. My mind drifted."

Devon smiled as he slid a pen into his pocket and closed his laptop. "I think we've focused on security enough for one morning since it isn't just Bella drifting off."

Lucas glanced at Bella, whose head rested on her fist as she stared unblinking at the display.

"These are critical details," Simone insisted.

"Agreed." Devon smoothed her ruffled feathers. "But perhaps a better discussion for the three of us. It's enough for the rest of the cadre to understand the final outcome. We've been at it awhile, and I'm satisfied with your plans. I would suggest the ideas you've scrapped be considered as backups. We'll require a constant shifting and rotation of security protocols. I want to keep Lorenzo guessing."

Simone nodded. "Shall we move on to the personnel assignments?"

Devon stood and stretched his back as he moved to the windows that overlooked the north side of the property. Stately oak trees dotted the landscape along with native brush, grasses, and comfortable modern cabins that housed Family members. "Let's take a break. I have messages to return. We can meet back here in an hour."

Lucas stood as the others filed out.

"Lucas, can I have a few minutes?" Devon turned from the window and poured a cup of coffee. He held up the carafe, and Lucas nodded. Devon poured a second mug and took both to a small seating area at the far end of the conference room.

Lucas followed, wondering what type of dressing down he

might get for not paying attention. He took the offered mug and sat. "I'm sorry for being distracted during the meeting."

Devon chuckled. "I was having a hard time paying attention myself. Simone and Sergi can become rather narrowly focused when discussing security. Especially now while we wait for Lorenzo to make a move."

Lucas relaxed. Not a dressing down then. "I fear it might become difficult to keep Oasis a secret."

"I do as well, which is why we're establishing more defense perimeters. Simone has also taken to heart Decker's suggestion of using rogue shifters. She's been working with him and Remus on the list of rogues and has interviews set up."

That surprised him. "Really? I thought she would consider it and then decide against it."

"After the last mission, I think she's finally come to trust Remus and his motives. Shifters bring a whole new dimension to security. And, if Lorenzo comes, he won't be prepared for wolves. With his inability to accept their cunning intelligence, it will take time for him to modify his attacks. Our job will be to stay one step ahead of him and keep him guessing."

"The rogues should love having the space to run and track. And they won't be afraid to attack. It's a perfect solution."

"I agree. Now, the reason I asked you to stay behind. It's time to get back to our search for Philipe Renaud and the *De første dage*."

Lucas straightened. He'd been planning on asking Devon but had decided to wait until the afternoon battle training. "It's been on my mind."

Devon smiled and sipped his coffee as he studied Lucas, almost making him squirm. "No doubt. I should probably include the rest of the cadre in this discussion, but I'd prefer to review the plans one-on-one. We know time is of the essence. While Cressa and I were in San Francisco the last three days, we were able to obtain a passport for her."

"Passport? You're leaving the country?"

"I haven't told the rest of the cadre yet. Cressa will tell Ginger later today. During Lorenzo's ball, just before the sirens went off, she met with the Oslo twins."

"They were there?"

Devon nodded. "Apparently, they've been getting close to Lorenzo with an interest in current Council matters and word of the Poppy. But who they really work for is House Aramburu."

"Aramburu? They haven't been heard from in ages."

"Yet, it appears they've been keeping up on Council politics from their homeland. They've extended an invitation, and I've accepted."

Lucas sat back—stunned. House Aramburu was, at one time, an extremely powerful House. From what he'd read, their homeland had been one of the largest among the Houses. But centuries ago, they had shuttered their gates and remained removed from vampire society. There were only rumors as to why.

"When do you leave?"

"In a few days. Security will become tighter during my absence, and we want to keep the fact I've left the country a secret. We'll be traveling on one of Remus's planes."

"That's a good idea."

"But until then, I'd like to hear your thoughts on the search for Philipe and the book. And this must be done quickly. I want a tentative plan by tomorrow. I understand whatever you come up with needs to remain fluid based on your discoveries, but let's have a framework to start with. You'll leave in two days."

Lucas scratched his chin and stared at his mug of coffee. No time like the present. "About that. I have a special request."

I STROLLED the path to the lake, stopping occasionally to smell a flower or watch a bee collect pollen before flying to another bloom.

I ran my hands along the tops of the tall grass that was allowed to grow wild.

We'd only been at Oasis for three days, but somehow, the lake had become our special place. It was a peaceful spot several yards from the path. It bordered a tiny cove where the ducks hung out. Sometimes I'd catch a few with their tailfeathers poking straight into the air as they searched for food in the weedy bottom of the shallow water.

I caught the hint of red through the grass. Lucas always brought two blankets. One to lay on and a second one we'd roll into a shared pillow. I hurried my steps when the scent of something grilled tickled my nose. The picnic basket sat in the middle of the blankets, a bouquet of jasmine lying next to it.

Before I reached the blanket, someone grabbed my waist and hauled me behind a tree. I giggled as the manly scent of the woods hit me.

Lucas.

His lips were on mine before I could take another breath. I hugged him tight, reveling in the warmth of his body and the tingling sensation that swarmed over me as his hands roamed freely until they landed on my ass. Then he pressed me against him as his kiss deepened.

When we came up for air, he didn't release me but held me against the tree.

"If it was evening, I'd have you stripped before you whispered my name."

"Why would we wait for evening?" I teased.

His brows wiggled. "You are daring, Miss Morrison." He stole another kiss.

"Everyone's in meetings or training. Who's to see?"

He chuckled and stepped back, pulling me with him. "Security is doing sweeps through the entire property. Not that I mind, but word will get back to Simone."

I sighed. "She really needs a date."

This time his laughter filled the air. "Come on, before the brie gets cold. The insulated container won't keep it warm and gooey for long."

The fact he said "gooey" made me gooey inside. I don't think he'd ever used the word before he met me.

We ate the brie with rosemary crackers, sipped raspberry iced tea, and shared a grilled roast beef sandwich stuffed with sauteed veggies. Then we lay on the blanket, our heads on our makeshift pillow, holding hands, and staring at the cloudless blue sky as birds twittered around us.

After ten minutes, he sprang up. "I almost forgot." He scrounged in the picnic basket and tossed me a small plastic container.

I popped the lid, already knowing what was inside. Sure enough—duck food.

I laughed and jumped up. "Let's go."

He sighed, but he was grinning when he chased after me. We sat on a patch of grass while I tossed pellets to the ducks, who devoured them within seconds.

"Devon and I spoke this afternoon."

I threw a few pellets to a duck who wasn't getting his fair share. "Oh." I tried to keep my voice light. I knew what was coming, though I'd hoped for more time before he left, but he was obsessed with tracking down the book. "How long will you be gone?"

He glanced at me, then took a handful of pellets and tossed them one by one into the water. The ducks paddled furiously as they tried to gobble each one up before another duck got to it.

"You always seem to know everything happening in the Family. Did Cressa say something?"

"She didn't have to. I know how important the book is."

He slid an arm around my waist, and I leaned my head against his shoulder. "Devon and I spoke about the book this morning. We reviewed the locations of all the Renaud libraries and annexes in the States and came up with a short list of which ones should be visited. A handful are close to some of Philipe's known contacts."

"That makes sense he'd have friends near the libraries. Will you try to reach out to them?"

"I'd be foolish not to, assuming they're willing to talk to me."

I laughed, but it came out strangled. "Who wouldn't want to talk to you? You're kind of irresistible."

He released the container from my tight grip and put the lid on. Then he turned me to him. Our eyes met, and I did my best not to tear up. It wasn't just that he was leaving. He'd left on other assignments since we'd been seeing each other. But Lorenzo was out there. He had to know Devon would be sending someone to the libraries.

"You're not going alone, are you? The partner requirement is in play when one of the Family is traveling, right?"

"It is." He glanced over my shoulder, and I couldn't begin to imagine what he was thinking—or not telling me. "I thought maybe you'd be my partner."

I stared at him and tugged at my right ear. I couldn't have possibly heard that correctly. "I don't understand."

He grinned, and a lock of blond hair fell over his forehead. "Now, I always thought you were smarter than that."

I gave him a soft punch. "I'm smarter than you know."

"Yes, you are. So, are you up to being my bodyguard?"

I shook my head, wishing it was that easy. "Devon wouldn't allow it."

"He's fine with it. But he wants you in extended training sessions until we leave in two days."

I studied him, waiting for the punchline. This had to be a joke. But I couldn't read past that stoic vamp look that was better than any poker face. "Why would he think I was the right person for this?"

"Because Sergi and Simone said you were ready."

Now the tears came, and he pulled me to him. I had no words

—other than Sergi and Simone must have been smoking something. He kissed me and wiped the tears away with a thumb.

I went rigid, and his eye quirked. "What?"

"I kind of worked out a trade with Anna." I explained the deal I made with her as a way to make friends.

"That's perfect. We can work her into one of your training sessions. If she's going to delve into the history books, ask her to give you the detailed background of House Renaud and House Aramburu."

"Why those two?"

He shook his head. "I've already said enough. Fresh ears. I want you to learn from the books, which is the way Anna teaches. We can compare notes on our way to Boston."

"Boston?"

"I hope you like lobster and clam chowder."

Chapter Four

THE ONE THING I'd liked about Oasis over the coastal manor house was that it was single-story. No stairs to climb.

When the training sessions started, I found out I'd been misguided.

The Oasis manor had an immense basement that included the panic room Anna had mentioned, a kitchenette, multiple entertainment and gaming rooms, more bedrooms for the regular staff —humans and vampires—and the training room that took up a quarter of the floor space.

That, of course, meant I still had to battle stairs after each two-hour session. With the training I'd undergone the last several weeks, the two hours shouldn't affect me as much as it did, but Sergi had increased the skill level and intensity. Fortunately, stairs led directly from the gym to the solarium where the pool and hot tub were located.

After my first extended training with Sergi, I soaked in the hot tub for fifteen minutes before dragging my limp body to my room. In keeping with the agreement I made with Anna, I collapsed for an hour's nap before meeting her back in the basement. For me, it was more of a cool-down as I taught her the defensive skills I'd been taught. She remembered some of the moves from her previous training, and I took the punishment when she made a strike or flipped me over, which built her confidence and gave me bruises.

It was worth it at the end of the hour when she stuck out her fist for our first fist bump with a smile on her face.

Afterward, we went off to our rooms for a shower before meeting in the library for my history lesson. Anna had searched for the best conference room, but Simone suggested the library since it was rarely used that late in the afternoon and books wouldn't have to be shuffled back and forth.

"I've been racking my brain on the best approach since we only have a couple of days together." Anna gave me a peeved look as if the compressed timetable had been my doing.

"Sorry. I had no idea Devon would let me go with Lucas."

"No matter. A couple of days of training is better than none at all, I suppose."

It hadn't surprised me that she might enjoy the training sessions, and I considered her concern. "Why does your training have to end just because I'll be traveling for a couple of weeks?"

She stared at me like I had bats flying out of my ears. "You're the trainer."

"There are far better trainers in the manor than me. I'm sure we can find someone to fill in while I'm gone."

She shrugged then dropped a large tome on the writing desk.

I stared at it. "I don't have time to read this in two days."

She tsked. "You and Cressa are like two peas."

I laughed. "Well, at least you've had practice."

She grinned, though didn't comment. Instead, she pulled over a rolling whiteboard she'd taken from one of the conference rooms. Then she placed two pads of paper and three pens on a side table I'd use for a desk.

"For notes. Now, open to where the bookmark is."

I leaned over the book that was at least a thousand pages thick and found the slim marker. When I opened it, I grinned. Printed across the page in two languages—one I didn't know and the other English— read The Houses of Aramburu, Renaud, Trelane, and Venizi.

"This is perfect."

"I'd considered asking Cressa to join us since she could use a refresher on House Aramburu before leaving for Spain, but that would dilute your training. So, I'm working with her in the mornings."

"She didn't tell me."

"It just started today." She turned and began writing the names of each House across the top of the whiteboard. Then she wrote bullet items under each name. "This is just basic information on each House to give you what Cressa calls the speed-read version."

I held back my chuckle, remembering Cressa's pain with Anna's need to start centuries in the past and provide minute details on everything. We'd laughed over wine when she spoke of those early days at House Trelane. Evidently, that training had paid off—painless or otherwise.

For the first half hour, Anna went over additional information about the Trelane, Venizi, and Aramburu Houses. The last half hour was spent solely on House Renaud since that was the mission I was going on with Lucas.

"The House Renaud's homeland, as you know, is in France. But the Family is global, mostly in the States, Europe, Australia, and the Middle East. In the States, they consider New Orleans the home library as that's where House Renaud was established in the early 1700s. The second oldest son operates the House. The oldest son remains in France running the European branches."

"What about the Father?"

"He's an ancient. A thousand years old, give or take a century. From what I've heard from various sources, he prefers to roam the main library outside their French estate and carries on phil-anthropic pursuits."

"Wow, that's really hard to get my head wrapped around."

Anna laid down the marker and dragged one of the heavy chairs next to me. "For being raised around vampires, I have to admit, some of these ancients and the things they've seen, the changes in the world, is mind-boggling. If you ever meet one, treat them as if they're as old as they look rather than their true age. It will save you some embarrassment."

"Good to know."

"Since we only have a few minutes left, let me point out some areas to take note of. Since you've already been to one of the libraries with Lucas, you probably already know the basics: the interior floorplan is the same in each library, although the inventory will be different. The Renauds are meticulous in the maintenance and recording of the inventory within each collection, and you must have special dispensation from the curator to remove any of the inventory."

She pushed the book toward me and tapped a finger on it. "I'd like you to read as much as you can on House Renaud. We'll go over your questions tomorrow, and I'll provide any other pertinent information you'll need before you leave. Then we'll delve more into Aramburu."

I sighed. "We're still doing the etiquette thing?"

Her lips twitched. "Did I not fist bump this afternoon?"

I sighed, rolled my eyes, and dragged out a long, "Yes."

She grinned. "Don't worry. Only the bare minimum of utensils will be involved." When I snorted, she shook her head and gave me an excellent school principal stare. "But there are things you should know as a Blood Ward if you want a vampire to believe that's what you truly are. Lucas tells me you did a fine job at the San Francisco annex, but it's possible you'll attend functions or visit other Houses in Lucas's quest. You need to be prepared for everything."

I nodded. She was right. This wasn't my first assignment for the House, but for some reason, it seemed like a test. I'd be foolish to not take her instructions to heart. And neither of us said a word when the last fifteen minutes ran to thirty.

AFTER LUGGING the huge tome to my room, I collapsed on the bed. A knock at my door woke me in darkness. The sun had already set.

"Come in." My words were drowsy as I raised up to my elbows.

Cressa peeked around the door. "I didn't mean to wake you."

I sat up and rubbed my eyes. "Just a bit of a nap."

She tiptoed around the clothing and other items strewn around the floor and glanced at the book on the bed. "A nap? Or did the reading bore you to sleep?"

I grinned, jumped out of bed to stretch, and grimaced from stiffened muscles. "Maybe a bit of both. The book isn't really boring, just difficult to read with the older style of English and cramped writing. I guess paper was precious a thousand years ago or whenever it was written."

"Are you focusing on House Renaud?"

"Yeah. I mean, that's where we'll be spending most of our time. It makes sense I should know as much as I can about them." I glanced out the window. "Did I miss dinner?"

"I was coming to get you before I headed downstairs. Lucas thought you might have passed out from the extended training." She quirked her lips. "And Sergi wants a word with you."

I rolled my eyes as I scrounged for a dress. I picked a cobalt-blue sundress from a chair, sniffed it, then shook it out. "What's his complaint this time?"

"Actually, I think he wants to commend you."

I was removing my leggings when her words hit me, and I lost my balance, managing to fall into a nearby chair. "Stop joking. What does he really want?"

"I'm serious. Anna asked him if he would continue the defensive training you've been teaching her. Actually, she asked if the training could be made available to any human that's interested."

"What?"

"I guess he and Devon never heard about the deal you struck with her. Simone was irritated for about a nanosecond and then considered the coming war. The three of them thought it was an excellent idea."

My cheeks grew warm. It was great they wanted to do that for the staff, but I didn't want the attention. "It was just a way to give Anna something to do. She seems out of her element here."

"Sergi wants to observe your next training so he can understand what you've been teaching."

"That's a nerve-racking thought. But, yeah. If it helps everyone, I'm game."

I pulled the sundress over my head then zipped up the side. After I checked my hair and added a bit of mascara, I linked my arm with Cressa's as we exited the room. "Are you excited about going to Spain? I mean, is Devon going to let you do some sightseeing?"

"So he says, assuming he believes we're safe, and Gregor Aramburu, the House leader, says it's okay. I'm hoping he does. I've always wanted to see Madrid."

"Really?"

"Okay, maybe not Madrid specifically, but definitely Europe. And before I forget, can you leave the book with Anna after you leave? She's using other material for reviewing Aramburu, but I'd like to reread their section of the tome at least once."

"I'll be sure to leave it in the library. But it would be easier to just grab it from my room since I'll be sleeping with it for the next two nights."

We laughed as we made our way to dinner. Before we made it to the dining room, Devon and Lucas met us in the hallway.

"Just the women we were looking for," Devon said. He waved us down a different hallway. "Let's talk in one of the studios."

Lucas gave me a nod and followed behind us. Cressa seemed more curious than concerned, so I relaxed the shoulders that had been creeping up my neck.

Devon directed us to chairs that circled a small coffee table with a lovely sculpture of what I guessed to be a wood nymph. "I thought we should talk before dinner. There's a change to your itinerary, and before we go over it, I want to assure you that I trust every member of the Family. But, in speaking with Lucas, Colantha, and Sergi, we want to keep the reason for your trip confidential. If what we suspect is truly in the book, Lorenzo might still be monitoring it."

"We were also thinking about the custodian Lyra remembers seeing the day before her accident. The one she thought was having an affair with Philipe." Lucas hadn't taken a seat. He leaned against a wall, hands in his pockets.

"Has she remembered her name?" I asked.

"No," Devon replied. "And considering the not-so-friendly welcome Lucas received from the curator in San Francisco, we don't think she'll be willing to share the name."

Lucas nodded his agreement. "With the curator being new to that location, it's possible she's not aware of her or her relationship with Philipe. And we don't want to draw unwanted attention to the custodian."

"So, how do we find her?" Cressa asked.

"There's one possibility." Lucas ran a hand through his hair and glanced at me. I wasn't sure why, but I nodded and gave him a smile. "The custodian I spoke with at the annex might be willing to help me out. I got the sense he was concerned by the information the curator gave us. Like he knew she was lying. He might have worked there in 1925 or has access to the names of the custodians at the time."

"So, we go to San Francisco first?" I asked.

Devon nodded. "But we need to minimize the ability for anyone to follow your movements. Sergi will be creating multiple identities for you. We'll need to update your photos for proper IDs, and I'd like that taken care of after dinner. As far as the mission itself, it will be up to you to follow where the leads take you. Sergi will be your single point of contact for any assistance you need, but I want specific check-in times established."

"What if the vamps that attacked us are there again?" The attack had been an adrenaline rush at the time. Afterward, it had shaken me. It all worked out, but I wasn't sure I could have disabled the vamp who attacked me if Lucas hadn't been there. I glanced at him, and his slow smile spoke volumes. It gave me more assurance than I expected. If he believed I could do this, I wouldn't let him down.

"You know what you have to do. You've been trained for this." Devon stood and laid a hand on my shoulder. "Lucas has confidence in you, and so do I. Finding this book is critical to our success."

I nodded, unable to string words together.

"We'll see you at dinner." Devon nodded to Lucas, and they strode out.

I stared at the wall where Lucas had been leaning. He'd been so confident. Not just about the mission, but about my role in it. I took Devon's words to heart, though it wasn't easy to align what I felt in my heart with what I heard in my head.

Cressa put an arm around my shoulder and gave me a squeeze. "That little chat just made it real."

I snorted. "Ya think?" I leaned into her, and she leaned back.

"I never meant for you to get so involved in Family business."

"I'm not sure when it happened, but somewhere I crossed the line. Maybe it's my need to pay Devon back for everything he's done for me. I mean, he could have just given me money and told me to find a new start someplace else."

"He wanted us to have each other. His way of ensuring I didn't lose my best friend. I doubt he understood exactly where the path to remove his censure would take him. I don't think any of us would have considered war."

I stood, fluffed my hair, and tugged at my dress before straightening my shoulders. "Enough wallowing. Lucas and I can do this. We'll find the book or Philipe."

"But not at any cost." She hugged me. "I can't lose you, so watch your backside and listen to Lucas. If all else fails—run like hell."

Chapter Five

LUCAS WATCHED the entrance to the San Francisco annex of the Renaud Library before returning to his scan of the parking lot. He reached for Ginger's hand.

"I think it's best if you stay in the car while I go in."

"Should I keep the motor running for a quick getaway like they do for bank robberies?" she teased.

Her eyes were enormous and darted about in her own search for the vampires who'd attacked them in the parking lot a couple of weeks earlier. Her knee bounced, a ball of pent-up energy just waiting to be directed someplace.

"I think you can keep the engine off, but you should be in the driver's seat." He didn't want to scare her, but she was already aware of the stakes. The vampires that had attacked them could have been Lorenzo's. If they were, they might still be there. Lorenzo had been quiet since the raid on his island and the rescue of his long-term prisoner—a powerful dreamwalker who'd been kidnapped and held in a cell for a century.

"Do you think the same custodian is still in there? Maybe today's his day off."

He grinned. She still had so much to learn. "Custodians don't have days off. Not in the same way as humans."

"Sounds like they need a union."

"You're still thinking like a human. You know vampires can go long periods without sleep or rest, and custodians have a passion for their work. But they're given time once a year for a sabbatical, which can last up to three months."

"Wow. Let's hope he didn't leave on one of those. Or, based on your previous meeting with the curator, wasn't forced on one."

"Now *that* matches my concern."

"On the other hand, if you speak with a different custodian who isn't aware of your meeting with the curator, maybe they'll be more willing to give you the information you're looking for."

He lifted her hand to his mouth and gave it a gentle kiss, his thumb caressing its tender skin. "A wonderful suggestion."

But he required more from her before he tested either possibility. He pulled her toward him until he could kiss her properly. A hot, urgent kiss. A kiss a soldier gives his lover before going into battle. It might seem overkill for a trip to the library, but these were no longer normal days. And while Lorenzo and the Council might not know it, House Trelane was already at war.

"I won't be long."

"You better not be. Don't make me come in there, daggers blazing."

He laughed. "I think the visual of that alone is enough to see me through."

He strode with his head down, occasionally lifting it to track anyone who might be lurking about. The visitor parking had several cars so he wouldn't be alone, and whatever might be going on within House Renaud in regard to the *De første dage*, they wouldn't tolerate a vampire attack within the library where other guests could be disturbed or inventory damaged.

The receptionist at the front desk greeted him with their usual spiel, and he quickly moved through the first floor and down the main staircase to the third. He spent ten minutes walking the stacks in search of the custodian but came up empty. One custodian stepped around a corner for an instant, but she wasn't the one he needed. Ginger's suggestion of speaking with a different custodian was an excellent plan B, but he wasn't there yet.

He jogged up the stairs to the second floor, which held more books. He had checked every aisle, circling the floor twice before seeing a custodian enter the floor from one of the many doorways. Odds were with him that this might be the vampire he sought, and he hurried toward them.

"Excuse me," Lucas called.

The custodian turned, and Lucas released a sigh of relief.

"Can I help you, sir?" When the custodian drew near, his eyes widened in recognition. He glanced behind him, then stepped into one of the stacks, crooking a finger for Lucas to follow.

When they were halfway down the aisle, the custodian turned on him. "Do you know how dangerous it is for you to be here?"

"I have a good idea."

"There is no more I can tell you of the book."

"That's not why I'm here. Ms. Renaud made that plainly obvious." Lucas glanced down the aisle and through the bookshelves to ensure they were alone. "You didn't get into trouble, did you?"

The custodian sighed. "No. Our new curator doesn't pay much attention to us, and we pay her little heed. Now, what can I do for you? It's best you don't stay long."

"I'm searching for a young female custodian who worked here in 1925. She would have been a good friend to the curator at the time."

The custodian's eyes went wide, and then they squinted into two dark stones. "You play a dangerous game."

"And these are dangerous times, though I would bet the majority of vampire society isn't aware of how dangerous."

"Come with me." The custodian scurried down the aisle, away from the door he'd originally entered. When he reached another door, he used his card key for entrance. They rushed down a flight of stairs to a landing and a door that should lead to the third-floor stacks. The custodian kept going until they reached the next level, the walls made of stone rather than finished drywall. He moved quickly down two other hallways before coming to a door labeled Storage Room 422. Using his card key again, the diminutive vampire led Lucas in. Overhead lights came on automatically, everything sensor controlled.

The room was the size of a small apartment filled with filing cabinets and racks of artifacts. A lone computer sat on a counter at the far end of the room. The custodian typed in a password and immediately brought up a long list of names.

"I wasn't here in 1925. I came a few years after Philipe Renaud moved to the Los Angeles library, but I heard nothing but wonderful things about him. The mission of the library was his only motivation."

"You don't happen to know where he is now?"

The vampire shot him a quick glance. "No. I'm not sure anyone does."

"He's still alive, isn't he?" Lucas's heartbeat picked up. He wasn't sure he wanted to hear the answer.

"As far as I know, yes. The rumors suggest he suffered a psychic break and is recuperating at one of the asylums, possibly in the homeland. Others say he walked out of his office and never returned, only giving notice that he was on permanent sabbatical."

"Do you know when this happened?"

"It's been decades now. Let me think. The current curator in Los Angeles has been there since just before World War II, or perhaps a bit earlier. I don't usually follow human affairs but sometimes it's easier when tracking time."

He continued with running computer searches while Lucas considered the information. That wasn't long after Guildford's meeting with Philipe. The timing was suspect, but without any other information, he tucked it away for further consideration.

"Here we go. 1925. Are you sure about the year?"

"Yes."

"There were two female custodians at the time. I know this first one. She works at the St. Louis branch now. The second one I don't recognize. Fiona Blackwood." He tapped a few more keys. "Oh yes, she was quite young when she worked here, barely a hundred years old."

"Does it say where she's working now?"

"It appears she's no longer a custodian, but her last location was at the Los Angeles library."

Lucas had expected as much, and any hope of a lead died.

The custodian opened a drawer and took out a pen and a slip of paper. He wrote a couple of lines, shut off the computer, and slipped the note to Lucas. "This is her last known address. This is all I can do for you."

Lucas nodded and tucked the paper into a pocket. "Will they be able to trace your actions?"

He shook his head. "I used a different ID and password. I might be old, but I have what the humans call tech savvy."

He was still grinning as he led Lucas back to the second floor. Before he turned away, he grabbed Lucas's hand. "The winds of change can be turbulent. But the truth shall set us free." Then he disappeared through the door where Lucas had first spotted him.

Lucas strode out of the library, once again keeping his head down. There hadn't been any suspicious-looking vampires on the first floor, nor did anyone seem to be waiting for him outside. He also didn't see the rental they'd come in until it pulled up in front of the steps.

He grinned. A bank robber's getaway. When he shut the door behind him, Ginger immediately drove away, maintaining a normal speed out of the parking lot and through the front gate.

They were a block away when her patience gave out.

"So. Are you going to keep it from me until I beg?"

Lucas chuckled. "She's not a custodian anymore, but I have her name and last known address."

~

THE COFFEE SHOP in the Embarcadero was loud and crowded with tourists. The perfect spot to relax without looking over one's shoulder. Lucas was lucky to find two stuffed chairs in a back corner, and Ginger had sprawled over one with her white mocha latte.

"Lyra was right." She dropped her head back with a silly grin on her face.

He couldn't hold back his own smile. Regardless of the seriousness of a mission, she always found something lighthearted to share. It released the tension in his muscles and took his mind off the problem—at least for a little while. "Right about what?"

"That the custodian and Philipe had something going on."

He snorted out a laugh. "Did you ever consider he might have requested her assistance at the new Los Angeles branch because of her experience and skill?"

She giggled and gave him a wink. "I think her skill is exactly why she moved to L.A."

His smile drew glances from a couple of women. Or maybe it was the light blush that warmed his cheeks. He'd never known a woman who could make him blush—except her. "Don't give me ideas. We have a plane to catch."

"Aren't we going to L.A. to see if she's still there?"

"Sergi is running a background check and should have preliminary information by the time we get to Boston."

"Why don't we wait here? We'll be clear across the country and have to come back."

"We have to come home eventually."

She kept an eye on him while she took a long sip of her mocha. Then her eyes lit up. "You don't think she's there anymore."

"I agree there was a relationship between them. Whether Philipe left at a request from his family, or he simply ran, he would have taken her with him. Maybe Sergi can find a trail through her. While we wait to see how that plays out, we might as well check a couple of the other libraries. We'll be close to New York where there's not only a library but one of the contacts I have for Philipe. I'll try to arrange a visit."

She shot up, a bit of mocha spilling over the side. "We're going to New York?"

"I was going to go over the itinerary when we were on the plane."

"I didn't pack for New York."

He snorted. "My apologies. I should have considered that."

"It's not funny. I didn't bring the right dresses."

He held back his smile, though it was difficult. Her expression was somewhere between a pout and annoyance, and for some reason, it stirred his cock. "I think we can manage a short shopping trip. Either city, your choice."

She leaned over, and he met her halfway for a kiss. "You're way too good to me."

"You deserve it. Now, finish your drink. It's time to catch a cab."

Chapter Six

"WELL, THAT WAS A BUST." I dropped my purse on a side table and draped my linen jacket over a chair before heading to the bar. I selected a merlot that was already open and poured a glass. "Do you want a drink?"

"I'll take a glass of wine." Lucas removed his tie and laid it over my jacket. "At least we were able to confirm the *De første dage* was listed for restoration in Boston and here, just like on the West Coast."

"I suppose." I handed him the wine then took a seat overlooking Manhattan and the river beyond. "I was hoping Philipe's college friend would know more. He could be lying, but he seemed pretty concerned he hadn't heard from him in a couple of decades."

Lucas opened his phone. "I have a message from Sergi. Check your burner."

I jumped up and pulled it from my purse. "I didn't even think to check. I have coordinates." I gave them to him, then picked up my wine before I sat on the arm of his chair, looking over his shoulder as he typed the numbers into his GPS tracker.

"Hazel Green," Lucas said.

"Where's that?"

"Alabama, about seven hours from New Orleans."

"Why not just go home?"

"You're assuming the custodian is still with Philipe or that they haven't moved again." He set the phone down and took my glass.

"True. I suppose even with the size of New Orleans, it would be difficult to hide there for decades."

"From Sergi's message, she's been moving every few years." He pulled me onto his lap facing the windows and placed his hands on my shoulders, his fingers gently kneading.

I leaned into it. "That feels so good."

"Your muscles are a knot. You need to relax. We still have a long way to go. You knew this wasn't going to be easy."

"I know. I'd feel better if someone had spoken to Philipe in the last decade." I lowered my head as the massage deepened, the warmth of his hands spreading a light tingle through me.

"Our focus needs to be on his contacts now. If we're close to a library, we'll stop in just to confirm the pattern is consistent, but it's no longer our top priority. The Renaud family will have heard of our visits."

"But they haven't stopped us. You said this last curator was friendly."

"And appeared honestly perplexed with the discrepancy in the records. But it's best we don't take any chances." He pulled down my dress zipper a few inches, slipping the straps down my arms, his massage now working its way across my entire back.

"Do you think there might be some members of the Renaud family breaking the rules?"

"I would rather think it's more about keeping something potentially dangerous from reaching any of the Houses. The Renauds taking sides in Council politics would be almost as earth-shattering as telling the vampire world that dreamwalkers still exist."

Featherlight kisses followed his hands that continued to work the knots. A couple of minutes later, the zipper was pulled all the way down and my bra was unhooked.

"Am I getting a full-body massage?"

"You need to relax before dinner." He moved his hands farther down my back as the dress fell to my waist.

His fingers traced my spine, his thumbs releasing pressure points, and as good as it felt, it was the stirring between my legs that demanded my immediate attention. I wiggled, feeling the press of his cock against my ass.

"Dinner in New York. It's pretty exciting."

"I guarantee it will be memorable." He reached around to cup my breast, his massage no longer focused on my muscles.

I leaned back, letting my head drop to his shoulder, and I closed my eyes. His fingers tweaked my nipples as he kissed the soft spot between neck and shoulder, dragging the tips of his fangs up my neck until they nipped at my ears. Then he moved a hand south, his knuckles brushing against my ribcage and over my belly, sending shivers of delight following his touch.

His fangs scraped along my back from shoulder to shoulder. A finger slipped under my lace panties. And I thought I'd come undone.

He teased me until I couldn't think. But I could feel. I sensed his need as he lifted me onto him. His strong arms wrapped around me, and he hugged me tight, gently rolling us back and forth until he was fully sheathed.

But he didn't stop. And I let the ripples of desire and my own hunger for him wash over me until I was nothing but raw emotion.

Then he pulled me off him. "Don't worry, baby. Just turn around." The shock to my system was short-lived as he helped me get settled before he pulled me onto him. Now we were face to face. His eyes glowed with his inner beast, which only made me want more of him.

I couldn't look away, and for a moment, I thought he might be mesmerizing me. He pressed the flat of his hand on my belly then ran it up my body, goosebumps erupting in his wake, until he stroked a thumb along my neck. The glow in his gaze never diminished, only growing hotter. I was witnessing his desire through his eyes. I wasn't sure how long I could hold everything in as I let the sensations ripple through me.

Then his lips were on mine, his tongue searching as his kiss deepened. Our rocking motion became frantic, and we gripped each other, afraid to let go, needing the soft embrace of skin-on-skin. My first cries of release shook me; the second wave spread a heat through me that made me gooey inside.

His arms never let me go, even when his body stiffened, and he let out a low growl that always made me smile.

We collapsed onto the soft carpet, his body covering mine, his lips pressing light kisses along my upper back.

There were no words for how he made me feel. His warm foreplay, his ministrations after sex. Without words he made me feel cherished, his hands now roaming over me in long, languid movements.

We never spoke of emotions—feelings. What could either of us say? Our relationship was problematic, so we shoved it away, living only for the moment. And then he curled me into him, his arm possessive as he tightened his hold.

And for the moment, I felt safe from the world.

WE WALKED ALONG 5TH AVENUE, stopping frequently as I window-shopped. He laughed as I pointed out one outrageous dress after another, assuring him I would look marvelous in each of them. We were still laughing when we rode up the elevator, his hands roaming over me.

"You were right." My hands did some of their own perusing as I squeezed his ass.

"About what?"

"I won't forget that dinner. It was so romantic."

Dinner had been at a penthouse restaurant that overlooked Manhattan. Candles lit the table, and the bucket of champagne kept the alcohol flowing. The meal itself was five-star, and I rubbed my tummy. The espresso afterward took the buzz away, and the walk back helped settle the food. I was ready to get busy again. This time we were going to take full advantage of our king-sized bed.

We'd made two steps out of the elevator before Lucas pushed me behind him. I hadn't seen anyone, but I didn't waste any time pulling the dagger out of my clutch. I stepped to his right as he moved into a defensive posture.

Two vamps waited at the end of the hall. They didn't look friendly. I couldn't believe they'd be so bold to attack us in a hotel where humans could leave a room or step out of the elevator at any moment. The vamps moved toward us. They didn't appear to be in a hurry, and there were no visible weapons, but they strode shoulder to shoulder, sneers on their faces.

We were in close quarters in the hallway. There wasn't any room to spread out. And we couldn't work back-to-back with a frontal attack. I considered Lucas's options, but I didn't have to think past the first one that came to mind. He'd take them both on, wanting to keep me out of it. There wouldn't be time to argue about it, so I fell back a step, putting distance between him and me.

I'd let him attack because these vamps were obviously falling for his defensive posture ruse. As soon as he dropped one, I'd make sure they stayed down until Lucas finished them both. We couldn't take a chance of leaving them injured. They'd most likely grab the first human they found to make a blood donor out of them— possibly taking too much and leaving the human nothing more than a husk.

When they were about thirty feet from us, Lucas ran. I chased after him, still keeping a decent gap between us. The vamps weren't expecting it, but they had quick reflexes. Lucas spun and kicked out, catching the chin of one vamp. He ducked as the second vamp swung his fist. The vamp missed, which took him off his stride, and Lucas struck the back of his knee. The vamp went down.

The first vamp was already coming at him, and I raced for the second vamp, kicking him in the head before he could stand. He must have seen it coming, and while he took the hit, he grabbed my foot and twisted it. I went with the twist, but it still hurt like a mother. I held back a scream so I wouldn't alarm Lucas. I hit the wall but held onto my dagger, so when the vamp came at me, I struck out, slicing his chest. Blood smeared his shirt, but it didn't stop him.

He grabbed me by the hair while gripping my hand to pull the dagger free. Instead of trying to pull away, I stepped toward him and kneed him in the groin. Who would have thought such an old trick would work so well? He went down, and I wrenched my knife free.

I was getting ready to stab him when his eyes went wide just before his head slipped from his shoulders.

Time seemed to freeze. Blood sprayed everywhere. I glanced down and stared at his head. His eyes, still wide in surprise, stared at the ceiling.

All I could think was—there went the carpet.

Lucas grabbed my arm and turned me around.

"Are you okay?" He shook my arm. "Ginger?"

I looked for the other vamp, and his headless body was slumped against the wall—his head a few feet from him.

"Where'd you get the sword?" I glanced up the hall but didn't see anyone. Then my gaze traveled back to the headless vamps.

"Apparently, they brought one to the party. I'm guessing they were hoping to take our heads back to whoever sent them."

"Now what?"

"We need to get rid of the bodies."

"And the blood?"

"Security will scratch their heads over it, but without bodies, there isn't much they can do."

"The cops will get the names of every guest on this floor."

"Our aliases can't be traced."

I stared at the head near my feet. "Then how did they find us?"

"I don't know. Open the door to our room. We need to hide them there until we can get them in the car."

I ran down the hall to grab my clutch and searched for the card key while not thinking about the dead vamps. Lucas already had one vamp over his shoulder, waiting for me to open the door.

Once the bodies and heads were in the bathroom, we stripped out of our blood-spattered clothing, my heart breaking over the waste of a brand-new dress. We stuffed the blood-stained clothing and towels into two laundry bags, dropped a head in each, then changed into traveling clothes.

It was close to three a.m., and the hotel was quiet. We took the elevator down to the parking garage, and I waited, keeping an eye out for hotel security as Lucas pulled the rental around. I packed our bags into the back seats while he went upstairs to get the first vamp. He brought them down one by one via the stairs and piled them into the trunk.

Lucas was familiar with New York and found a quiet pier where he dumped the vamps and the laundry bags into the deep, dark waters. Then he drove us to the train station.

"Now what?" I asked. My nerves were shot, and a bone-chilling cold came over me, creating an unstoppable shiver.

Lucas turned the heat up high and put an arm around me. We cuddled the best we could with a console between us. "We'll catch a train to D.C. One of Philipe's contacts is in Maryland."

"Do you think they followed us from Renaud's library?"

"Maybe. But I didn't sense them, and I've been watching."

"Did you contact Sergi?"

"Not until we can get new burners. I don't want to take a chance."

I leaned my head against his shoulder and gripped his hand tighter as we waited for the morning commuters to arrive so we could vanish from New York within a sea of humans.

I had so looked forward to that king-sized bed.

Chapter Seven

TALL TREES SURROUNDED the stately manor that resided on ten acres of a landscaper's dream just outside Frederick, Maryland. The front gates had been left open, and from what Lucas could observe, security was light. He'd heard of House Beall, but it had fallen to a shell of its former self over a century ago. He strode to the front door then paused when he realized Ginger wasn't next to him.

She had stopped to smell the roses that lined the front walk. When she noticed him watching, she scurried to catch up. "Sorry. I couldn't help myself. They're so beautiful."

"I don't mind. I didn't want to knock until you were with me."

She stepped next to him and smiled at something behind him. He turned to find the door opened and a petite woman dressed in a pastel-pink pantsuit staring at Ginger before looking beyond her.

"Those are prize-winning roses. They were our father's favorite." She stared at them for a moment longer then glanced up at Lucas. "Can I help you?"

"I'm sorry to disturb you. My name is Lucas Maynard with House Trelane. I was wondering if Carmen was at home."

"What does House Trelane want with my daughter?"

"Mother. Don't be rude." A woman, who appeared close to Lyra's age, pulled her mother away. "Please come in."

The older vampire gave her daughter a tolerant look, but it turned suspicious when she eyed Lucas. Then she sniffed the air. "You brought a human with you."

"My Blood Ward."

"I see." She turned to her daughter. "In the sitting room, if you please. Try not to be long." The woman tottered down the hallway and disappeared around a bend.

"I'm sorry about that. She's not fond of visitors."

"We're sorry for the intrusion, but we have urgent business. Are you Carmen?"

She tugged her sweater closer and nodded. "You said you're from House Trelane?" She led them through a door to the right where a brightly lit room welcomed them. "Can I offer you a refreshment?"

"I appreciate the offer, but we won't be long."

Lucas and Ginger sat on the couch, and Carmen took one of the stuffed chairs across from them.

"This might be a sensitive topic, but we're looking for Philipe Renaud. My understanding is that you're one of his friends."

At the mention of Philipe, she paled, and her posture turned rigid. "That was many years ago."

"Within the last decade?"

She considered the question. "About that time. Maybe a year or two earlier. I don't have a point of reference to be any more accurate."

"That's alright. We don't need exact timeframes."

"I've spoken to Fiona since then. Maybe five years ago." She laughed. "It's about time for our next check-in."

"Check-in?"

She waved a hand and appeared more relaxed. "A turn of phrase. I knew her decades ago. And ever since she went off with

Philipe, it's only been phone calls, and those are rare. About every five years I hear from her. It's become a joke between us."

"Is she alright?" Ginger asked.

Carmen glanced at her as if she'd forgotten Ginger was in the room, then she gave her a soft smile. "That's so sweet. Thank you for asking." She ran her fingers up and down the arm of the chair as she stared at something beyond them, the movement barely audible to Lucas in the quiet room. "I think so. She's more reserved than she used to be. I thought maybe she was having an argument with Philipe, but whenever I mention him, she becomes as bubbly as when they first met." She laughed and shook her head. "I've never seen two vampires more in love. No. The stress was coming from someplace else. Or maybe she was just really tired."

"Do you know where she was calling from?" Lucas asked. And, as he expected, that's when her suspicion returned.

"Why? You didn't mention why you were looking for Philipe."

Lucas glanced at Ginger, and she nodded. He hadn't wanted to bring up the book unless he had to, but if Philipe and Fiona were still hiding after all this time, he would need to be specific to get a decent answer.

"We believe he has knowledge of or possibly possession of a book we're searching for."

"You mean something from the Renaud Library?"

"I mean something that used to be in the Renaud Library." And now that he'd gone this far, he might as well go all the way. "It appears to be missing."

Her shock appeared genuine. "You must have received incorrect information. Nothing ever goes missing from the Renaud Library. Nor is it ever misplaced."

She was a true believer, just as he had been, and it wouldn't be easy to change her mind. He could tell her about the multiple book facades that claimed it was in restoration at the four libraries he'd personally visited. But she would have to see it before she would believe it.

"I'm sorry to have wasted your time." He stood, and Ginger rose next to him. "It's good to hear the two of them are doing well."

Carmen stood. "I'm sorry I couldn't have been of more help."

He'd only taken a couple of steps before a tingling bell sounded. He turned, but not before he saw Carmen's gaze fill with confusion. She made to turn for the door when the bell sounded a second time.

She raised a finger. "Just give me a moment, please." She strode toward a desk in the far corner of the room and, keeping her back to them, picked up the handset of an old 1940s-style black telephone.

"Yes." The pause was brief. "Are you sure? Yes, of course." She hung up and heaved a breath before turning toward them. "This might sound strange, but my grandfather wishes to speak with you."

Now it was Lucas's curiosity that rose. "I'm sorry. I thought your grandfather had died some time ago."

"No. He's still with us. Please, come this way." She led them toward the back of the house, then turned down a hall that ended at a set of double doors. After removing a key from her pocket, she inserted it into a panel to the left of the doors. The doors slid sideways to reveal an elevator.

He took Ginger's arm as they entered. When he turned around, Carmen waited outside. "Aren't you coming?"

"He'll want to speak with you alone."

And the doors closed.

~

"ARE you sure this is a good idea?" Ginger asked, her gaze hitting every part of the elevator. She squeezed her purse against her chest.

"I don't think they plan on attacking and holding us hostage." Lucas grinned. She'd stoically faced two vampires a mere twenty-four hours ago and helped him dump their bodies in the Hudson River. But she was nervous about seeing an ancient.

He could understand her trepidation, but it was hard to get past his own curiosity. Old man Beall was supposed to be dead and buried based on everything he'd heard. And that information was close to a century old.

A bell chimed as the doors opened, and he blinked. The elevator had brought them to a library. And it wasn't a cozy one with paneled walls, darkly upholstered furniture, a hearth with glowing embers, and stuffed bookcases that lined the walls. Though there were plenty of bookcases.

This room stretched for a good hundred yards and was as wide as the house. The bookshelves ran floor-to-ceiling, and there were several rows of them in addition to those that lined the walls, only leaving space for long, thin windows to brighten the immense room. Lucas spotted three rolling library ladders, and there didn't seem to be an empty slot on a single shelf.

Statues and ferns filled the spaces around multiple seating areas, each adorned with a sofa and two side chairs in a variety of colors. This was the most elaborate home library he'd seen outside of the Renauds', and it would take a lifetime to go through all the books.

A male voice came out of nowhere. "Please continue through the library and take your first hall to the left. My room is at the end."

Ginger jumped and scanned the ceilings for the speakers. Lucas didn't see those, but he found the cameras. There must have been a similar setup in the sitting room, where the old man had seen and, most likely, listened to their conversation with Carmen.

Lucas pulled Ginger's arm through his and guided her according to the given directions. When they reached the door, Lucas knocked.

"Come. Come."

The voice was deep and commanding. Lucas had been

expecting something wispier from an ancient who was supposed to be dead.

When they entered, Lucas had to force himself not to shy away from the vampire in front of him. He knew Beall was an ancient of at least a thousand years. But that didn't explain his shriveled appearance. Lucas focused on the eyes, which were such a deep brown they were almost black, filled with a sharp intelligence that belied the body that held them hostage.

"Sit on the sofa over here. It's difficult for me to get around when I'm not in my wheelchair, and sometimes I just need to get out of the damn thing." He gave Ginger a long perusal. "Blood Ward. Come here, girl."

Ginger seemed glued to the floor, but after a short pause, she gave Lucas a sidelong glance before moving toward Beall. Lucas took the opportunity to follow behind her to get to the couch.

"Give me your hands." His were an odd shade of ivory with long, bony fingers that ended in perfectly manicured nails. "I'm not contagious."

That seemed to wake her up, and she gripped his hands. "I'm sorry. That was rude. It's just that I haven't seen a true ancient before."

His laugh was coarse, and he choked a bit before his voice returned to its normal timber. "I'll tell you a secret. Most of them look more like your young vampire here. Now, squeeze my hands. Harder. That's it. And let me look in your eyes, and don't worry, I'm not mesmerizing you."

He stared at Ginger for some time, then released her hands and waved for her to take a seat. His voice took on a teasing note. "An interesting choice for a Blood Ward. She seems more suited for battle."

Ginger sat straighter at the comment, and Lucas chuckled. "You're not far off."

The old man slammed a fist on his chair with more strength than Lucas expected for his fragile state. "I thought so."

Then he turned serious as he stared at Lucas. "I'll ask that you keep this conversation confidential. As far as the world knows, as you stated earlier, I'm almost a century dead now. The truth of the matter is that I have the wasting blood disease that impacts our species. As you know, there's no cure, only a long, slow death as my own blood eats away at me. Doesn't matter how many humans share their blood with me or what type it is, it immediately turns my own blood against me. Not even the beast can help. I'd rather no one knows. It's not heritable, but should someone discover the reason for the reduction in our fertility rates, I don't want Carmen living under what many would call a curse."

"They'll never hear it from us."

The old vampire seemed appeased. His gaze became unfocused for a long moment before he turned his dark eyes on Lucas. "You're searching for the *De første dage*."

Lucas blinked. "Yes. How do you know about it?"

"Because I was on the Council when it was decided to have it hidden within the bowels of the Renaud Library."

Ginger reached out and gripped Lucas's hand. Not wanting to interrupt Beall, he squeezed her hand and simply held on as the ancient vampire continued.

"They didn't think anyone outside the Council was aware of the book. It wasn't until Guildford Trelane—over a thousand years later—asked about it. That was when I received the first calls. A couple of other ancients, ex-Council members, were worried that someone had asked about it. Poor Philipe had no idea what Pandora's box he'd opened."

Ginger snickered at Beall's casual reference to Cressa's alter ego, and Lucas almost bit his tongue to keep his grin in check. The old vampire had no idea how close his comment was to the truth. Not only was Pandora the alias Cressa used when she was a thief, but the fact she was also a dreamwalker is what started Devon down this dangerous path.

Lucas covered the moment with a clarifying comment. "I understand the title means "the first days."

"That's correct."

Beall had been almost gleeful in finally sharing knowledge of the book with someone—an outsider. Now, he'd become tight-lipped. If he wasn't going to say it, Lucas wouldn't spoil the opportunity.

"And do you believe what's written in the book could shatter vampire society and bring about a civil war?"

Beall's eyes squinted as he tapped a bony finger on the desk. "How committed is Trelane in finding the truth?"

"And what side of the line does House Beall sit?"

The old vampire laughed until he wheezed, and Lucas thought he might have to call someone. Beall sipped water from a nearby glass and waited a moment. "Forgive me. Sometimes my lungs can't seem to keep up with me." This time he took a larger gulp of water, wiped his mouth, then studied them both.

It went on for so long, Lucas was surprised Ginger didn't start bouncing a knee, but she had released her grip on him and sat as still as any vampire.

"We were once a powerful house, a strong ally in battle. Now, the House is focused on education, which is where my grand-daughter spends most of her time. Her mother is so busy social-izing she wouldn't notice bombs dropping unless they hit the manor. My son squandered his inheritance and then got his fool self killed. And with the slim chance of any future heirs, House Beall will most likely die with me."

"What will happen to Carmen and the rest of the household?" Ginger asked.

"House Pearson has committed to support the Family through marriage. They need our name recognition in order to move higher within the aristocracy. As traditionalists, House Pearson sides with House Venizi. Carmen isn't happy about it, but I have to consider the safety of the entire Family."

"I see. And would you consider an offer from House Trelane?"

"You're not looking for a wife, are you? And with such a beautiful Blood Ward by your side."

Lucas grinned. "I don't think a marriage proposal will be required. That does appear to be a Venizi trait. We can offer protection in the way of a small security force residing at the manor. Your daughter and granddaughter are free to continue their own pursuits as long as the House remains loyal to Trelane."

"And what would Trelane ask for in return?"

"Everything you know of the book, and if necessary, your support of House Trelane with the Council."

Beall eyed him then leaned back to stare at the ceiling. Silence descended for a solid five minutes before he lowered his gaze to meet Lucas's. "And you have the power to make such an offer?"

"I'm cadre."

The old vampire's brow lifted. "I'm sorry. I wasn't aware."

Lucas waved him off. It wasn't standard procedure to declare being part of a House leader's cadre, but it was well understood that the cadre had the power to make commitments on behalf of the House. "You might have locked yourself away, but you've been keeping your eye on the Council, and you're aware of the building tension between the old ways and the new. The shifters are restless. From what little I know of the book—it will either rip vampire society apart or pave the way for its future. We're betting on the latter and preparing for the former."

Beall grinned, his teeth a stark white against his sallow complexion. "To be young again and ready for battle." He shook his head. "It doesn't seem that long ago."

Lucas would have loved to spend days with this ancient and hear his tales of war. Being that old and a House Leader, he would have seen his share of them. He glanced at Ginger, who still hadn't moved. At first, he was concerned at her frozen profile, but there was a sparkle in her eye and that look of curiosity he knew so well.

Beall coughed and interrupted his thoughts. "There are many

things in the book that could initiate either outcome you've stated, but I'm afraid I can't provide the specifics within the pages. What I can share is why the book was created, or at least, what was told to the Council of the time." He shifted in his seat and rang a bell. "If you don't mind, I need some tea."

Within several minutes, a female servant brought in a tray with a tea service. She glanced at Lucas, ignoring Ginger, and he nodded. The staff believed her to be a Blood Ward, and as such, didn't deserve a choice unless Lucas requested it. Archaic, but Ginger didn't say a word.

Once the tea was served and the servant left, Beall sipped his tea and considered his words.

"Before I begin, I'm going to ask you to suspend your personal beliefs on what I'm about to share. Where many humans believe the folklore of King Arthur so do many vampires believe the myth of dreamwalkers." He paused as he studied Lucas, whose face remained blank, then flicked a glance to Ginger, before nodding. "Good. I believe the rest of my story will then appear more plausible to you. Thousands of years ago, dreamwalkers walked the earth alongside vampires. The two species were what you might call interconnected—a symbiotic relationship that served both species. During a time before that relationship matured, the two species were at odds, which resulted in a great war. After several years and more deaths than one could count, a truce was called. It was during their negotiations that the two species discovered something within themselves that could benefit the other. The truce was sealed with the Dagger of Omar. Many don't believe this dagger exists, but if it did, it would add validation to what was written in a book that would begin a new day for both vampire and dreamwalker. The book, as you know, was called *De første dage*, the only recorded document that specified the agreement between species."

Lucas sat back, and Ginger scooted closer, reaching out for his arm. "Do you know what the benefits were that were shared between the species?"

Beall shook his head. "I have my suspicions, but I never had the benefit of reading the book. And no, I won't share an old vampire's musings. You'll have to discover that on your own. I'm not one to start rumors, especially around something that can get one killed."

"And the reason why the book has been hidden?" Lucas asked the obvious question, and as much as he wanted confirmation, he knew he wasn't going to get it. But Beall's words were enough to read between the lines.

Beall drained his teacup and reached for the teapot. Ginger rose and picked it up, refilling his cup and refreshing theirs. "Thank you, my dear. You're very kind." He gave Lucas a wink. "And properly trained. I should expect nothing less from House Trelane. Guildford was always particular about the kindness of his Blood Wards to do the right thing."

Lucas bowed his head, accepting the compliment. He'd owe Ginger a fancy dinner as compensation for her performance today.

After finishing his second cup, Beall continued. "The species lived comfortably together for centuries until certain members of the Council began to fear the dreamwalkers. From what I heard, there had been a few bad apples among the dreamwalkers, but it was enough. These members convinced the majority of the Council that there was a better path without the dreamwalkers. The rumors and fear spread rapidly, which is one reason I don't barter in rumors."

"And what happened?" Lucas asked.

He shrugged. "There are dozens of answers—maybe more—to that question. But I'll sum it up for you. In all your years as a vampire, have you ever been told of dreamwalkers, let alone met one?"

Lucas shrugged and hedged his answer. "Not once in all my earlier years."

"Yet, if I had to guess at your mission, this book is something you'd search for even without Trelane's support."

Lucas allowed a small grin to show. "I'm a student of history, and other than this one elusive book, there's nothing else written about dreamwalkers in the Renaud library that I'm aware of."

"And yet it seems Trelane is hanging his seat on the Council on this very book."

"Let's just say he's building a rather strong case."

A light glow hit Beall's gaze, and he grinned. "I see." He steepled his fingers and gave Lucas a long, appraising stare. "Then I'll leave you with the one piece of information I feel confident in sharing. The last I heard—and this was about a year ago—Fiona was in Fayetteville, Tennessee. She's your best hope in locating the book."

Chapter Eight

THE PUB WAS reminiscent of what I thought a pub should look like. Not the fancy ones intent on encouraging the happy hour crowds with electronic dart boards and flashy video games. The food would be the typical fare you'd find in any chain restaurant regardless of the name on the building.

This pub was dark, smoky, and narrow, with dark-green walls and tables with wooden bench seats with tall backs so you weren't staring at the back of someone's head in the next booth. A scarred and drink-stained bar ran the length of the building against the wall to the left.

In the far-right corner, two men stood next to a pool table with a single red lampshade hanging over it. They watched a third man take a shot, and they leaned to the left as the ball rolled toward the pocket as if they were encouraging its progress. When it hit the edge and bounced away, their moans could be heard above Johnny Cash singing about a boy named Sue. Music my father listened to when we lived in Nevada before the family moved to Seattle.

Lucas selected an empty booth in the middle of the room and sat so he could watch the door. Neither of us expected vamps to make a move in a human bar, but we weren't taking any chances.

He'd already checked the back exit and ensured we had a clear path to it.

After leaving House Beall, Lucas drove south until the sun was close to setting. He didn't want to put the House in jeopardy by staying too close. I wasn't sure it made a difference, but Lucas had taken a state highway that headed the same southerly direction as the interstate, hoping to stay off the vamps' radar.

"What do you think of Beall's story?" I asked the question because he hadn't wanted to discuss it while driving. It didn't happen often, but sometimes Lucas required complete quiet to untangle a knotty problem or work through a strategy. Basically, he was in his head, and his blank expression was his "do not disturb" sign.

"His story carries the startling authenticity of the truth." He stole my leftover pickle and took a swig of beer. "I'm disappointed with the Council...something that's becoming more common the further we pursue Devon's mission."

"You expect more from your government? It's not much different on the human side." I nibbled at my fried cod, pleased at how tender and juicy it was, while glancing at Lucas's salad. Only with vamps would the male be eating a salad while the female human was stuffing fried food in her mouth. My only excuse was that comfort food reduced my stress levels. I was going to gain an easy five pounds before this trip was over.

"The only thing I've learned is Remus has been right all along, though I shouldn't be surprised. It matches Devon's vision."

"Of a combined Council?"

"It's only fair. Equal representation."

"That would only be true if the dreamwalkers get their fair number of seats."

Lucas grimaced and stabbed at his salad, piercing the tender leaves as fiercely as if they were enemy combatants. "And that will be a hard sell with the current Council."

"Not if we find the book, and Beall gave us the best lead we've had so far. Except it doesn't match what Sergi gave us."

"But it's close enough."

"What do you mean?"

"You need to start using your GPS map. Though the two cities are in different states, only fifteen miles separate Hazel Green and Fayetteville."

"I must not be getting enough sleep. I should have known to check that out during our drive."

Lucas shrugged as he chewed, giving the room a quick scan. "I've been thinking about how the vamps are finding us."

"You think they're tracking us rather than just tailing us?"

He nodded and pushed his plate aside. He hadn't been eating well and hadn't sourced a blood donor since the morning we'd left Santiga Bay. But in his current mood, he wouldn't take my concern to heart, so I'd wait.

He finished his beer and looked at the check. "I think we need new supplies. A couple of streets over, there was a grocery store and one of those places that has a little bit of everything. Let's stop there on our way out of town in the morning."

"At least we have a destination."

He left cash on the table and kept a hand on the small of my back as he steered me out the rear exit of the pub. We circled the building to find three vamps positioned around our rental. Lucas pushed me back until we were out of sight.

"It's not too far to the hotel. Did we leave anything critical in the car?" Lucas peered around the corner.

"No. Everything is in the duffels we left at the hotel."

"Let's walk back and hope there aren't any vamps waiting for us."

"You think they've been tracking the rental?"

"Maybe. Worst case, we check into a different hotel and then regroup in the morning."

We traveled the backstreets, and halfway there I was thanking the heavens I wore my comfortable boots that were good in a fight. I might start sleeping in them. When we got to the hotel, we went directly to the bar, which was busier than I expected—until Lucas mentioned an insurance convention. We found a lone table in the middle of the group, and he left me there while he checked the room. I wasn't happy about him going alone, but his mood hadn't improved, so I didn't push.

I nursed a vodka martini and flirted with a group of salesmen while I waited, hoping to fit into the crowd. But as time ticked away, I worried about Lucas. He'd been gone twenty minutes when he finally strode through the crowd, casually putting an arm around my shoulders. The salesmen collectively sighed and lifted their drinks. Lucas bought them another round on our way out.

"What took so long? I was getting worried." I put an arm around his waist as we walked through the lobby, keeping an eye out for anyone who appeared suspicious.

"I checked all the floors and the staircases. Our room looks the way we left it. I think we'll be safe for the night, but we should reconsider our transportation."

"Can the hotel get us a new rental?"

"That might be best. I'll report the other one stolen."

When we reached the room, we secured the door, placed our daggers within easy reach, climbed into bed, and spent the next few hours channel surfing. By two in the morning, we were both still a little wired, knowing three vamps were out there.

Lucas lowered the volume on the TV and shut the lights off. We cuddled next to each other, my head resting against his shoulder. I couldn't stop glancing toward the door, watching the doorknob to see if it turned.

"Neither of us is going to get much sleep tonight." I held his hand. A simple gesture, yet I grew strength through his return grip.

"Let's give it a try while we wait for morning. We have a long drive tomorrow and can take turns napping in the back seat."

"Then we should get a real pillow. The duffels aren't a great substitute."

He chuckled. "Add it to the list." After a few seconds, he kissed my temple. "It was a good thing I showed up in the bar when I did. I thought I might have to fight my way to your table."

I poked him in the ribs. "You weren't jealous by the attention I was getting, were you?"

He rolled over, surprising me with a rather passionate kiss. "I was insanely jealous."

I giggled. The conditions weren't right for us to get busy, but that didn't mean we couldn't flirt.

"I have to admit, I thought insurance agents were a bit more straightlaced. But I bet they'd still be partying if the hotel bar didn't shut down at one a.m."

"I think you'd turn heads at a convention for priests."

"Now that's just the sweetest thing to say."

We both laughed, and he hugged me tighter. "You know I never meant for you to get so deeply ingrained in the Family business."

"You make it sound like you work for some mob boss."

"Some days it feels like that. Minus the drugs, extortions, and sex-slave trading."

"Cressa said the same thing just before we left for San Francisco. But honestly, what was my life before this? I was living in the Hollows. Even with Bulldog's protection, every day was a toss-up as to whether I'd get caught in a drive-by shooting. I thought I knew how to protect myself, but these last weeks, I learned I wasn't anywhere near capable." I nestled deeper into his strong arms. "But I am now. I might get a bit wigged out with the fighting and the decapitations, but I think I'm handling it pretty well."

He kissed the top of my head. "You're handling it beautifully. And you were perfect with Beall. He liked you."

"I wish there was a cure for him. I can't even imagine what he's gone through these last hundred years."

"No one is immortal. Some of us just live a lot longer, but it doesn't mean our end won't come eventually. Now, let's try to get a couple hours of sleep."

I snuggled against Lucas and closed my eyes. I didn't know where this relationship was going or how long it would last. What had started as curiosity of what it would be like to fuck a vamp had turned into something much deeper. He had become a significant part of my life. When Devon had been readdicted to Magic Poppy and was stuck in his beast form while the House faced sanctions, Lucas had considered going rogue if the inevitable happened. Afterward, once everything had returned to normal, he'd told me what he'd been planning at the time. If he was forced to go rogue, he would have asked me to go with him.

And as soon as he told me that—even with having to leave Cressa, as painful as that would be—I knew I would have said yes. That realization had shaken me to the core. I'd never been as close to a human male as I was to Lucas, and for now, there wasn't any possibility of letting this vamp out of my sight.

AN EARLY-SUMMER STORM hit us the next afternoon. The rain came down so hard, Lucas turned off the highway and drove a couple miles to a sleepy little town and found a bar at the edge of it. The plan was to grab a meal and wait out the storm.

They were cheap burgers, the meat questionable at best, and I studied Lucas when he pushed the plate away after a couple of bites.

"You need a blood donor." It was difficult to tell how pale he was in the dim glow of the bar light, but it had been almost two weeks since we'd left Santiga Bay, which was when he'd last fed.

"I'll take care of it when we get to New Orleans. I'll be fine until then." His tone was defensive, and I let the matter drop.

"I think I saw a grocery store a little farther down the street.

Why don't we pick up some fresh fruit and vegetables? We can snack on them until we get to a larger town and find you a better meal."

He squeezed my hand. "That's a great idea." He fished in his pockets. "Some solid sleep would help. Damn. I left my wallet in the car."

"I can get it."

He pulled me back when I stood. "I'll be back before you know it. Eat your fries. They're somewhat edible."

I laughed. He hated french fries. He wasn't much for any type of cooked potato. But I was like that with tomatoes unless they were on a burger. I watched him walk out the door. He might be paler than normal, but he still had his vampire swagger going on.

After five minutes, I began to worry. I fished in my purse, breathing a sigh when I found the emergency stash of cash Lucas had given me several days before. Exhaustion was taking its toll on both of us not to remember it.

I dropped a twenty on the table and raced out of the bar. The torrential downpour had lightened to a heavy rain. Lucas had parked at the far edge of an expansive dirt parking lot, out of sight of the street. The bar was probably the only one for miles, and while the lot looked dismally empty now, it was probably jam-packed on the weekends.

After checking the street to make sure no one was lurking, I kept my head down as I rushed to the car, only lifting it to confirm no one was following me. I was halfway across the lot when I saw the bodies.

I ran the rest of the way, slipping on the mud but managing to stay on my feet. My heart pumped so fast it was difficult to catch my breath.

Red pools of blood had mixed with the heavy rain and mud, leaving a macabre scene.

Two of the vamps were headless. My heartbeat escalated to a

jackhammer staccato. The hair appeared dark rather than Lucas's blond hair but, being wet, I couldn't be sure.

Please. Please. Please. Don't be Lucas.

I wanted to close my eyes, but I forced myself to look at the faces.

Thank the gods. They weren't him.

I almost collapsed with relief, but I had to find him.

Lucas lay at the back of the car, face down in a puddle. He couldn't drown, but it didn't stop the panic when I noted how red the puddle was. He grimaced when I turned him over, and I leaned over him to shield his face from the rain.

"Lucas. Lucas. Can you hear me?"

His arm barely lifted an inch before it fell to his side. His clothes were sliced in dozens of places. It was impossible to tell how bad it was, but the cuts had to be deep if he could barely move.

I glanced around the parking lot, thankful the rain kept people indoors. Or at least kept their heads down.

Think. Damn it. Think.

A cool chill swept over me as I slowed my breathing.

What would Cressa or Simone do?

I took off my light jacket and covered Lucas's face then turned to the two dead vamps. I found the keys to the rental in Lucas's pocket and opened the trunk. My steps were slow as I approached the first headless body. I'd helped Lucas move two bodies in a similar condition a couple of days before. I could do this.

Before dealing with the bodies, I grabbed all the weapons I could find, whether lying in the mud or on their person, and dumped them in the trunk. Next was checking pockets for wallets. Neither had any identification on them. They might have left it in their car, wherever that was. But they were carrying money, and I took it all.

I stood and surveyed the lot. We had parked by a small stand of trees, which turned out to be the best spot to dump bodies. I dragged the first one under the canopy, then leaned against a tree as I struggled for breath. The mud hadn't made it any easier to move the dead weight. Once the second body had been laid by the first, I collected their heads and dropped them in between the vamps. I had no idea which head belonged to which body, and it didn't matter to them now. The local sheriff would have a headscratcher with this one.

Next was how to get Lucas in the car. I tried to rouse him, but he was barely conscious. It had been difficult enough to drag the vamps. Lifting Lucas into the car would be next to impossible. I pulled out my dagger, and without a second thought, slit the fleshy part of my hand below my thumb.

I pressed it to his lips. "Drink, baby. Come on. Some nice donor blood. You need your strength. We need to get you in the car." I held his head up and after a long minute, I felt the pull and a tingling sensation as he began to drink.

He must not have realized who he was drinking from; otherwise, he wouldn't have drunk so deeply. Maybe I was wrong because he'd only taken a few swallows before he stopped. Though he might have passed out. I glanced at my cut. It was going to hurt like hell. I hadn't thought this through. I'd sliced my best hand for wielding a dagger. Sergi trained me to use both hands, but my right hand was the strongest.

I glanced where the dead vamps had laid. So much blood. Then it hit me, shocking my brain like jump-starting a battery.

Blood worked both ways. Human blood nourished vamps, but their blood carried healing properties. I found a fresh pool of Lucas's blood where it dripped onto his jacket. I pressed my hand into it, not sure how long it took. After a minute, I wiped the blood away and checked the skin. The cut was no longer bleeding, and it was beginning to scab over. The skin would be pink in another minute. Crazy.

Lucas stirred. "Ginger?"

"I'm here, baby. Do you think you can stand long enough to get in the car? We can't stay here."

"The others?"

"You killed two. If there were more, they're gone."

"Just the two." His breaths were short rasps.

"Don't talk. Let's get you in the back seat so you can lie down."

I opened the back door, then squatted behind his head and pushed him to a seated position. He was lethargic, but with some inner strength that I attributed partly to the beast and the rest to my blood—meager as the amount was—he half stood, half crawled into the back seat. He rolled over and collapsed before he got his legs in.

I raced around the car and yanked open the passenger door. I grabbed him under the arms and pulled him the rest of the way in, then stuffed the softest duffel under his head before closing the door and rushing back around to push the rest of his legs in to get the door closed. The last thing I could think to do was confirm no evidence had been left behind other than the pooled blood. Footprints were already fading into the mud.

Once in the driver's seat, I checked to ensure my purse was on the passenger seat and Lucas's wallet was in the console. I drove the car over the area where the fight had gone down, covering as much of the scene as I could before turning for the street.

The rain was still heavy, and there wasn't a single person in sight. Even the street traffic was light. The gas gauge showed more than half a tank. I took a slow left turn out of the parking lot and kept within the speed limit as I headed for the main highway.

"Lucas? Are you with me?"

A groan would have to satisfy for now. We'd barely had the rental for one day, yet the damn vamps were still tracking us. Until I found out how they were doing it, we were in grave danger. I considered calling Sergi, but he was hours, if not a full day away.

He'd have to fly commercial since Lorenzo was probably monitoring Devon's jet.

I had to remain focused. Stay calm and leave the emotions on lockdown until we were safe.

First things first. Find a secure location and check Lucas's wounds. Then find a way to get the vamps off our trail.

Chapter Nine

I PULLED off the interstate at a truck stop and parked near the semis. Sunset was still a couple of hours away, and the rain had reduced to a constant drizzle. Somehow, sitting in the middle of the trucks, we seemed protected from prying eyes. An illusion, but it kept me focused. I watched the truckers as they moved about, some going in and out of the attached diner, others carrying small duffels that most likely held a towel, a change of underwear, and a dopp kit.

Other than the truckers, the lot was quiet. I got out and climbed into the back, sliding Lucas's legs over so I could sit. Blood dripped onto the carpet. I took a moment to center myself, readying myself for the next step.

His eyes were closed, but he was breathing, as shallow as it was.

"Lucas? Are you awake?"

A mumble was his only answer.

Taking a deep breath, I started at his legs, searching for each injury, assessing which were minor and which were life-threatening. The worst-case scenario was that he would lose enough blood that either his beast would rise, or he'd bleed out. A vamp could eventually die of that, but I didn't know how much blood Lucas could lose before there was no coming back.

His pants were bloody, but there weren't any cuts or holes in the fabric. I tenderly lifted his shirt, though it was more like prying it off. Dried blood had mixed with both congealing and fresh blood. Our last bottle of water had rolled under the front seat. My hands were too bloody, so I used my shirt to grab it and twist off the cap. I soaked the shirt so I wouldn't create more damage.

When his shirt peeled away, I gasped. His chest looked like a tic-tac-toe board, lines crossing everywhere. Most weren't too bad, but there were four deep cuts and two holes that probably pierced one of his kidneys or maybe his liver. My anatomy wasn't the best.

But I knew enough. Lucas might be safe in the car, but he was bleeding out. My first priority was to stop the blood loss. I dug through a duffel, yanking out the few shirts we had left. Using the last of the water, I cleaned his chest, then used two shirts to staunch the bleeding. If I couldn't lift his body, I wouldn't be able to wrap the makeshift bandages tight enough to keep pressure on the wounds.

I applied the pressure manually for five minutes then cut my palm, giving Lucas more blood. His pulls were weak at best. I would need to give him blood more frequently, but unless I stopped the bleeding, it would be an endless cycle until I was too weak to give more. I sealed my cut and sat back.

I held his hand, murmuring words of love and support as I considered our options. The first thing was to take stock of myself. My clothes were covered with blood. I had to change. I grabbed leggings and a T-shirt and stepped out of the car, leaving the door open to cover me from onlookers as I quickly changed.

Once dressed, I slumped in the front passenger seat, mental fatigue overtaking me. But after a couple minutes of silence, I pushed it aside and picked up Lucas's wallet, pulling out the cash. I added it to what was left of my emergency funds and the money I took from the dead vamps. We were flush. Thank heaven for small favors. We were a long way from New Orleans, where Lucas could get a blood donor, but I didn't think he'd make it in his current condition. And those three vamps were still out there. We needed a safe place to hole up until Lucas was strong enough to stay conscious and walk. Fighting strength would be out of the question without a healer or several blood donors.

The truck stop would provide basic supplies. Then a thought struck. Up to now, I'd been trying to think like a vamp. We were up against vamps who thought like vamps. I had to switch up the game. Lucas was of no help. We had to rely on my skills. The survival skills I'd learned on the streets—cold, hungry, and on the defense from street thugs.

Instead of channeling Sergi, I needed to channel Harlow.

Soft murmurs made me turn around, and I squeezed through the gap between the front seats to get closer to Lucas. He kept repeating a single word, and once I understood what it was, my brow rose.

"Rosalynn."

LUCAS MUMBLED. A burning ache like fire. The beast stirred. The darkness returned.

"Hold your arm up. You'll never defend your neck that way." Marcus swung, and Lucas ducked, bringing his sword up to take a stab at Marcus's stomach. "Better."

Marcus swung again, and this time Lucas blocked it, keeping his elbow raised. Sweat leaked into his eyes, burning them, but he didn't back down.

"Lucas!" His name squealed from a young girl, and he took a moment to glance back in time to see her take a tumble.

The flat edge of a blade hit him on the shoulder. The force was so powerful it brought him to a knee, and then a sword touched his neck.

"If I've told you a thousand times, brother, don't let anything distract you—even Family." Marcus shoved his sword into the sheath that hung at his side. "If you're dead, who will protect them?"

"Understood." Lucas rose and brushed the dirt from his knee then turned to watch Rosalynn, his five-year-old sister, pick herself up and continue her run to him. He grabbed her as soon as she reached him and swung her in the air, her giggles bringing a smile to his face.

"You got me killed, little sister."

"You're funny," she said. "It's only practice."

"I've told you before, Rosalynn," Marcus lectured. "There's no playing during practice." He marched past them before Rosalynn turned and stuck her tongue out.

Lucas mussed her hair and kissed her cheek. "You smell like strawberries."

She nodded vigorously, her cheeks plump with a smile. "We picked them and ate them. But we saved a few for you."

"Well, that was kind of you."

"I know." She giggled as Lucas strolled toward the woman waiting several yards away.

"Hello, Mother." Lucas bent and kissed her cheek.

"I'm sorry about Rosalynn. She's such a precocious child I don't know what to do with her half the time." Kathryn Maynard held out her arms, but the child held tight to Lucas.

"She's not bothering anyone. I should have known not to turn around. Obviously, I need the distractions to help with practice." He waved her arm away when she attempted to take her daughter a second time. "I'll take her back to the house. I need something to eat before I challenge Marcus again."

"You need to train while you're hungry," Marcus yelled over his shoulder as he picked up his armor and walked off.

"Yes, I know. In battle conditions, no one knows when their next meal will come." Lucas stared after his brother, trying to remember when he'd become such a hard man. Being the oldest was never easy, especially with their father.

"Let me take her. Your father will be home soon." She worried her hands as if they couldn't settle unless she was holding something.

"Don't worry so much. Let me spend time with my sister. I want to pick some apples from the orchard. How about a nice apple tart for dessert?"

His mother glanced around then nodded, giving a last look at her daughter. "That should temper your father's mood. But don't be too long."

"Yes, Mother." He kissed her cheek and turned away, Rosalynn's head resting on his shoulder.

Once his brother and mother were out of sight, Rosalynn's head popped up. "Can we play hide and find?"

"Can I hide first?"

"No, silly. I hide, and you try to find me."

He chuckled. "Of course." He'd barely set her down before she took off. "The orchard, remember?"

"I know." Her voice filled with childish annoyance. She ran with abandon, stopping to pick up a wildflower here and there.

They spent an hour in the orchard, and he returned to the manor with a full basket of apples and a sleeping sister nestled in his other arm, her head on his shoulder. His father's stallion was being led to the stables, and Lucas detoured through the kitchen, handing his basket to an excited cook.

He rubbed his hands together. "I thought I'd have to ask one of the gardeners to bring me a bushel. You're too good to me."

"Nonsense. But you better save me an extra tart."

"For you, always."

Lucas took the back stairs to the nursery and laid Rosalynn on her bed, covering her with a light summer quilt.

He heard the yelling before he reached his father's study. Magnus Maynard was in another one of his foul moods. Nothing new there, and Lucas would catch hell for pampering his sister. He didn't care. Sisters were meant to be pampered. At least, that was how young girls in the Houses of his friends were treated. But their House leaders weren't as strict as his father, who always seemed to have something to prove.

"There you are. From what I hear of your training, you would do better with more time on the practice field than playing nurse-maid to your sister." Magnus poured wine into a goblet and drank half of it down.

Lucas glanced at Marcus, and though he caught a flinch from him, his brother showed no other emotion. Brian, his other brother, wouldn't meet his eye. Lucas sighed. Being the youngest male in the manor seemed to be a curse. His brothers had almost thirty years of battle training over him, yet he was supposed to be their equal. Until he could best one of them, his father would never give him a rest.

"I can do both."

"That's the job of a governess. Is that where you've set your sights? To be a babysitter."

"You know as well as my brothers my goal is to be cadre."

His father laughed, and after taking another long drink of wine, he choked, beating his chest to clear his airway. "You might be useful to another House someday, but cadre? I can't think of a House that would take on a bookworm."

His brothers didn't dare glance at him. He didn't have to read minds to know they thought the same thing. It was the early nine-teenth century, and knowledge in the art of war, politics, and the economy would be just as important if not more so than who had the strongest army. But his father would never see that.

"Spending time at the Renaud libraries is not wasted time. And a strong House leader will recognize the importance of knowledge as well as might for a strong cadre." Lucas stood his ground as his father whirled on him.

The strike was expected, as was the power behind it, and while Lucas staggered back, he didn't fall.

Though his face was red with anger, Magnus laughed. "Well, at least you can stand on your own two feet this time. I suppose that's something." He turned to Marcus. "Double his training until you're satisfied he can defend the House with honor." He flicked his fingers at Lucas.

"Go. Perhaps your mother needs your services in the drawing room."

That got a chuckle from his brothers, and Lucas, his cheeks tinged with anger, bowed his head and made his escape. He was still fuming when he reached the library and stomped to the sideboard to grab the decanter of whiskey. He drained half the cup and welcomed the slow burn. After taking two deep breaths, he walked along the bookcases. For all his bluster, his father had read some of the books, but he preferred talk of the old days as he walked through battle scenarios with his brothers and cadre, all battle-hardened men.

Lucas found a book that fit his mood and dropped into his favorite chair. In front of the slow-burning fire, the late spring evenings still cool, and with drink in hand, he lost himself in the political intrigue of King Henry's court. His father might not believe in him—and at one time his respect mattered—but Lucas had learned something more important than swordplay. It only mattered if you believed in yourself.

Chapter Ten

"WHERE ARE WE?" Lucas managed the same few words each time he woke before losing consciousness for another couple of hours.

"In a motel. Just rest." I gave up my attempts to feed him blood while he was coherent. He refused to accept it. It was easier to feed him while he was out. His subconscious—or more likely his beast—wasn't as squeamish about taking my blood.

By the time I gathered my purse and took a last glance around the room, he was sleeping again. Besides his meager bandages, he was naked under the covers.

Before leaving the truck stop earlier that evening, I'd bought water, two sets of sweats—one for him and one for me—what bandages they had, and a pen flashlight. It wasn't enough, but it was a start.

Fixated on how the vamps were tracking us, I crawled under the rental car and made my way along the frame, inch by inch, running the flashlight along every nook and cranny. We had already ditched everything we'd packed for our trip, including our nice suitcases, in exchange for duffels, new clothes, and cosmetics. Lucas had rented another car, yet the vamps still found us.

Did the vamps have time to plant a tracker? If there was something to find, my money was on the car. With Lucas bleeding in the backseat, time pressed in, and I was giving up hope of finding anything until I spotted a lump on the far side of the fuel tank. I ran my hand over it, and after tugging hard, it fell into my hand.

I ran the flashlight over it and watched a tiny red light blip on and off. It was definitely a tracker. *Fuckers.* I took the time to run over the car again and, thirty minutes later, determined there was only the one.

I'd considered going through each piece of clothing, shoes, and the duffel itself in search of other tracking mechanisms, but who was I kidding? I'd already tossed all my favorite clothes days ago. So, after changing into my new sweats, I gathered everything else and threw it in the truck stop's dumpster.

I stared at the tracker and considered crushing it. Other vamps might already be monitoring us, and I glanced around the parking lot, not really expecting to find any, but that didn't mean they weren't out there. I needed to throw them off our track, and then I remembered something from some TV show. If I glanced in a mirror, would I see a diabolical smile?

I wandered the parking lot and scanned the license plates of the big trucks. Then I found the perfect one. Idaho. Close enough. Maybe they'd think we'd given up and were heading home. I glanced around, and not seeing anyone, attached the tracker inside the front wheel well of the semi.

With a satisfied grin, I fell into the driver's seat, but another thought sobered me. All the attacks had involved two vamps. But there had been three at the last hotel before Lucas was injured. Where did the third vamp go? Or was that an entirely different group? Maybe they used one vamp to manually track us while the other two stayed behind to take us out. When the vamp doing the tracking didn't hear from them, two more were sent. It was possible that Venizi, or whoever was sending them, used vamps from allied Houses. The answer to that would require Lucas's experience.

I shook my head. It didn't matter now. The tracker was gone. I had driven the back roads until I found a town with a fair amount of restaurants and stores, and grabbed a room at a bearable motel. Now, as I took a last glance at Lucas lying on the bed, I hoped I was doing the right thing. The TV was tuned to a classic movie channel, and when I closed the door, I hung the "Do Not Disturb" placard on the doorknob.

The town was large enough to have a twenty-four-hour combination grocery and hardware store. I bought two sets of clothes for each of us, two sets of sheets and towels, a new duffel, toiletries for both of us, first aid supplies, a cooler, a case of water, two gallons of orange juice, cookies, fruit, and veggies. The orange juice and cookies were to restore me after I gave blood. If it was good enough for the Red Cross, it was good enough for me. After I packed everything in the car, I realized I'd forgotten something and ran back in and bought a new burner phone.

When I got back to the room, Lucas was still sleeping, and his major wounds still leaked blood.

"Hey, baby. Can you wake up?"

No response.

I hauled everything in from the car, set up the cooler, then began working on his injuries. The minor cuts seemed to have healed, which gave me hope, but the deeper ones still oozed blood. Once I had new bandages in place, I took the old shirts and towels and tossed them in the tub, wishing I'd bought detergent. I filled the tub with enough cold water to cover the items and left them to soak.

I crawled into bed next to Lucas and cut my palm.

"Wake up, Lucas. It's time to feed."

The call to feed must be instinctual because his lips tightened on the cut, and he drank. A flutter of hope rose as each suckle was stronger than the last. He just needed rest. If I only knew how long we had before someone else tracked us down. We were miles from the closest interstate, but we couldn't stay long. At this point, we were nothing more than sitting ducks.

~

THE VOICE SOOTHED HIM.

When he tried to open his eyes—he didn't have the strength.

Before Lucas could give it another thought, sweet honey touched his lips. He didn't question it, clasping his mouth around the soft skin. A familiar scent floated around him as he suckled the life-saving blood. Then the beast took over, and he fell into the memories.

Lucas dropped into the chair across from his bed, the opened letter still in his hand. A tear escaped down his cheek. He didn't bother wiping it away as he stared out the window, not noticing the Spanish moss rustle in the breeze as it hung from the large oak trees. Nor did he hear the twilling of birds as they flitted among the branches. The scent of magnolias and the humid air had no impact on him. He might as well be in a vacuum that matched the silence echoing in his ears.

The bastard had done it.

He had destroyed his beautiful sister. She had endured a strict and sheltered life with little love from their father. And now, she'd been traded in marriage to a stranger from an allied House as if she were nothing more than a fine piece of china to be displayed on a shelf. Their father completely disregarded her desire to marry another—a vampire from a strong House who loved her as deeply as she did him.

But he was a mere second son. Not the eldest like her newly betrothed in the Bertrand House. Lucas had begged her to ignore Father's wishes. In reality, Magnus Maynard couldn't force her, but the rebellious child of his youth had been battered with verbal abuse into a submissive female who would do what was expected of her.

From the spare letters he received from her, she'd been the young sister he'd known in her childhood. Her happiness and love for Eric were plain to see in her words. He briefly wondered how Eric had taken the news. Had this been less civilized times, Father's decision could have precipitated a war between the Houses.

He slowly crunched the paper into a ball before letting it drop to the floor. He barely heard the knock on the door and ignored it when it opened. He assumed it was his valet as it was nearing dinnertime.

"I take it you received bad news. Was it from home?"

Lucas jumped up and turned, bowing his head to his new House leader, Girard Lafitte. He'd been in his service for barely a year and was still getting his footing. "Yes, sir." He noted Lafitte's glance at the crumpled letter on the floor. "Not the best news but nothing that would impact House Lafitte. I'm sorry it distracted me from my duties."

Lafitte studied him. "Grab your jacket and follow me."

Lucas did as ordered, trailing after his leader as they strode down the stairs, through the house, and out the front steps. Two saddled horses waited for them. Lucas mounted the one the stable boy handed him and waited while Lafitte issued instructions to the head of his cadre.

Then Lafitte took off without a word, and Lucas followed. He hadn't failed to see the sheathed swords that had been attached to both saddles. They rode for twenty minutes, and as the horse cantered behind Lafitte, Lucas swayed to its rhythm. His anger rode just beneath the surface, but it began to fade as his attention gravitated to the beauty of the passing landscape. The sticky warm air caressed the restlessness in his soul.

He shook off his melancholy when he glanced at his House leader. His view of the road they traveled immediately shifted. With only the two of them, Lucas's role had elevated to bodyguard should they run across an enemy force. Although it was rare these days, it wasn't unheard of, and he gave his new responsibility his full attention.

When they came to a glade next to a lake, Lafitte stopped near a tree and dismounted. Lucas remained on his horse and studied the tree line along the edge of the glade. After a couple of minutes, he was satisfied they were alone. He jumped down and looped the reins over a branch. His brow rose when Lafitte removed his sword. So, this was to be a training exercise. He drew his own sword but held it down, waiting for Lafitte's command.

Lafitte stalked to the middle of the glade, turned, and lifted the sword so it was directly in front of his face. Then he swung it in a wide arc toward the ground.

Lucas performed the same opening sequence, and then they danced.

Lafitte's movements with his blade were swift and decisive, whereas Lucas focused on the precision of his footwork. He moved effortlessly between one form and another. That alone had gotten him out of trouble on numerous occasions. He gave the same care to his measured strikes.

Lafitte lunged, but Lucas blocked and parried with a stab. Lafitte had anticipated the move and jumped back, then attacked with a powerful strike that Lucas barely dodged. They circled each other. He'd been a decent swordsman by the time he'd left home. He was sent to House Lafitte as a trade his father made in exchange for a debt owed. Just another child to use for barter.

An image of his sister crying in her bed resurfaced, and Lucas advanced, the anger making his strikes come faster. Lafitte matched each attack, returning them with equal force. They continued their match until their shirts were wet with sweat from the thick air of the bayou.

Lucas had no idea how long they battled before he fell to his knees, a stitch in his side and his breath heavy. "I surrender."

Lafitte dropped into the grass next to him, tossing his sword aside. "Thank the heavens. I wasn't sure how much longer I could stand."

Lucas glanced at him, and when he saw truth in his leader's gaze, he did his best to hide any emotion.

Lafitte smiled as he drew his arm over his forehead, wiping away the sweat. "I don't remember you being quite that good when you first arrived."

He chuckled. "My father and older brother would agree with you. But the same pattern of training doesn't improve one's abilities. It tends to make them lazy."

Lafitte nodded. "An excellent observation. Something my cadre is quite adept at."

"I'll learn much here."

"And what have you learned this afternoon?"

Lucas considered his words. "Two things, I think. The first is that I can't change what I don't control and what has already happened. And second, a sword fight is good for depleting hot emotions."

"This is why I was so quick to accept your father's proposal. Not to speak ill of the vampire, but he made a bad deal."

"Oh?"

"You are the smartest of your Family. Skill with the sword might have been important a hundred or even fifty years ago, but now? Of course, fighting techniques are critical to protect me and my Family, but war is rare. We are moving into a future where the necessary skills are for business and trade. More so than it's ever been. Industry will be our future."

He stared at Lucas for a moment. "Your father also has the reputation of a man who stands on a hill of sand. His loyalties shift with each step he takes. It's best you remove yourself from that stigma." He stood and brushed off his pants. "We'll soon be moving to my New Orleans manor."

Lucas perked up at the news. Living at the Baton Rouge estate was a luxury, but there was little to do outside his duties and training. Fortunately, Lafitte kept a huge library where Lucas spent most of his free time. But New Orleans was the primary manor for House Renaud, and the largest Renaud Library in the States resided there.

Lafitte must have read his mind. "When you're not on duty, I would like you to spend time at the Renaud Library. I know its purpose is to report on the past, but over the decades, I've learned there are many things to gain from our history. Ingenuity will sort its correct adaptation to modern problems. Like sorting cream from the milk. I believe you have the intellect to be one of those conduits. I want you to study the past and find those lessons that will strengthen House Lafitte.

"I've always wondered why our Family history began as neighbors to House Renaud. But it's simple, really. Many vampire Houses believe that brawn or the size of their army will determine their status and longevity. But they're wrong. Knowledge is the key to survival regardless of who is in power." He shook his head and gave Lucas a rueful smile. "My children say I talk too much. But I argue that I'm the one everyone seeks out at parties."

Lucas returned the grin. "I'm told parties are good for the soul."

"Really? Who said that?"

He thought about it, then chuckled. "I think it was my grandmama."

Lafitte threw his head back and laughed. "Ah, my young vampire, that's another reason you're fitting in so well here."

When they reached the horses, Lafitte took him by the shoulders. "I heard about your sister's betrothal. By your reaction to the letter you received, I assume you also know and are unhappy with the news. There's nothing I can do to help you. You will need to come to terms with this on your own."

He stepped back and gave Lucas a thoughtful look. "Let me leave you with this one bit of information. I know Mason Bertrand quite well. We have the same thoughts about the future and are strong allies. I don't know whether love can grow between him and your sister, but know that he is a good and righteous man who will treat your sister well. He bears no fools, and while this marriage has strengthened his bond to your Father's House, he won't grant access to her if it causes her any pain. She will be protected."

Lucas swallowed. He hadn't known how much he needed to hear that. She would be safe. He blinked back tears and nodded. "Thank you for that, Father. I will be forever grateful for those words."

They rode back to the manor in silence. When they handed off the reins to the stable boys and jogged up the steps to the manor, Lafitte patted him on the back before walking through the door.

Lucas stopped and turned around to view the old plantation. This was a foreign land to him, but for the first time in his life, he had a home.

Chapter Eleven

SERGI STARED out Devon's office window. He never understood why Devon looked out the window so often when making a decision. His own office had no windows. He preferred an environment with no distractions, especially when he was stuck on a particularly difficult issue.

It was also a small office where visitors were limited to two at a time. Devon had offered him something that matched his standing as cadre, but it would only encourage more visitors. The more visitors, the more they tended to linger. He enjoyed his privacy too much for that.

But with Devon out of the country, Simone at Oasis, and Lyra working with Colantha to ease Hamilton's transition from his long imprisonment, Sergi was in charge at the coastal manor.

For the first time, he understood the comfort of allowing his mind to wander as he took in the blooming flowers and the birds that hovered at the feeders. The ocean view didn't bring him the peace it brought to so many others, but it provided the necessary distraction.

Lucas had stopped reporting three days ago. His last cryptic message advised he was in Maryland and had received valuable information. That was enough for Sergi to narrow down three different Houses Lucas might have met with. From the list of Philipe's contacts Lucas had shared before leaving, Sergi had a fair idea of which House. But he hadn't decided whether contacting them would be prudent. Not yet.

Where would Lucas have gone from there? They had been in New York prior to Maryland, so he had to assume either west or south. New Orleans would be a possibility if the information Lucas obtained pointed to House Renaud. If Fiona was their target, they might head to Hazel Green, the location Sergi had given them.

The other possibility worried him the most. What if Lucas had been injured? Or worse? Surely, if Ginger hadn't suffered the same fate as Lucas, assuming they hadn't simply gone silent for another reason, she would have reached out to someone. If she had contacted Cressa, he would have heard from Devon by now. She might have contacted Harlow, but he couldn't see what Harlow could provide that the Family couldn't. Unless she required help from someone with no connections to vampires.

That idea didn't sit well. If he hadn't come to know Ginger as he had, he would assume she'd call the manor immediately if she were in trouble. Of all the humans in the Family, she was the most unpredictable. He snorted. That was saying something considering Cressa and her penchant for making her own decisions.

There were too many possibilities to start considering the worst. Perhaps a look at the map would give him a better idea of what Lucas would have done next. He didn't get any further than waking the computer when the office door burst open.

Simone stormed in, slamming the door shut behind her. "Where's Lucas?"

He motioned for her to take a seat. "I don't know. His last message from three days ago put him in Maryland."

"That matches the information I just received from our security team at House Lewis."

"Lewis." Sergi's brow lifted. "Virginia?"

Simone nodded. "The team has socialized with the Houses in the surrounding states."

Sergi nodded. "To keep abreast of any tension between them. And, of course, with their proximity to D.C., the lobbying alone can become problematic."

"The team leader received a call from an acquaintance from another House asking why someone from House Trelane would visit House Beall."

"That confirms one question. House Beall is on Philipe's contact list. How did our team respond?"

"Basically, that it wasn't any of their business. Then he reported the incident." Simone adjusted her royal-blue caftan and scratched at her matching blue braids piled on her head. He never understood why the tough-as-nails Somalian vampire always dressed like a runway model when not in her guard attire but assumed it was all her time spent in New York and Milan. "I know Devon spoke to you privately about Lucas's assignment. With the House on lockdown, it seemed wise to bring it to your attention."

"To be honest, I was just considering what steps I should take to find them. They've been followed by vampires since New York. Though they might have been following Lucas since Boston and simply didn't make their presence known."

"Or they were waiting for a more opportune time to attack."

Sergi nodded and leaned back in the desk chair, finding it more comfortable than his. Perhaps it was time for an upgrade. "He was taking security precautions, which could explain why he's gone silent."

Simone considered it. "Can you show me his route so far?"

"I was in the process of bringing up the map when you arrived." He used Devon's computer and pushed the display screen sideways so they could both study the image.

Simone pulled her chair closer to the desk. "I assume you're using the old code for messages."

He nodded. "It requires making some educated guesses. From what I can tell, their first stops were at Renaud libraries in Boston and New York. The book was listed in the card catalogs, and the false book identified it as being out for restoration, just like at the other libraries. From there, he'd been meeting with Philipe's contacts, though he didn't share which ones. I can only guess which Houses by the direction Lucas is traveling."

"And you said the first attack was in New York."

Sergi nodded.

Simone grunted. "That would be standard practice. Monitor until you have a feel for your target and then wait for the right moment."

"So far, they've come at Lucas in pairs and were easily dispatched, but we have no idea whether it was Venizi or the Renauds. Though a third player could be involved that we haven't considered."

"They're being tracked."

"I believe so. I'm just not sure how. My best guess is that they have multiple teams."

Simone considered it, her fingernails tapping a quick staccato on the desk. "Half the teams run surveillance. Plant a tracker if they can. The B teams go in for the kill."

"After New York, Lucas began proper security measures, but the back of my neck itches. I don't like it."

"Where would they go after Maryland? Who's the next closest contact on his list?"

"There are two in Georgia if he's heading south. One in Savannah and one outside Atlanta."

"He could have reached those in a day. In three days, he could have been in New Orleans. Is it possible they headed west or back north?"

"There were contacts in Ohio and Missouri."

"Too many possibilities. Are any of these contacts in Houses allied to House Trelane?"

Sergi brought up the list of contacts with their locations. "They all belong to small Houses or are registered rogues. House Beall in Maryland is the largest, and that's not saying much. But I believe they have the strongest ties to us. You should also know I tracked down a female custodian who worked with Philipe in 1925 and might still be in contact with him. Her last known location was Hazel Green, Alabama."

"Do we have Family in the Southeast? I haven't checked the current mission statements."

Sergi nodded. "We have a team of four that went to Saratoga to help a House with their security issues. They need another day or two to finish up, but I can have them reassigned now."

"What are Bella and Jacques up to?"

"They've been dividing their time between the upgrades to the existing safe house and fortification of the new ones."

Simone rubbed her forehead. "I should have known that. It's not that I don't agree with Devon's lockdown orders and ensuring everyone works in pairs, but it depletes our resources in getting things done."

"Where are you with the rogue shifter interviews? That should release some resources to put toward the safe houses."

"I had my last one yesterday. I have a meeting with Decker this afternoon, which was my main reason for driving out. If all goes well, they should be in place by the end of the week. I have rooms being assigned."

"You're thinking we should send Bella and Jacques south?"

Simone sat back and considered the map. "With Renaud being the center of this, the path appears to lead to New Orleans. Ohio and Missouri seem rather arbitrary, but perhaps that's the point. Can you track the rental car?"

He shrugged and checked his tablet. "I started an hour ago but it takes time with the number of aliases I created for him. The most recent rental was reported stolen in a small town south of Maryland about three days ago."

"He must have abandoned the car and rented a new one. Then they went off-grid." Simone studied the map, and Sergi waited for her suggestion, which didn't take long. "Let's get Bella and Jacques to New Orleans. At least they'll be within easy reach."

"Agreed. I'll contact Bella now."

Simone stood. "I want to check on Lyra. Anything I should know before I go up?"

"So far, all has been quiet. And I realize that doesn't mean everything is good."

Simone snickered. "Until this war with Venizi is over, nothing will be good. Just better or worse than the day before."

Sergi couldn't agree more. He texted Bella before returning to stare at the map. If Ginger had been injured, Lucas would have told him, and would probably have returned home or found a healer. But Sergi didn't see Lucas going dark for that.

What if Lucas had been injured? What would Ginger do? He was still considering that fateful scenario when a knock came. Bella stuck her head in.

"You wanted to see me?"

"That was fast."

"I just left the safe house and was on my way to the new one."

"Come in. I want you to take a look at this." He filled her in on his discussion with Simone and their deliberations on where Lucas and Ginger might be.

Bella sat back, arms crossed over her chest as she studied the map. She appeared almost casual in her assessment, but her leg bounced with boundless energy. "If he picked up valuable information from House Beall, then maybe he's getting close to something. That would explain an increase in attacks. Whoever's sending the teams of vampires might be getting nervous, and they're most likely increasing the size of the teams. Lucas could be hiding, waiting them out."

"Why wouldn't he check in?"

She shrugged. "If they don't know how they're being tracked, maybe they're not confident with the burners."

"That's a possibility. What if one of them is injured?"

Bella slid him a glance, knowing quite well the other reason no one reached out was because they were both dead. "You want me to go find them?"

"It's a long shot at best. But if we get word, I'd rather they have a friend close by."

She nodded. "Am I taking Jacques?"

"Yes. Keep a low profile. Simone and I agree they're most likely heading south. I sent you the list of locations where they might be headed in addition to where their last rental car was ditched. Maybe you can pick up a trail."

"Doesn't Lucas have a friend in New Orleans?"

"Two, actually. Lafitte and Romero, but he's closest with Romero."

"Do you think he'll mind if I reach out?"

"No. I'll give him a heads-up and send you his favorite meeting spot. He's not aware of the book as far as I know."

"Understood. When do we leave?"

"There's a red-eye that leaves in four hours. I'll have the flight information and your list of aliases within the hour."

"Got it." She rose and was almost to the door when Sergi stopped her.

"If Lucas is injured—"

With a feral smile, Bella finished his statement. "Then the only thing standing between him and a team of vampires is a human female."

Chapter Twelve

THE BEAST HOVERED between wakefulness and sleep. The healing had begun, but the beast was hungry. It felt his master stir, but it wasn't his time.

It needed more rest. More healing. More blood.

It roared with hunger for the sweet nectar.

Unable to rise, the beast growled with impatience. Too weak to take control, it slumbered in the darkness and waited for blood.

LUCAS PUSHED past the line of men and women lined up at the side entrance to the restaurant. "Make way. If you wish to meet with Romero, you need an appointment. Otherwise, stand back."

"Some of us are here for you, honey. What time do you get off?" one woman shouted through the crowd.

He blushed and glanced back at Romero, who grinned at him. Great.

"What's your name, hot stuff?" another yelled.

Once they were inside and several feet from the door, silence overtook the group of four as they made their way to their usual table at the back of the restaurant. Romero held court four nights a week at the establishment, and he paid the owner handsomely for the service.

Romero slapped him on the back. "Seems my new bodyguard might require one of his own."

Lucas didn't say anything as he performed a sweep of the room in coordination with the other two bodyguards. When he finally nodded to Romero, assuring him the room was clean, his new House leader laughed.

"You need to relax a little. There's nothing wrong with smiling at the women, who obviously find you quite charming. I must say, I'm a bit jealous."

"Sorry, Father."

Romero rolled his eyes. "Again, with the Father stuff. If you have to be so formal, at least say sir. Although I prefer Romero."

"Yes, Romero." Lucas held out the chair for him. After Romero took a seat, he added, "And I find females are just as likely to carry a dagger and can be just as skilled at using it."

Romero's laughter filled the room. "Someday you'll have to tell me the story of how you discovered that. Until then, tell the chef I'm ready for the first course. And tonight, I'm in the mood for a Bordeaux. I'll take my first meeting once the meal is served."

"As you wish." Lucas was uncomfortable using Romero's first name, so for now, he would avoid salutations until required. He strode to the kitchen, constantly scanning for a threat. After seventy-five years of service to House Lafitte, he found himself at a new House, though he was no stranger to Romero, who was a good friend to Lafitte. Three strong Houses, including House Renaud, might seem too much for New Orleans, but the Houses had strong ties to each other going back centuries.

Two months ago, Lafitte had asked him to a private dinner. The two had grown close over the years, and Lucas had become a trusted sounding board for Lafitte, though he wasn't cadre. Lafitte waited until they nursed brandy on the patio to ask if Lucas would be interested in moving to another House as an exchange. It was common for Houses to trade one or more vampires for another, depending on the needs of the House and the experience and knowledge of the vampires.

Romero had recently taken over as leader of his House, and due to his business interests, sketchy as some of them were, and his work with the local vampire community in granting favors and services, he required a strong collection of bodyguards.

Lafitte understood Lucas's desire to one day be part of a cadre, and it could be decades away, if not a century or more, if he remained part of Lafitte's House. Lucas had been happy in his service to the House, but not many leaders would care enough to find opportunities for those under them.

So, the deal was struck. Romero was a modern vampire in every way and treated his Family well. And while not part of his cadre, being a personal bodyguard was considered an esteemed position. It was a valuable skill for his resume.

After delivering the message to the kitchen, he returned to his post, standing behind Romero, while the other two bodyguards took positions to the left and right. After four hours of an extended meal and several meetings, Romero shook hands with a young female vampire, promising to look into her issue at his earliest convenience.

They left through a back exit where the limo waited outside. Romero was a well-known player, even among the humans, which was evident by the handful of groupies waiting outside, but there was little time for them to call out before the limo pulled away.

"Landon, I'd like to go to the club." Romero settled back and poured a glass of scotch. "Lucas, I have an assignment for you. I understand you spend quite a bit of time at the Renaud Library."

"Yes, sir."

"How familiar are you with vampiric law?"

"I've reviewed all the volumes and understand the basic tenets. I would say my knowledge runs wide if not deep."

"Father was the legal expert in the House. With him gone, I'll need someone to fill that gap. Genevieve, the last female I met with this evening, requires assistance with the laws involving property. She's having a contentious battle with a small House over it. Can you refresh my knowledge in that area by Friday?"

The request shocked but also pleased him. Vampiric law was an area he'd become interested in after reading hundreds of history texts during his service with Lafitte. "That shouldn't be a problem."

"Excellent. Now, let's all relax before heading home."

The club was one of Romero's favorites. The owner didn't discriminate and allowed humans, shifters, and vampires to congregate. It was high-end and fiercely patrolled by in-house security to prevent fighting or other unpleasantries—like taking advantage of the humans. Romero had a private lounge on the second floor that overlooked the club.

Once Romero was safely in his lounge, the bodyguards could take a break. Not that they ever took a real break, but with the in-house security and privacy of the lounges, Romero encouraged them to have a few drinks and bring in women if they chose.

That evening, Romero chased the other two bodyguards out, suggesting they find someone to dance with. "I love coming to the club to watch the crowd enjoy themselves without actually having to be included."

"It's probably the closest you can get to being among others while letting your guard down. So to speak." Lucas sat back, accepting the glass of scotch the attendant handed him before exiting.

Romero chuckled. "Exactly. Now, why don't you try that?"

Lucas shifted uncomfortably, which made Romero's smile widen as he shook his head.

"I asked the others to leave because I wanted to speak with you privately."

Lucas hadn't been with the House long enough to know whether he should be worried, so he just nodded.

"You've only been in my service for a few short months, but I'm quite impressed with you." He waved his hand before Lucas could respond. "I'm aware of the House you were born into, but I take Lafitte's recommendations quite seriously. You've risen above the difficulties one faces being the youngest male in a House. I gave you the assignment to study vampiric law not just to assist in House matters, but to strengthen your assets."

"I appreciate the opportunity."

"We'll also increase your training in martial arts. You've developed excellent fighting skills, especially in hand-to-hand, but I think they can be improved."

"I agree. Not many of Lafitte's guard has that skill."

"I'll introduce you to the Baron. He's a master black belt in several disciplines. He's out of town a great deal, so scheduling will be difficult, but you might find me a worthy opponent in the training room."

Lucas lifted a brow. "Now I'm intrigued."

"Excellent."

A knock at the door made them both turn, and Lucas gripped the arms of his chair in anticipation of defending Romero. The in-house security man stationed at the door popped his head in. "Sorry to disturb you, sir. There's a Devon Trelane asking to join you."

Romero jumped up. "Yes, yes, let him in."

Lucas stood, unaware of the vampire. Trelane strode in and quickly scanned the room before grinning widely at Romero. The two vampires hugged, slapping each other on the back. Romero grasped Trelane's forearms while giving him a long appraisal.

"You're looking good. What brings you to the South?"

"A small matter for a friend. I head back home in the morning, but since I was close to New Orleans, I had to stop by."

"Of course. I would have been hurt otherwise. Have you seen Lafitte?"

"I had dinner with him."

"Excellent. And how is it assuming leadership of the House again?"

"More difficult than I imagined."

Romero chuckled. "As you should have expected."

Trelane shook his head. "I did, but I'd hoped my father's legacy and my alliances before my...shall we call it a detour...would have been enough of a foundation. But, House by House, the meetings are becoming friendlier."

"Gossip spreads quicker through the Houses than the scent of jasmine through New Orleans."

Trelane slapped Romero on the arm. "And this time, it's an added benefit to my long list of atonements."

Romero turned to Lucas. "My apologies. Let me introduce you to my newest bodyguard, Lucas Maynard. Lucas, this is Devon Trelane, leader of House Trelane."

The name clicked. "Guildford Trelane's son?"

Trelane smiled and held out his hand. "The same. And I believe you're one of Magnus's sons."

"The youngest."

Trelane glanced at Romero. "Interesting."

"A recent acquisition to the Family from Lafitte's House."

Lucas received another studied appraisal.

"Quite interesting." Trelane took a seat on the other side of Romero as Lucas poured him a scotch.

The conversation turned to current events within various Houses, which Lucas soaked in. Not being part of a cadre meant this depth of information was only disseminated through assignments or word of mouth among Family members. Even then, it was diluted by rumors and suppositions. To hear two House leaders discuss strategies, politics, and relationships was like a gift from above. When they included Lucas in the conversation and listened intently to his comments, he couldn't help but sit taller.

They were laughing in response to one of Trelane's stories when the bodyguards returned a couple of hours later, each with a woman—one a vampire and the other a shifter, if Lucas had to guess.

Romero looked at the bodyguards and smiled. "Why don't you take the limo and head home." He glanced at Trelane. "You have a car?"

Trelane glanced at his watch. "Yes. It won't be a problem to drop you home."

The three of them spoke for another hour before Trelane stood. "I have a plane to catch at sunrise. Shall we call it a night?"

When they exited the club, the streets were quiet with dawn a couple of hours away.

"I drove myself. The car is just down the street." Trelane led the way.

Romero sucked in a deep breath. "Even at this hour, the scent of jasmine and beignets fill the air."

Lucas brought up the rear as the two leaders strode side-by-side. He scanned the shadows. They made it two more blocks before he heard the footsteps—hurried and coming from behind them.

The three turned as one to face four vampires who spread out as they slowed their approach. If they were surprised to see Trelane, they didn't show it. Lucas wondered who they'd come for.

Each side took a moment to size up the situation, then time stilled as they waited for someone to make the first move. Trelane didn't appear to be in a waiting mood, and a dagger slipped into his hand as he charged the two in the middle.

Romero raced off to his right while Lucas turned toward the vampire on the left, who carried a sword. They had come to take heads and nothing less. Lucas ran straight for him, then ducked as soon as he saw his opponent lift his arm. He barreled into the vampire, hitting hard with fists to the midsection before slamming one into a jaw. The blade fell from the vampire's grip, and Lucas kicked it away.

The vampire shoved Lucas off, landing a blow that knocked him to his knees. When the vampire kicked out, Lucas blocked his leg, knocking his adversary off-balance. The few seconds gave him time to get on his feet and take a quick glance at Trelane and Romero, who were holding their own. One of the opposing vampires had taken a dagger to the kidney and was trying to remove the blade, which was just out of reach.

Lucas stepped back when another strike came and, pivoting, swept the other vampire's legs out from under him. He stabbed him in the gut, aiming for the liver. Lucas ran for the sword he'd kicked away. He must have missed the liver because he heard the vampire two steps behind him.

He grabbed the sword and, still on his feet, twisted, swinging his weapon like a bat. The vampire wasn't expecting it, and his eyes went wide seconds before his head toppled to the ground.

With a lust for blood, Lucas turned to find Romero finishing off his opponent. Trelane had taken the sword from the vampire who was struggling to get on his hands and knees, blood dripping heavily from his midsection. Trelane didn't waste time. He swung the sword like an executioner meting out justice.

Lucas turned to the last enemy vampire, who managed to stand and pull a dagger from his boot. He wanted to take the vampire's head, but instead, slammed the side of the blade against it. The vampire dropped to his hands and knees, clearly dazed.

Romero staggered to Lucas's side, blood leaking from his left arm. He managed to check the injury before Romero pushed him away. It was a deep gash but not life-threatening and would heal fast enough.

Trelane picked the remaining vampire up by the back of his shirt and pushed him against a nearby building. "Who sent you?"

The vampire smiled, his teeth red with blood. "Venizi sends his regards."

Without a second hesitation, Trelane stepped back and swung the sword, and as the sound of metal hitting stone reverberated around them, the head bounced and rolled a few feet away. Trelane turned to Romero. "Sorry, my friend, for bringing trouble to your door."

Romero's eyes glowed an electric green, and he grinned at his friend. "I can always count on you to show me a good time." He spat on one of the dead vampires. "I'll be sure to let Lafitte know where Venizi can pick up his vampires." He glanced around and pointed to the alley. "There should be a dumpster down there."

Lucas wasn't surprised Romero would call Lafitte. As the largest House in New Orleans, Lafitte had to be told of Venizi's transgression of entering the city without acknowledgment. Without any witnesses, the Council would never officially hear of the incident, but Venizi wouldn't be welcome in the city for some time—if ever.

They worked together and piled the bodies and heads into one of the dumpsters. Venizi wouldn't bother collecting them, so they'd either end up in the landfill or the police would eventually file them away as unexplained murders of unknown indigents.

Romero wiped his forehead. "I assume they thought you'd be alone."

"I suppose I should have brought a bodyguard."

Romero slapped him on the back. "You've always been one to live dangerously."

Trelane turned to Lucas and held out his hand. "You have my thanks, Lucas Maynard."

Lucas shook it. "Any time, Mr. Trelane."

Trelane laughed. "I think you've earned the right to call me Devon."

Chapter Thirteen

INCREDIBLE PAIN.

He'd felt worse, but the pulsing, burning ache deep inside made it difficult to focus on when that might have been. The beast was restless. And they were both hungry.

His memories were dull and clouded, and he couldn't remember what he'd been doing before waking. What was the last thing he remembered? It was difficult to think past the pounding in his head—a red flag that he was low on blood.

Ginger.

Where was Ginger?

His first instinct was to sit up, but he couldn't move his body. He was weak as a newly made vampire. That wasn't good. Think. They'd had lunch, or what passed for food, at a small-town bar. He'd gone outside. That was it. He'd forgotten his wallet.

Vampires had been waiting for him.

His eyes opened, and though he couldn't move his head, he glanced around the unfamiliar room. A cheap motel. That was unfortunate. He could have used the room service attendant for blood except for the problem of not being mobile.

A warm body moved next to him, and he managed to nudge

his head enough to see the dark-brown tendrils spread across his chest. He released a breath he didn't know he'd been holding. She was here. Something was going his way. His arms were plastered at his side, but he lifted his head again, this time with more movement. It was only for a few seconds, but it was enough to see the bandage on his upper left arm. The rest of him was covered with a blanket.

He'd also caught more details of the room. A shopping bag sat on the table by the window, a cooler was on the dresser across from the bed, and, in the corner, a duffel had been placed on a suitcase rack.

How did he get from the parking lot at the bar to this motel room? He closed his eyes, and bits of memory stirred. Someone dragging him. Ginger begging him to take a step. Blood dripping into his mouth, then him sucking the sweet nectar that tasted of her.

His eyes shot open. She'd fed him with her own blood.

She moved. It was subtle, but he recognized the signs of her waking.

Then her head popped up. "Lucas?"

She pushed herself up and stared down at him. Her face still scrunched from sleep, her gaze full of worry, but then she smiled.

Somehow, he knew everything would be alright.

She ran a hand over his face and pushed a loose strand of hair away. "Morning. It's good to see you awake."

When he didn't say anything, her smile faded. "Can you hear me? Can you talk?" She picked up his hand and released it. It fell on the bed with a thud. "You still can't move."

He licked his teeth and the roof of his mouth. "No." His throat was raspy, and she twisted around to grab a bottle of water.

"Will water help?"

He nodded, irrationally pleased by the small movement.

She knelt and strained to lift his upper body to stuff a pillow under him. After she drank the first few sips of water, she tipped the bottle to his lips. He drank two small swallows before she took it away and dried his chin and neck where the water had dribbled.

She waited a minute, mumbled soothing words, then lifted the bottle once more. He was allowed the same small amount as before, and she repeated drying his face before setting the bottle aside.

When she turned back, she gripped a dagger.

His eyes went wide.

"Don't bother trying to avoid this. You have major injuries that are still leaking blood. You're obviously too weak to do anything more than open your eyes, and the jury is still out on whether you can speak. We've spent too much time in one place, and I can't move you anymore. You need to be able to walk. Or crawl. I'm not particular. But you will not fight me on this."

With her lecture firmly stated, and his voice not strong enough to protest, she sliced her palm and held it against his mouth. He'd never wanted to take blood from her. A dangerous path indeed. But they were in survival mode, so he took what she offered.

The beast didn't argue when her palm reached his lips. And it was the beast who suckled. At first, with hard, deep pulls, then slowing—the taste of her blood intoxicating. During it all, she ran her hand through his hair. Then he remembered nothing at all.

The next time he opened his eyes, the TV played a black and white movie, the volume set low. Ginger hunched over the table, a large to-go cup, most likely coffee, within easy reach. She stared at a travel map and occasionally scratched something down in a notebook. Every so often, she would peer through the sheer drapes at the parking lot—either daydreaming or watching for vampires. Probably both.

As if sensing eyes upon her, she turned to him, and that smile that seemed only for him lit her face. "Hello, sleepyhead."

"Where are we?"

"In a small town about fifty miles west of Durham." She stood and stretched. Her sweatshirt rose above the waistband of her leggings, giving him a view of her belly.

He groaned with frustration at not being able to hold her. At not being able to protect her.

She climbed onto the bed and knelt next to him, peering down with a questioning stare. "You seem better."

He lifted his arm and managed to set it on her knee. "More motion than the last time I woke. How long was I out?"

"This time? About two hours."

"Since the attack?"

"A couple of days. Do you want to try to sit up?"

After some effort, most of it supplied by Ginger, Lucas leaned against more pillows with a better view of the room.

"I'll check your bandages in a couple of hours and feed you again."

He opened his mouth then reconsidered when she planted her fists on her hips. Her eyes squinted with the same look his sister gave him when she was ready for a fight.

"Will you lie next to me?"

Her spirit changed instantly, and without another word, she settled herself next to him.

"How safe are we?" It was time for him to know how much trouble they were in.

"I found a tracker on the rental car. If the vamps are following it, they should be on their way to Idaho, but I imagine it didn't take them long to figure out they got punked. I dumped our duffel and everything in it and started over. I think we should get a different rental once we decide on our destination."

"What happened in the parking lot?"

It took a moment before she spoke. When she did, everything spilled out so fast he had a hard time keeping up. He listened without questioning, from the moment she found him in the lot, to hiding the two dead vampires, getting him in the car, then covering their tracks and finding a cheap motel in a small town off the beaten track. This wasn't the first time she amazed him. Her actions weren't from Sergi's or any other vampire's playbook. They just didn't think the same way as humans. Standard procedure when being chased by an opposing force with deadly intent would be to continually change cars and find the fastest route to an allied House, which, if driving, would be the interstate, not the back roads.

"What's the map for?"

"You need blood donors or a healer. Preferably both. I figured New Orleans, but I don't know what Houses might be between here and there that could help. I've been reviewing various routes. The smaller state roads are the best, but they take longer."

"Have you contacted Sergi?"

She bit her lip. "I was worried someone might be able to trace the call, even with the new burner I got. And I didn't want to give away our location."

He nodded. Chances were slim anyone could trace the call, but that didn't make it impossible. She was alone, and he was nothing but dead weight at the moment. He couldn't fault her decision.

"You're doing everything right. We'll contact him once I'm mobile."

She relaxed, and they sat in silence. He breathed in her essence, freshly washed with a soap scent he didn't recognize. This moment reminded him of the occasional mornings he could sleep in. They would lay in bed together, talking about random things that didn't mean much of anything, yet revealed a bit more of themselves to each other. And though he couldn't move, this was the safest he'd felt since they'd arrived in Boston.

"Tell me a story."

She snorted. "A fairy tale, perhaps?"

"Something about you. I know your mother is alive and living in Seattle, but you've never mentioned any siblings."

She tensed for a split second. If he had to guess, it was a reflexive response she'd never completely been able to erase. He recognized it because he carried a personal familiarity with the sensation.

"I have a brother and sister, both several years older than me." She moved away to sit against the headboard, her knees pulled up, but her arm still pressed into him. "My dad called me their love child because they'd had me late. Mom thought it was funny, but my brother and sister became uncomfortable any time it was mentioned. It might have been for some other reason, but I cringed every time Mom or Dad said it. It was as if my brother and sister weren't made out of love but for some requirement, like checking something off a list."

She hugged her arms around her knees. "I guess it sounds kind of petty now, but I never felt like they wanted me around. One of them always had to babysit me rather than go out with their friends. Most of the time, it was like I didn't belong. At that early age, a few years is a huge gap between siblings. I don't know. It's kind of hard to explain. But I rebelled." She released a sharp laugh. "They say the youngest in the family tends to be the wildest. So, I guess I fit the pattern."

He wanted to hold her and share words of comfort. That she belonged somewhere now. "I don't think it's petty. To a child, those things stay with them. It's hard to shake."

"It sounds like you might know something about that. You don't talk about your family."

He shrugged. "Not much to tell. Two older brothers. One younger sister and another who died not long after her birth. As the youngest male, it was expected of me to go to another House. Find a place for myself."

Ginger curled into him again, her head resting on his shoulder. "You miss your sister."

He was going to deny it as he so often did. But Ginger was someone he wanted to share everything with. The only one. "I miss Rosalynn a great deal. But I didn't leave on friendly terms with the family."

"Rosalynn?" He'd felt her tense when he first said the name but, as she repeated it, she relaxed and laid her head against his shoulder. "Rosalynn is your sister." Another moment passed before she squeezed his hand. "It's a beautiful name."

"For a beautiful baby sister, who was like my shadow. But, similar to you, my brothers were much older than me, and while there was an age gap between me and Rosalynn, we shared many happy times together." He smiled as he remembered his sister's childhood, but then an old anger poked at him. Maybe he wasn't ready to discuss something that happened so long ago. "She's married now to the eldest son of another House. My father didn't have the sense to arrange business relationships with other Houses in order to make ours stronger. He fell upon old traditions of marriage between Houses to build strength and close allies."

"You didn't approve of the marriage."

"She was in love with someone else at the time. From what I knew of her beau, he was in love with her as well. But he was only the second son of a House, and though it was a powerful House, it wasn't good enough for Father. My sister had a tender heart and had been raised to do what she was told."

"Is she happy?"

His heart beat painfully at her simple question. And it reignited the shame he'd locked away. "I don't know. I've written, but it's been some time. I know she's comfortable and well-cared for, but happy? I hope so."

She gripped his hand. "That's so sad. I don't think I'd have the strength to marry for the sake of someone else's convenience."

"You would have stood up to your father. Of that, I have no doubt."

"Oh, absolutely. And that's the obvious way of showing strength. But to do what you believe your family needs at the expense of your own happiness is its own kind of strength. Whether we agree with the practice or not."

He hadn't considered his sister's actions from that perspective.

Regardless, was it fair to force that burden on someone for such a high sacrifice? "I don't think Lyra would have agreed so easily if Guildford had agreed that a union with Venizi was necessary. You walked away from your family to find the peace and freedom to become your own person. I think everyone should have the right to do that."

"But sometimes it comes at a cost that not everyone is willing to pay. And some are still paying for it."

"Are we talking about Rosalynn or you?"

Though she didn't respond, her scent changed. There was more to the story that she wasn't comfortable sharing. Was she embarrassed or unsure what he'd think? He didn't want to push and changed the topic to something he'd always been curious about.

"How did you meet Cressa?"

She sat up and leaned away again. Their discussion made her jumpier than he'd ever seen her. One minute, needing comfort, the next, needing distance. Then it hit him. When the story was about her, she pushed away, still touching, yet retaining her space. Perhaps a flight response. Then, she snuggled back when it was his turn to reveal something. As if she wanted to reassure him she was there.

And there he was, unable to hold her when he sensed she needed it the most.

"We met at the Lowdown."

"That's the bar near your apartment."

She nodded. "It was Bulldog. Cressa was new to the Hollows and, being a single white girl, he was all about safety in numbers. Or maybe it was to help me."

"In what way?"

She picked at her nails, then chewed on one. He hadn't seen her do that since the first day they'd met. This was going to be bad, but he couldn't think of anything she could have done that would make her any less dear to him. But he gave her the time to tell the story in her own way.

"When I first left Seattle, I drove south, stopping to see the cities and sights along the way. The only trips our family ever took were down the coast to the same city every year. I wanted to head someplace warmer without all the gray skies and rain. I don't know why I stopped in Santiga Bay, but it was a decent-sized city on the coast, which I still love. The coast, I mean." She relaxed at this part of her story. A good time for her. "I thought I'd stay for a bit then move on. I found a decent job, but the edge of the Hollows was the only place I could afford, and it was a tiny studio at that.

"The job was great until the company ran into hard times and had to let some of the staff go, which, yep, included me. It didn't take long to land another job. The pay was half of what I'd been making, and it was tough to make rent each month. I found a second job but it still wasn't enough. Mom wanted me to come home." She wiped at an eye. "I felt like such a failure. Of course, I was too proud, or too stupid, to tuck tail and go. I had a boyfriend. God, what a mistake that guy was. Before I figured that out, I let him move in to share rent. He ended up buying a bunch of stuff that turned out he couldn't afford. I thought he was dealing weed or something, and to my shame, I didn't complain about the new furniture, big screen TV, or bitchin' entertainment center. Not until one day when he wasn't home and the loan shark came calling."

She wiped a tear away and didn't look at him, preferring to stare straight ahead.

"Turns out, the asshole went out for that proverbial pack of smokes and never came back. He'd run off when he couldn't pay the loan shark. But there I was in an apartment full of the remnants of his loan, and I ended up on the hook for the debt."

Lucas didn't have any words. He understood how loan sharks worked. They didn't care who paid them as long as they got their money. With Ginger at her most vulnerable, she was an easy mark.

"So, there I was, owing a debt with interest compounding daily. I'd never see my way clear, and Sorrento knew it. The only chance I had to make the payments and eventually pay down the loan was to dance at one of his clubs." She sniffled and turned her face away. "When I met Cressa, I'd been working at the club for a couple of months. It was another four months before she found out why I was dancing there. She was already Pandora. Had been long before she moved to the Hollows. She asked me to move in with her because she had a spare room. Said she could use help with the rent. Then she did the unthinkable."

"She spoke with Sorrento and took over your debt."

She whipped around so quickly, Lucas reflexively flinched. It was one of those good news with bad timing moments. His ability to flinch was a sign the healing was almost complete and he should be mobile soon. But the timing was bad.

Ginger's eyes widened, and she leaned back. "Oh, my god." Her expression quickly changed, and she lowered her gaze to stare at her chewed-up nails. "I wasn't going to do anything."

"I know that." He touched her arm. "Seriously, you took me by surprise. Did you see me flinch?" He found distraction was the best policy in these situations.

A small grin appeared. "I did. I think that's why I was so alarmed by your reaction." Her smile widened. "How long before you can completely move?"

"I don't know, but it should be soon. Maybe by morning."

"You should take more blood before we go to bed." She must have thought he'd refuse because she forged ahead. "Don't argue with me. I need you up, and if not in fighting mode, strong enough to get in and out of the car on your own. Then we can get moving. I'm getting this itch that we've stayed too long as it is. So, you're getting blood whether you want it or not."

He couldn't help but grin. He wasn't sure if his facial muscles changed, but he could feel the grin just the same. "Yes, ma'am."

She growled. "Just look at us. We're sharing the most

depressing stories of our lives. No wonder we're on edge. From now on, not one more sad tale. Not on this trip. Deal?" She held out her hand as if to shake on it.

"You're kidding, right?" He tried to lift his hand, but the single flinch had drained his reserve.

"Too soon?" She crooned and stepped off the bed. "I didn't hear that we had a deal."

"I'll think about it."

"Do you think you'll be okay for a few minutes while I run over to the diner? They're pretty quick with the meals."

"Sure. I'll just lay about and appear menacing if anyone breaks down the door."

"That's the spirit." She gave him a peck on the cheek, then one on the mouth before prancing to the door. She gave him a cheeky grin before disappearing.

She didn't fool him. The fact she could flit between being sad to having such an upbeat attitude was what made Ginger so special. And that was before adding in her compassion. She still hurt inside and wasn't happy about the debt Cressa took on. The debt Cressa now owed Devon. He'd wait until he was fully healed and back to his fighting strength. Then he'd find a way to make that pain go away. He owed her that much.

Chapter Fourteen

BELLA STRODE out of the jetway and into the busy New Orleans airport with Jacques at her side. She didn't stop to scan the crowd but continued toward the exit, her messenger-style bag slung over her shoulder, a small duffel at her side, and the pounding of her military-style boots muffled on the carpeted floor. Jacques waited a beat then followed behind with a single duffel, staying within a couple paces of her.

She didn't expect anything to happen at the airport with so many people around, but it was a standard protocol the two of them used. When they walked one in front of the other, they had more visibility to scan the crowd for trouble. In this case, vampires who might be waiting to follow them.

Sergi had called ahead and arranged for a rental car to be waiting for them at curbside under one of her aliases. Friends in all the right places. She thanked the shifter, who handed her the keys then bumped fists with her before running to a waiting car. Once they were gone, she dropped her bags in the back seat while Jacques did the same before sliding behind the wheel.

"It's been some time since I've been here," Jacques said as he pulled into the stream of cars exiting the airport.

Bella pulled out her tablet and brought up a map. "Follow the exit for I-10 East. It will take us straight to the Quarter." She kept the tablet open and pulled down the visor, thankful for the makeup mirror, which she positioned to watch the cars behind them.

"What time did Sergi set up the meet with Romero?"

"Nine this evening." Jacques glanced at his watch. "We have time to check the library."

She tapped her fingers on the tablet. Lafitte had been advised of their arrival, so he shouldn't be sending any cars to trail them. Sergi gave her the green light to visit the Renaud Library and look for the *De første dage* as long as they weren't being followed. Time to bait the hook.

"Circle the neighborhood a few times. Let's get comfortable with the streets and see if we shake any tails. Then I'd like to get checked in."

He nodded, and they drove in companionable silence. They had been partnered for so long, the Family teased them as if they were an old married human couple. While the sentiment was accurate, their relationship wasn't intimate—at least not at the level one would suspect. In reality, they were more like two siblings who shared every detail with each other.

After thirty minutes of driving around the Quarter and nearby neighborhoods, Jacques pulled into the hotel parking structure, ignoring the valet so they'd have quick access to the car if needed. Once checked in, Bella stared at the Mississippi River from their twelfth-floor suite, letting Jacques handle logistics.

"I informed Sergi we arrived and weren't followed. He says the library is still your call. No word from Lucas."

When she didn't say anything, Jacques stepped behind her and rubbed her shoulders. "He's fine. If they've been running into trouble at each stop, they're probably lying low until the trail is cold."

She bent her head to the left and then right as Jacques

continued to work his magic at relieving her stress. Lucas was a well-trained soldier, and Ginger had improved quickly with Sergi's training. However, while Ginger had been put into precarious situations in the past, Bella wasn't convinced of the human's stamina as the attacks increased.

"I won't be able to sit in this room for another eight hours. Let's check the library and see what dust we kick up."

He slapped her back. "That's the spirit, ma chère."

"Ugh. You're not going to start speaking French everywhere, are you?" She picked up her messenger bag and strode to the door.

He followed behind, chuckling. "Only to those who understand it. How often do I get to speak it otherwise?"

"Only every time you find Devon alone while he's drinking cognac. Even Cressa knows to leave the two of you to jabber away."

She smiled as she headed for the elevator, knowing he was grinning ear to ear. He enjoyed annoying her, and if nothing else, it took her mind off Lucas.

"WHAT DO YOU THINK?" Jacques asked.

Bella scanned the half-full parking lot at Renaud's Library. "I think we're in luck that it's busy."

"I agree. I don't see anyone in the vehicles. Do you?"

"No. If they have anyone watching, they might be inside. That's where they were when Lucas and Ginger were followed in San Francisco."

"Then perhaps we avoid the tea room."

Bella snorted as she exited the rental. She took another scan of the area, this time focusing on the trees and the VIP parking lot where several other cars and two limos were parked. "Maybe they're having a conference or a special luncheon."

"Even better. It will make it easier to see if we're followed."

She couldn't disagree, and they took a leisurely stroll up the steps. Jacques handled the receptionist while she monitored the activity on the first floor. A group of vampires stood down a side hall where a table had been set up in front of one of the conference rooms. That confirmed one special function in addition to three small gatherings in the tea room, all of them in full conversation. Nothing that warranted alarm bells.

Jacques stepped next to her and handed her a map. He pointed to the back cover where special events were listed. "The conference is a lecture on tracing one's ancestral roots. There's another one scheduled at three p.m. for changes in vampire law over the centuries."

She chuckled. "We should have brought Anna."

Jacques smiled and directed her toward the stairs.

"I didn't know you were familiar with the libraries."

He shrugged. "It's been a long time since I've been in one. My birth Family was always interested in learning more about our ancestors. I spent a great deal of time running through the stacks."

"I'm surprised you and Lucas haven't visited one together."

"Just because I spent many hours in one doesn't mean I found it interesting. Except for the books that spoke of battles, of course."

"Of course."

They took the stairs down to the third floor and went straight to the card catalog. Bella let Jacques flip through the cards while she watched his back. She'd noted several guests on the second floor, but other than themselves and one custodian she'd spotted down one of the rows, the third floor appeared empty.

"Got it." Jacques stepped past her and turned right down the second aisle. He slowed a third of the way down, tapping his fore-finger against each shelf and then each book until he stopped. He pulled down a book from the second shelf and, shaking his head, opened it to show her the fabric-lined cavity with a single note.

"Don't tell me," Bella sneered. "It's out for restoration."

"Yep." He closed the fake book and reshelved it.

"That pretty much closes the book on whether we have a conspiracy."

"It's hard to read it any other way. This is the main Renaud Library in the States. The only question is whether the entire Family is involved or a specific faction."

"Let's see if we catch a tail back to the hotel. We need to update Sergi."

AFTER BELLA ENJOYED a late lunch with Jacques on the suite's balcony, they played gin rummy. Jacques always carried a deck of cards. He had once shared that it began when he was a chauffeur in his last House. He spent most of his time sitting around and found a deck of cards easy to carry while providing sufficient entertainment.

She assumed the cards were only part of the story, and it explained why he preferred to drive on their assignments. If they went out together during their time off, he let her drive. She thought it curious, but after working with him for so long, she'd come to understand what it was really all about. He still considered himself a chauffeur and not the invaluable team member he'd become.

He believed the only reason he was allowed to participate in Devon's cadre meetings was because of her. If Devon didn't think he belonged because he brought no value, it wouldn't matter that Jacques was partnered with cadre, he wouldn't have gotten into Devon's office. And the kicker was—Bella had no idea what to do about it.

When it was time, Jacques drove them to a tea house along Lake Pontchartrain. They were directed to a table for two in one of the back rooms with tall windows that overlooked the water. Along the opposite side of the room, Bella noted the vampire who sat on one side of the table while a couple sat across from him. With three bodyguards surrounding him, it was obvious Romero was holding court.

Jacques ordered an appetizer and a bottle of wine then gazed at the lake while Bella studied Romero.

"From what Lucas told me once, Romero spends his days caring for the Family businesses, but at night, he runs his side job of granting favors." Bella wasn't sure what Lucas saw in this vampire to remain in contact with him, even if he'd been in service to his House. "From what I understand, the small favors are to help the average vampire who has issues the Council wouldn't be interested in reviewing. I don't know if I believe it."

Jacques held his answer until after the server decanted and poured the wine.

"Lucas has a great deal of respect for Romero," Jacques said. "On one hand, he could be telling you what he believes because he's seen and heard it himself. Or, if you want to play the other side, his respect for the vampire is blinding him to reality."

She took a sip of wine then rolled her eyes, irritated she picked up the habit from Ginger. "I can't tell you how helpful that was."

He grinned. "Anytime. I have many opinions to share."

She snorted. "Let's not go there."

They nibbled on their appetizers and were finishing their last sips of wine when one of Romero's bodyguards flagged them over.

Jacques assisted Bella into her chair, and when he sat, he turned toward her, letting Romero know she was the one in charge.

Romero didn't miss a beat and waved at his bodyguard, who poured a brandy for them, giving Bella a gentle smile that reminded her of what a handsome man he was. No doubt an excellent negotiator and possibly a manipulator as well.

"This is a beautiful location." Bella returned his smile.

"A better venue than before. When Lucas was in the Family, I held court at a restaurant off the Quarter. Unfortunately, my clients weren't fond of the crowds." He gave an indifferent shrug. "One does what they must, and I find I enjoy the tea house. And the safe environment soothes my clients." His brow rose. "I don't believe we've met. I understand you're from House Trelane?"

"That's right," Bella answered.

"I would have expected Lucas."

"That's why we're here."

"I see." Renaud's pleasant smile disappeared, and he waved away his guards. Once they'd moved to a back wall, he asked. "Is he alright?"

"We hope so. He was searching for a particular book at the Renaud libraries. His interest seems to have drawn too much attention. The wrong kind. It's been three days since he's checked in."

Romero's brows furrowed, and he blindly stared at the table. "Do you know what book he was searching for?"

She glanced at Jacques, who shrugged. Great. This was on her whether to divulge the information. Devon said they were at war, and the book was a critical part of his plan. When Devon returned from his trip to Spain, he would call on his allies. It was a risk divulging the name of the book, and Jacques's words played in her head. Was Lucas unbiased enough to see his friend for who he was? It surprised her how quickly the answer came without any hesitation. She trusted Lucas with her life, as she did with Jacques and each of the cadre.

"*De første dage.*"

Romero remained still as a frozen lake, but the beast showed itself with an instant flash of yellow. She hit paydirt, but would Romero play along or play dumb?

He called his bodyguards back. "I have three more appointments. I'd prefer to discuss your request in a more private location. Is your hotel room suitable?"

It was Bella's turn to be surprised, and she did her best to hold it in. "Of course." She gave him the name of the hotel and their suite number.

"Would one a.m. be too late?"

She gave him a wicked grin. "Is it ever for a vampire?" When he returned her smile with a lusty one of his own, she stood. "Until then." She bowed her head in deference to Romero's status and strode out of the restaurant, Jacques following two steps behind.

Once they were a couple of blocks away, Jacques said, "It appears your gamble paid off."

"We'll soon see."

"You don't have high hopes for it?"

"I'm hoping he has useful information to share rather than use the time for his own fishing expedition."

Chapter Fifteen

LUCAS WOKE AND GLANCED AROUND. Same motel room, and from the slow breathing of the warm body next to him, Ginger was asleep at his side.

They'd had a horrible fight after they'd shared their family stories. He needed blood, and Ginger, dagger in hand, was ready to bleed for him. He refused on general principle though he was quite aware she was his only viable blood source. But he'd taken enough from her already.

After fifteen minutes of back-and-forth arguing, she grabbed her purse and stormed out. He heard a car door slam before it screeched out of the parking lot.

If she meant to make a point, it worked. He didn't like being left defenseless in the room with no idea when she'd return. Worse, she was alone with no backup.

She returned thirty minutes later, still pissed off. Her silent glare was enough for him to wait for her to speak first.

He wasn't sure if he should have been irritated or fascinated by her rationalization as she lectured him.

"I feel fine. I'm not lightheaded. My brain is functioning at top speed, and I've bought everything I need to keep it that way. I have plenty of water, orange juice, cookies, and the makings for a simple spinach and tuna salad. I can give you more blood. And you know you need it. Where else are you going to get it from? You can't even stand."

She towered over him with a fist resting on her hip. Her dagger was still gripped in her other hand, and she tapped it against the side of her leg in a steady rhythm.

He was too tired to continue their argument. His healing was primary, regardless of his growing irritation. "Bring me your arm."

She gave him a suspicious look. They didn't argue often, and when they did, she rarely gave in easily, but she also knew when to back off. He expected part of the issue was her revelation about her debt, but if he brought it up, it would only make things worse, so he gave her a weak smile.

"There's no reason to keep cutting yourself. Let me feed directly from your wrist. It won't hurt as much."

"Oh." She sheathed her dagger and extended her arm to his mouth.

His pierce was quick, and though she flinched for an instant, she leaned into him after the first two pulls. Her blood was heavenly nectar, and if he allowed the beast to rise as it struggled for survival, it could drain her too far. The beast liked her taste as much as he did, which was why he'd relented to take her blood. He had to build his strength and remain in control.

He took more than he should have, reasoning that it was best to get a large dose to complete the healing. In a few hours, maybe less, they could be back on the road. With a decent organic meal and one or two more small blood donations, he'd be back to fighting strength.

After giving him her blood, Ginger had curled up next to him, her arm slung over his stomach, and slept.

Now, several hours later, relief flooded him as he bent one leg and then the other. His first thought was to wake Ginger, but she needed the rest. He was surprised she hadn't collapsed from exhaustion before now. Preferring the warmth of her next to him, he remained where he was and turned his attention to their next steps.

He didn't agree with getting rid of the rental. Not yet. It would take days for Sergi to find where Lucas had rented the last one, and he had all their aliases. If Sergi hadn't found them, no one else had a chance. Not through the rental agencies. And since they weren't visiting libraries or other Houses, they were as close to invisible as they could get.

The next issue was Sergi. He hadn't been updated for three days by Lucas's calculation. He would call the rental companies because he believed in following a strict process, but he wouldn't rely on that alone. Lucas had told him they were in Maryland in his last report. From there, Sergi would guess their route and send someone south. He might assume they'd go to Hazel Green in search of Fiona.

Without hearing from Lucas, Sergi might also suspect he'd been injured and would go to New Orleans. Sergi might have sent one of the teams from Savannah out to search for him.

Lucas had to stick with the mission. He would call Sergi once they were on the road, but first, they had to get moving. Ginger wasn't wrong about that. He grinned. They were close. His nose for books picked up the scent the minute Beall revealed his knowledge of the *De første dage*.

Ginger's light moan pulled him out of his planning. She was close to waking. He played with the edges of her thick mane of hair. She snuggled deeper into the covers in a vain attempt to hold onto sleep. He brushed his knuckles along her cheek, and she brushed her hand against his as if swatting away a fly.

One eye popped open, and it took a moment for her to focus on him. Her arm snaked out and grabbed his, which moved to grasp her hand. Her eye widened, a grin followed, and she popped into a sitting position with her hair haloed around her head. She'd forgotten to remove her mascara from the night before, and when she rubbed her eyes, it gave her a sultry, rumpled-in-bed look. The sheet had fallen to her waist, revealing her bare breasts.

He might have involuntarily licked his lips because her head tilted to one side, and her grin turned mischievous.

"It appears someone's strength is returning."

"I don't know what it means for my ability to stand on two legs, but I can move them. I'd like to check the bandages and see if the wounds have healed."

"Let me pee and brush my teeth, then I'll grab the first aid kit."

"At least your priorities are in order."

"Trust me. You'll be happy you waited." After brushing her teeth, but before the first aid, she put the small four-cup coffee maker to work. She poured two cups and brought them over with the kit.

She took her first sip, then started pulling off bandages. The first cuts had completely disappeared, leaving fresh, unmarred skin. So far, so good. She appeared to be removing bandages in order of severity. A small gap in the skin was all that remained of the last injury. It would heal on his own, but one more donation, which he planned on getting once they were on the move, would close it up. They would be vulnerable for another day.

"These look amazing compared to what you looked like that first day." She shivered. "Let's not repeat that. From now on, we move as a pair. Those had been Devon's orders, and the one time we didn't follow them, you got hurt."

"But I took care of the two vampires." He squared his shoulders and felt powerful in the small motion. He was proud for taking two heads—the fact it almost killed him was secondary.

"You almost got dead. Don't make me tattle to Devon."

"You wouldn't."

She considered it. "You're right. I wouldn't have to. I'd just have to mention it to Cressa. You know, just an off-handed comment."

"That's hurtful."

She kissed his cheek, but when he turned to catch her lips, she placed two fingers over them. "It's for your own good. Are you up for breakfast?"

His stomach immediately rumbled at the thought. "White omelet with spinach and a better cup of coffee."

"Ouch. I can only work with the supplies I'm given, but I wouldn't expect anything less from an espresso snob." She slung her purse over her shoulder and locked the door behind her.

He waited a couple of minutes in case she forgot something, then threw back the covers. He sat up, and while his stomach muscles screamed retaliation, he made it without any sign of blacking out. He bent one leg and then the other. They still seemed eager to cooperate.

He turned to the side of the bed, his legs following as if second nature. Which it was, and he couldn't stop grinning. He was moving.

Now, came the hard part. He leaned against the nightstand and pushed himself up. His legs wobbled, and he reached for the bed to keep upright. He stood tall and took several breaths, giving his legs time to remember their job.

His initial steps reminded him of his sister when she was a toddler. During her first week of attempting to walk, she made the most curious faces, as if she wasn't convinced whether standing was worth all the fuss. He hadn't thought of Rosalynn for some time, and though talking about her with Ginger had been painful, it released dozens of wonderful memories.

He used the edge of the bed to make his way toward the bathroom. By the time he made it there, most of the wobbling was already receding. His second test before Ginger returned was to refill his coffee cup and walk to the table without spilling a drop.

He released a heavy breath when he placed the cup on the table and sat. He pulled over the map Ginger had marked up and calculated where they'd been, where they were now, and the next step in their search.

When Ginger returned, she was so surprised to see Lucas sitting at the table, she almost took a tumble with the two cups of coffee she held close to her chest and the paper bag hanging from her arm. She set the coffees and bag on the far side of the table.

"You didn't wait for me." She sounded hurt.

"I had to see if I could do it on my own."

"And?"

"I was a bit shaky at first, and I admit the walk to the bathroom and bringing the coffee over was a bit taxing. But I'm past the danger zone."

She took two food containers out of the bag and passed one toward him. "I asked them to add some fruit."

He opened the container, and his stomach growled in appreciation. It looked good. He took the first bite and nodded. "Not bad for a diner, I suppose."

"I thought they might squabble about an egg white omelet, but they didn't bat an eye." She dug into her scrambled eggs and munched on bacon.

The coffee was better than what the motel provided, and he felt better once he pushed the empty container away. Neither had spoken while they ate, but Ginger picked at her food as she watched him. She was measuring his stamina, still the observant caregiver.

"I checked us out of the room."

He nodded. "That's good. I'd like to get back on the road. Do you have a cell?"

"Yeah, but I haven't used it for anything other than the internet."

"It's time to call Sergi, but I'll do that while we're on the road."

"Where are we headed?"

"Fayetteville."

"Not Hazel Green?"

"We've been given both cities as her last known location. They're fifteen miles apart by interstate. Fayetteville's a larger city, so we'll have more options for motels. We can start our surveillance in Hazel Green, and if we don't catch any leads we'll try Fayetteville."

"Which will be more difficult with it being larger."

"It does seem more daunting now that we're getting closer."

"You need a donor."

"I'm feeling better than I expected. The food helped. But you're right. And I happen to know a place where I can get a full feed."

She grinned. "You're not getting addicted to my blood, are you?"

"No. Just you."

Chapter Sixteen

BELLA LOUNGED IN A CHAIR, one booted leg thrown over the arm, as she reviewed the security changes Sergi had sent out that afternoon. It wasn't required reading. The updates would only be good for three days, and the chance of her being home before then was slim. But knowing what the old plan entailed could help her identify possible security threats once they returned. Anyone using an old protocol would be considered suspect. It was a rare moment for someone in the Family to get their procedures wrong. But it happened on occasion, which was why she waited for answers to the security questions before attacking.

Jacques squatted on a bar chair playing video games on his tablet, eating nuts from a can. The occasional groan signaled each death of his avatar.

She glanced at the time on her tablet, surprised to see it was a couple minutes past one. Romero was late.

The knock came on the heel of her thoughts. Still punctual considering he was a busy House leader.

She glanced out the peephole. Romero and two of the body-guards from the tea house stared at the door. She unlocked it and opened it slowly, peering around the door to confirm it was just the three of them. When she was satisfied they were alone, she swung the door wide. "Come on in."

The three vampires followed her to the main living area where Jacques now sat on one of the chairs framing the sofa. No tablet in sight.

Romero glanced around. "They've updated the decor since I've been in one of their suites." He wrinkled his nose, which turned him from handsome to absolutely adorable.

"Turquoise not your color?"

"Can't say that it is." He looked around and then at the hall that led to the two bedrooms. "Do you mind?"

"I'd be worried if you didn't ask." She waved for the body-guards to have a look around and ensure there weren't other vampires lurking about. Devon would have asked the same.

When the bodyguards returned, shaking their heads to confirm the rest of the suite was empty, Romero nodded toward the door. They exited, closing the door firmly behind them. They would station themselves in the hall to detract any unwanted visitors.

Bella waved Romero to the sofa. He unbuttoned his suit jacket and stretched out. His entire posture shouted sedate. She wasn't fooled. There was tension behind his eyes and a throb at his temple.

"Is there any update on Lucas?" Romero asked.

"No. The last we heard he was in Maryland."

"Maryland? There's no library there." Romero considered it a moment. "Is the book the only item Lucas is searching for?"

"He's also searching for Philipe Renaud."

Romero closed his eyes. "That makes sense. I wish he'd come to me first."

"Do you know where Philipe is?"

"He never gives his location."

"So he's not dead?"

Romero shrugged. "Not that I'm aware of, but I haven't heard from him for several months."

"Do you know how to reach him?"

"In a way."

Bella itched to get up and pace. The back-and-forth subtleties weren't her forte. She preferred the direct approach but didn't want to push a House leader. Perhaps a different angle.

"Would the House Renaud send vampires to protect their secrets?"

Romero's gaze searched the room before he refocused on Bella. "Every House has its secrets."

"Lucas has gathered information that points to someone in the Renaud Family who's not following the House's primary mission in the protection of all vampiric knowledge."

"That's a rather dangerous supposition. What led him to that conclusion?"

"Someone has been tampering with the inventory." She explained the fake book for the *De første dage* and its presence in the card catalog system at several libraries, including the home library in New Orleans.

Romero's color faded. "You're positive about this?"

"The first location the cadre checked was the Los Angeles branch. This was a couple of months ago, but, as you're aware, the House has since been distracted with other issues." She didn't have to mention the Boretsky incident since Sergi had visited Romero and Lafitte at the time. "Lucas recently visited the San Francisco annex where the fake book reflected the actual book was out for restoration but, according to the curator, the book had been moved to Los Angeles at the time of the 1906 earthquake. Besides the fact the Los Angeles library wasn't built until 1930, we know the book was in San Francisco in 1925. Lucas has since discovered the same fake book in Boston and New York."

Romero shot off the sofa and paced along the windows that

reflected the bright lights of the city against the backdrop of the dark Mississippi River. He ran a hand through the thick black hair, giving him a tousled bedhead look. When he turned back to Bella, he looked like a vampire who had finally come to a stark realization. "It's taken decades, but apparently Philipe's concerns were well founded."

Bella glanced at Jacques, who had shifted in his seat, more acutely attuned to the discussion. Now, they were getting somewhere.

"What secret is Philipe hiding? It has to do with whatever's written in that book, right? Something that could create a disturbance within the Council?"

"He never told me what was in the book. He claimed it was too dangerous for anyone to know. That just the idea of it could be enough to spur a civil war."

"Did it ever occur to you it might be the ravings of someone who'd spent too much time in the stacks and not enough time in reality?"

Romero laughed. "A sentiment from someone not comfortable with books?"

"I'm more of an action-oriented vampire."

"Devon always did prefer diversification in his cadre. Do you have anything to drink?"

Bella nodded to Jacques, who stood and went to the bar.

"Scotch or cognac?" he asked as he checked the bottles. "Looks like we have some top-shelf vodka as well."

"I'll take a vodka on ice." Romero sat down and accepted the glass Jacques handed him.

Jacques opened the fridge and pulled out two beers, handing one to Bella.

Romero took a sip then stared into his glass. "I take it Sergi's recent visit with the human woman, who was introduced as Devon's Blood Ward, somehow relates to this book?"

"Why would you assume that?"

"Well, let's see. I haven't seen Devon or Lucas for over a year.

Lucas calls, of course, but we never talk House business. Then within a span of a couple of weeks, Sergi comes to my court, and then Devon follows. Neither of them had business with either me or Lafitte. I know Sergi visited the library, I assume asking about Philipe."

"Let's just stop the dancing, shall we?" Bella stood, beer in hand, as she took Romero's previous position to pace in front of the windows. "I've been watching Devon and the cadre tiptoe around this book and the missing Philipe for a few weeks now, with everyone guessing what might be written in it. A book that is either hidden somewhere in the bowels of the Renaud library system or has been purposely removed. The search for answers has attracted a string of vampires with deadly intentions. But as I mentioned before, I prefer direct action over all this intrigue."

She stopped and turned to Romero. "Do you know what Devon considers my specialty?" When Romero shook his head, she continued her pacing. "I'm really good at distractions. Like a magician, I get everyone to look one way while the real trick is happening elsewhere. And when I think about everyone chasing after this book that claims to be out for restoration in several libraries—it smells like a distraction to me.

"We have a curator who gave false information about the book being someplace we knew it wasn't. If she had only gotten her dates right, maybe I could believe that Devon and Lucas have gotten worked up over nothing. But the fact that the Renauds not only have incorrect data in their inventory, which supposedly hasn't occurred once in the library's history, but that they've also managed to misplace a book tells me someone is lying.

"Now, how do we know they lied? Or worse, that someone altered the inventory? Because we know, firsthand, that in 1925, Guildford Trelane asked Philipe if the annex had the *De første dage* in the inventory. Philipe confirmed he found the book and they arranged a meeting. Trelane, along with his wife, daughter, and her boyfriend, traveled to San Francisco specifically to review the book.

We know, based on Lyra's own words, that Philipe and Guildford met. On their way home, the Trelanes are involved in a horrific accident that killed the House leader, his wife, and supposedly the boyfriend, leaving Lyra traumatized."

She glanced at Romero and was satisfied she had his complete attention. "Are you with me so far?"

He nodded.

"At some point after that, and who knows when since a hundred years passed before someone asked about the book again, Philipe disappears. Did he get worried when he heard about Guildford's tragic death, or was it because some other vampire came looking?"

She returned to her chair to perch on its edge. She rested her elbows on her knees, still holding on to her beer, and looked him in the eye. "Devon isn't going to let this go. And he doesn't care what it does to the Council or whether it creates a civil war. Venizi has been trying to silence Devon—hell, his entire House, for decades. Maybe longer. We need to find Philipe before someone else does."

Romero studied her then finished his vodka. "I believe this is where the players are asked to lay all their cards on the table. Yes, Philipe has a secret and is hiding to protect it. But he's apparently not the only one with a secret. If Devon is ready to go public with something, I want to know what evidence he has. And then, if it's warranted, I'll help you find Philipe."

Bella considered the request. It was back to trust. But there was one other thing she wanted to know first. Something she was sure would provide a link back to Venizi. Even if it wasn't enough proof to take to the Council—she had to know. "Tell me one thing. When did Philipe go underground?"

Romero ran a hand through this hair. "That's hard to pinpoint; let me think." His brows scrunched in thought, then his features hardened. "I don't remember the year; it's been a few decades. But one thing does stick out. It was about the same time Venizi began questioning Devon's seat on the Council."

Click.

That was the turning point. The catalyst. Venizi must have gotten wind of the book and dreamwalkers. Maybe Hamilton had cracked and given Venizi a breadcrumb he was able to follow. She was making wild-ass guesses, but she knew Venizi too well.

"You believe the two events are related." Romero scooted up on his seat until there was little space between them.

"I think it goes back farther. Either Venizi was aware of the book before Guildford's trip to San Francisco, or he'd been following Guildford and found an opportune time to take care of two problems."

"I don't understand."

"I know. That's because you're missing an important ingredient." She turned to Jacques. "What do you think?"

"He's a trusted ally, and he'll be told soon enough once Devon returns. We need to find Lucas and Philipe now."

Bella was taking a huge chance, but Jacques was right. And she'd been thinking along the same lines earlier that evening.

"What I'm going to ask needs to remain between you, Devon, and his cadre. At least for now. Are you willing to accept those terms?"

"I give you my word." No hesitation.

"What do you know of dreamwalkers?"

Chapter Seventeen

I GLANCED OVER AT LUCAS. We'd been on the road for an hour and for most of that time he sat silently in the passenger seat, staring out the front window. His head was somewhere, and I didn't bother him. My mind was elsewhere, too.

His words repeated in my head. He wasn't addicted to my blood—just me. Not the words every girl wanted to hear, but not every girl dated a vamp. I grinned and glanced at him, but he didn't notice me.

He didn't seem bothered by our fight the night before. I'd been childish about him taking blood from me, but I was getting that itch. The one I got every time I thought about my past. My mistakes. There was a time when that itch was enough to make me want to run. I didn't feel that anymore. Not since Lucas. The itch just created different side effects, making me cranky and stubborn.

In the end, he'd taken more blood than I'd expected. It had been an erotic moment. An odd thing to say, but there it was. The only question was whether my past would make him look at me differently.

I glanced over again then dropped my gaze to the phone in his hand. He hadn't made the call.

"Are you waiting for a particular reason?" I asked.

"What?" He glanced at me, then down at the phone. "No. Maybe."

"Like a Band-Aid."

He gave me a curious stare.

"You know. When you need to remove a bandage, it's easier to rip it off fast."

"You didn't do that with my bandages."

My cheeks warmed, and I kept my eyes on the road. But I felt his on me. "Special case."

He chuckled. "I see." He dialed the number then looked out his side window. "It's me. I'm alright. We ran into some trouble, but we're back on the mission." A long pause. "Yes." A sigh. "No, we have a lead on Fiona." Another long pause, and he ran a hand through his hair. "I understand." He heaved another sigh. "Fayetteville, Tennessee. We should be there by morning." Another long pause and, this time, his hand fisted for a brief second before releasing to rub his thigh. His tone held a note of irritation. "We know what we're doing. If you want to do that, that's your call. You know where we'll be." He hung up and dropped the phone in the console.

"That didn't go so well."

"He wants us to go to New Orleans and meet up with Bella and Jacques."

"And you don't agree with that."

"Why drive all the way there just to turn around and double back? It's a waste of time."

"Did Sergi agree with that reasoning?"

"It doesn't matter. Devon gave me the assignment. Sergi was assigned to monitor the situation, not make decisions when he doesn't have all the information."

"Alright." I wasn't privy to how the cadre worked, but Lucas didn't report to Sergi. This had been Lucas's passion since first hearing about the book. He knew what he was doing.

Lucas took my hand and squeezed. "I wasn't the youngest in my family, but I was the youngest male. Perhaps I'm just as rebellious as you."

I grinned and squeezed back. "Now, that's something I can work with. What do you want to do about the rental?"

He picked up the paper map with all their notes. "We need to make a detour. It's a bit out of the way, but we can pick up a new car, and I can get some blood. After that, we're going dark. Bella and Jacques will have to use their tracking skills if they want to find us."

I snorted. "That won't take long."

"I know. But at the moment, I'm not in the mood to make everyone else's life easier."

~

"So, why did we drive all the way here just for a new rental?" I crawled out of the car. I'd driven non-stop since morning, only stopping to eat and pee, and my legs refused to work.

Lucas had slept most of the way, and the blood I'd given him the night before continued to heal him. But he wasn't strong enough to wield a dagger or sword. And if he could, he wouldn't have the necessary speed required to fend off more than a single vamp.

"We're not getting a rental. Can you get me some water and maybe some fruit, if they have it?"

The convenience store was busy with humans, so it should be safe enough to go in alone. "What are you going to be doing?"

He was already striding toward the street, and he yelled over his shoulder, "I won't be long."

There he was going off on his own again. I doubted the vamps were aware of our location, but I wasn't born yesterday and wouldn't be surprised again. And that thought lasted about a minute as Lucas jogged across the street and walked into a local bank.

What the hell?

Sure, no problem. Just take some time to catch up on your banking.

Then I considered why a bank. The vamps he'd killed had a lot of money on them. Lucas still had his own stash. The money I'd spent on supplies barely touched it. Maybe he just wanted to be ready in case of another emergency.

I locked the car and marched into the store, turning my focus to simple shopping. I bought a case of water, two bottles of orange juice, bananas, apples, and, finally, road trip snacks for me. Ten minutes of staring out the car window dragged by before Lucas stepped out of the bank and hurried to the car.

"Let's go," he said as he closed the door. "At the light, make a right. There's a used car dealership a couple of blocks down."

"You're going to buy a car?" My voice squeaked.

"No one will be able to track us. Sergi included."

"Oh. I hadn't thought of that." It was a great idea to keep the bad vamps away, but he was making Bella's task harder to find them. Although, she'd most likely consider it an acceptable challenge.

An hour later, with what had to be the fastest sales transaction the salesman ever made while he unknowingly donated half a pint of blood, I drove out of the lot in a ten-year-old white panel van. There weren't a lot of conveniences, but it wasn't all bad. The van had an upgraded radio with satellite stations, drove smoother than I expected, and the seat was higher so I could see over the top of most cars.

We bypassed the interstate, found the state highway, and headed west. A few hours later, Lucas selected a small town for us to overnight. We picked up dinner from a grocery store and found a nondescript motel on the edge of town next to a diner. At least we'd have something hot for breakfast.

I eyed him as we ate premade salads while an old musical played on the TV. "You seem quite capable of slumming it."

He glanced up with a mouthful of salad and washed it down with a swallow of wine from a plastic cup. "You think I can only survive in five-star hotels?"

"They're the only ones you've taken me to." I held up my hands, fork waving. "Not that I mind. I just thought that's how vamps always traveled."

"It's common for the House Leader, cadre, and many others in the Family, but there are times when surveillance dictates other accommodations."

We finished the bottle of wine and watched TV until it was time for sleep.

"Come closer. I haven't been able to hold you for days." Lucas held the sheet open for me, and I curled up next to him, his arms holding me tight. "I owe you so much." He kissed my forehead, my cheek, and then my lips. It didn't last long, but it was passionate.

"Why do you think you owe me anything?" I asked.

"Because, my sweet angel, if you weren't as smart and quick as you had been that night, I'd be in the afterlife looking down on you, sad for all the days I would miss having you in my arms."

I clutched him tight, the import of his words reminding me of what I'd refused to consider. I'd almost lost him. And our mission was far from over. For the first time since Lucas mentioned it, I was happy Bella and Jacques were on their way.

WE'D BEEN WATCHING the same grocery store for three days. Thank god it wasn't an open-all-night store or we'd be sleeping in the van. At least I'd talked Lucas into buying an air mattress, just in case. The day before, we thought we'd found Fiona, but it wasn't her. At least, she wasn't a vampire, and Lucas assured me only vampires could be library custodians.

"How long are we going to try this approach?" I asked while picking through an assorted nut mix, searching for the last hazelnut before switching to almonds.

"At least a week. Bella will find us soon, and then we'll have more options. The store has a delivery boy, and I've been considering following him on one of his runs. Fiona might stock up on dry goods, but she'll eventually need fresh food. Whether she's with Philipe or not, she's been living on the run for too long to ignore its necessity. She'll also require blood and could take it from the delivery boy if he doesn't visit her often, otherwise, she'll need to come to town."

"So, either the delivery boy or some other unsuspecting human ends up their unsuspecting donor."

He shrugged. "A minute to mesmerize, take the blood, leave them with a pleasant thought, then send the human on their way. No fuss. No muss."

"What does it say about me that I'm no longer fazed by that?"

He grabbed my hand, kissed it, then stole the can of nuts. "It says that you're intelligent and understand more of how the world works."

"I guess."

"Think of it this way. When you were trying to keep me safe, not knowing how to stay hidden, what if you didn't have money to buy food, rent a room, or buy gas?"

Money had been one of the first things I took stock of once I checked on Lucas and hid the dead vamps. I didn't have to run through the situation we'd been in to know what I'd have to do. I would have risked the call to Sergi, but it would have been at least a day or more before he could get to us. Lucas had a credit card, but using it would have left a trail the bad vamps could have picked up. The bottom line was that I might have done something I wasn't proud of to keep Lucas and me alive.

"When you put it that way, I would have done things I thought I'd left behind in the Hollows."

"Survival is a strong instinct. It doesn't matter the species."

"I've never asked, but do you think this book can be as damaging as everyone believes? Cressa doesn't talk about it. Does it really hold the truth of vampire and dreamwalker history?"

"I can only guess at what might be in the book, but it must be something that could upend vampire society. Fiona and Philipe have been in hiding for decades. That either makes them extremely paranoid or terrified of the book's authenticity."

"My ass hurts. I think I'll run in and get us dinner. The store will be closing soon."

We ate our premade salads and fruit at the table in our motel room. I finished my glass of wine and disappeared into the bathroom after grabbing a bag out of the duffel.

I slipped out of my clothes, took a quick shower, and put on a skimpy nightie I'd found on sale. Cressa always said I could find a gem in a coal mine. It wasn't fancy, but it showed plenty of skin, which was the entire point.

We hadn't had sex since the night before he'd been injured. During our stakeouts, he'd take a break to run through his training program while I watched the store. He was back to his fighting speed, which told me he was ready for other vigorous exercises.

I grinned as I folded up my leggings and tunic and stepped into the room. He was head down studying a local map and making notes. I didn't know what he was hoping to find, but sometimes it was his general interest in learning rather than anything to do with a mission.

He didn't notice as I dropped my clothes on the duffel and stepped up behind him. I ran my hands over his shoulders, gently massaging them. He leaned into it, though partly by reflex, while he remained focused on the map. When I moved my hands down his back, continuing my massage, he dropped the pen as I moved below his hips.

Satisfied I had his attention, I moved my hands back up to his shoulders and down his chest while I nibbled at an ear and then his neck. When that didn't seem to be enough, I blew a soft whisper along the back of his neck.

He moved so swiftly, I gasped, then giggled when he lifted me in his arms. His gaze glowed an electric blue when he took in the nightie.

"You read my mind." His kiss was hot, passionate, and unforgiving.

I writhed in his arms, his lips never leaving mine as he laid me down, covering me with his body. I pushed at him, wanting to be the seducer, but he wasn't going to budge. And the molten heat sweeping across my body overrode any salient thought I had.

He pushed the strap off my shoulder and freed a breast. After that, I'm not sure I could recall anything else. It was all arms and legs and breasts and cock and heated touches. Lips and tongues, and the erotic feel of skin on skin.

I lost track of time, and we didn't come up for air until we were both damp with sweat, our breaths coming fast, our heart-beats pounding against each other's chest. It was raw and desperate. I wanted more, but we fell asleep in each other's arms. I'd take care of the next round in the morning.

Sometime later, a knock on the door made us both jump out of bed like someone had thrown the melted remains of the ice bucket over us. We dressed quickly before each grabbing a weapon. I moved toward the bathroom, hovering in my fighter's stance.

At this point, the nightie seemed an unfortunate clothing choice. I should have taken the time for leggings, but Lucas was too fast. He moved on silent feet and peered through the peephole. Then he laid his forehead against the door.

He glanced back at me, was going to say something, but a strange smile caught the corners of his lips. He opened the door and swung it wide.

"Hello, Rom."

A dark-haired vamp stood in the doorway, giving Lucas a

studied perusal. He gripped Lucas's upper arms, pulling him in for what I assumed was a brotherly hug when his gaze caught mine.

He stared as a slow grin spread across his handsome face.

I was still in my fighter's stance, dagger in my right hand, and in my nightie. My cheeks flamed with embarrassment at being caught like this.

He was still gripping Lucas, but his eyes never left mine when he responded to Lucas's greeting. "Ah, mon pote. Who do we have here?"

Chapter Eighteen

AFTER OPENING the door to Rom and seeing his gaze light up at Ginger, Lucas turned to see her as Rom might be viewing her. And that's when it hit him that he should have given her time to change. She hadn't shifted a foot as she stood there in her night-gown, dagger held in an offensive gesture, ready for an attack.

Rom would see a beautiful woman in a skimpy negligee grabbing a dagger he would assume belonged to Lucas. But to him, she was a striking warrior, even with her rosy cheeks. She held her stance while studying Rom, who wore his mischievous grin, before glancing past him to Bella and Jacques, who had followed him in.

They only gave her a quick glance, noted her dagger, and Bella nodded with approval.

"Well, I guess now it's a party." Ginger lowered her weapon and turned to the duffel, picking up the clothes she'd been wearing earlier. "I'll just change." She gave Lucas an annoyed glance. "You might want to put some coffee on." Then, dagger still in hand, she disappeared into the bathroom.

"Now, I know why you went silent for three days." Rom's brows wiggled before he turned serious. "All kidding aside, you look a bit pale."

Lucas greeted Bella and Jacques with a nod then busied himself with the coffee. "I'm mostly back to full strength, but I could use a decent blood donor. It's been nothing but sips since Ginger found me in the parking lot. But let's wait for her. I can tell you what she shared while I was healing, but you might have questions."

Rom took a seat at the table, Jacques relaxed in the nearby chair, and Bella leaned against a wall, always prepared to pace.

"I assume you weren't followed. I'm not up to changing motels again." Lucas scrounged in a shopping bag for the paper cups Ginger had purchased, unwilling to use the ones provided in the room. For someone who'd lived part of her life in the worst conditions, she'd become particular about certain things.

"Bella and Jacques are quite cautious." Rom pulled the map to him, analyzing it in a few short minutes.

"I believe you used the word paranoid," Bella replied in a droll tone.

Lucas chuckled. "It must have been a long drive from New Orleans. I assume that's where you came from."

"You have no idea." Bella strolled to the coffee pot. "Go sit. We'll need more coffee than this four-cup pot will provide." She picked up the package of coffee and a filter. "At least you bought something decent."

Ginger picked that time to exit the bathroom, nightgown and dagger in hand. "I can pop over and get breakfast and coffee once the diner opens." She dropped the nightgown in the duffel but placed the dagger on the nightstand. "What time is it anyway?"

"Three a.m.," Jacques said. "I suggested we wait for a better time before imposing."

Ginger laid a hand on his shoulder. "At least some of you have manners." Her annoyance was tempered by her cheery nature, though, by the glance she shot Lucas, she wasn't going to be so easily mollified. She straightened the sheets and bedcover, then plopped down on the edge, close to Lucas but within reach of her dagger.

Rom's smile grew wider, and he noted the placement of the dagger. He stood and walked to her. "I'm sorry for our rude timing, but I know how much Lucas enjoys surprises. My sincerest apologies." He gave her a slight bow. "I'm Romero. Leader of House Rousseau and a dear friend of Lucas." He held out his hand, and Ginger reached out to shake. Her eyes widened when Rom kissed it, and her head tilted to the side as she considered him.

"I'm Ginger Morrison of House Trelane."

Lucas couldn't hold back a satisfied smile, his chest filling with an unexpected emotion at how easily the words came for her. He caught Bella's second nod of approval as she poured the first cup of coffee.

"It's splendid to meet another member of Devon's Family, and apparently, a fierce warrior." He returned to his seat, taking the cup Bella offered. "I can tell from the way you held the dagger and your stance that you've learned from the best." He gave a side glance to Lucas. "But I would expect nothing less from Sergi."

Ginger crooked a smile, taking a cup from Bella. "Sergi is an exceptional instructor, but I try to model myself after Simone's finesse with a dagger."

"Touché." He sat back as he sipped·the coffee, holding her gaze for a bit longer before turning to Lucas. "So, tell me everything from the moment you arrived in Boston. Every detail will be important."

Lucas began the tale, and Ginger took over from the point where she found him in the parking lot. Bella's and Jacques's interest was piqued when she walked through details of hiding the dead vampires, misdirection with the tracker, getting to safety, and feeding Lucas small amounts of her blood as often as she could. Lucas finished the story from when he woke, and their decision to track Fiona.

Rom listened intently, leaving Bella to ask most of the questions. Once everyone was up to speed, Lucas asked a question of his own.

"I understand why Bella and Jacques are here. But why you?"

Rom ran a hand through his hair and let his gaze wander for a minute. "I know something of the book, and Philipe contacts me on occasion to let me know he's alive. I know he moved around, quite a lot in the early days, and spent time in Europe about thirty years ago. His list of personal contacts is quite small with the rare phone call. It's been a couple of months since he last reached out."

"You've never told anyone?" Lucas asked.

He shook his head. "You know how important it is to keep my contacts anonymous. Sometimes, and more recently, more times than not, it's a matter of life or death. When Sergi asked me about Philipe when he was in New Orleans a few weeks ago, I was shocked." He chuckled as he ran a hand through his hair again. "I knew at that moment everything would soon come to light if Devon was interested. That vampire is like a wolf on a hunt."

"You did a good job hiding it. Sergi wasn't convinced one way or another whether you knew more."

"You would have, though."

"Of course, but we've been through a lot together. Besides, I didn't spend those years as a bodyguard without paying attention."

Rom laughed. "Which is why you're now cadre of a great House."

Lucas didn't respond, but his old mentor's words pleased him. Ginger squeezed his shoulder and kissed his temple. He hadn't sensed her draw close.

She turned to Rom, understanding the protocol when a House leader was in the room. "The diner should be open. Is there anything special you'd like for breakfast? I'm sorry there won't be any beignets, though, even if there were, I doubt they'd live up to your expectations." Then she grinned. "But their cinnamon rolls aren't half bad."

She listened to everyone's orders, then stuck her dagger in her purse before striding to the door. Jacques followed, and when she glared at him, he shrugged. "You won't be able to carry it all."

It took a moment, and then she patted his arm. "I appreciate the assist." She understood he was following security protocols, and after the lecture she'd given Lucas on the same topic, she couldn't argue.

Once they were gone, Rom asked, "Can she take care of herself? I mean in a fight. It's apparent she's resourceful enough to keep you alive."

Lucas nodded, but he glanced at Bella, somewhat curious. "We've been in some sticky situations. She has skill. What do you think?"

Bella gave the question its due diligence. "She's a quick study and seems to have a second nature for reading a situation. In my opinion, she has more bravado than sense, but her only true weakness is being human."

"There's a way to solve for that." Rom sat back and twirled the paper cup.

"No." Lucas wasn't prepared for the veracity behind the single word. "That is a personal decision. An irrevocable one. She must come to that consideration on her own, of her own free will—if she does at all." He locked eyes with Rom. "I will not have it mentioned in her presence. I've never asked anything of you before, but I'm sincere in this request."

All humor fled Rom's gaze. "Of course, brother. It was said in jest and with poor judgment. It's easy to see the depth of feeling you have for each other. And mutual respect. That's difficult to find in any species." He held out his hand. "You have my word."

Lucas ignored it. "Your word has always been good enough for me." Then he took the proffered hand. "Thank you for taking time away from the Family to help us."

Rom's shake was firm, and he held it for a moment before letting go. "This day has been coming for a long time. Though I've never met a dreamwalker, I felt their presence within the city. Like wraiths flowing with the early-morning fog. Draped through the city as thick as Spanish moss. They won't wait much longer. There are times at the darkest hour, I can feel the tension building. No one else speaks of it, and sometimes I think I'm imagining it. But it's real. I don't know why I can sense it when no other can. Or perhaps they're as mystified as myself and unwilling to look the fool.

"I'm here to help you find Philipe, if it's possible, and Devon has my allegiance in his war. Don't look at Bella, she didn't say anything I wasn't already aware of. I've known Devon longer than you. It was easy to see during his last trip to New Orleans that he was at a boiling point with the attacks on his House. He's been more than patient, and now he's within striking distance of the vampire's holy grail. This will be earth-shattering news for most vampire Houses and could bring about a civil war. But most of its effects might be contained within a personal war between two powerful Houses. It would save many vampire lives."

Lucas sat back, his head reeling. Devon had understood this from the start. Not when he first began his mission to remove his censure, but when he first suspected Cressa was a dreamwalker. And then he discovered what might be contained within the *De første dage*. It all fit. Devon's entire life since his father's death.

Rom broke his musing. "It would have been easier to have met a dreamwalker before making such a commitment for my House, but I have to trust Devon knows what he's doing. Venizi has become too bold."

Lucas shook his head, still partially in his thoughts, which was why his next statement came out so matter-of-factly. "You have."

His gaze dropped to the map, but the lines became unfocused. Talks of war hadn't seemed real until now. Though he couldn't envision Devon's end game, he trusted his Father as he had Rom and Lafitte before him. Since Devon's declaration of war, he hadn't shared his inner thoughts with the cadre, and Lucas suspected he wanted to wait until he returned from Spain. House Aramburu was a wild card that could tip the scales or create further chaos.

He was so deep in his thoughts, he almost missed Rom's startled look. "What?"

Rom stared at him as if he was leaking brain matter. "You said you have. I want to know what that meant."

Lucas replayed the earlier conversation, unsure what he meant at the time. When he remembered, he grinned. "Dreamwalkers. You said you never met one, but you have." It wasn't often he knew something before Rom. In fact, it was damn rare, so he let his old House leader have a think on it.

Rom's forehead furrowed, giving a glimpse of the wrinkles that might form in another five hundred years. He snapped his fingers. "Cressa?"

Lucas laughed. "You're a bit slower than you used to be."

"Aah." He sat up, leaning his elbows on the table as a spark of the beast lit his gaze, his tone full of wonderment. "It all makes sense now. I found it difficult to believe Sergi would bring Devon's supposed Blood Ward all the way to New Orleans to see a Renaud Library when there are several closer to him. But I did believe him when he said his business had nothing to do with the New Orleans Houses." Rom paused as he continued to put it together. "Then why come to New Orleans?" He chuckled. "Don't tell me. They met with another dreamwalker."

When Lucas just grinned at him, he sighed. "I told you not to tell me. Sometimes, I think Lafitte rubbed off on you more than I first suspected." Then he brightened. "I think a trip to Santiga Bay is in order, just to ensure I understand the details correctly."

"You're always welcome, you know that. But I think Cressa has it in mind to return to New Orleans with Devon. That would be an excellent time for Devon to speak with the House leaders."

Rom nodded. "Including Renaud."

The entire idea exploded in his head as he considered what could be accomplished with a meeting of the New Orleans Triad—three powerful Houses.

Before he could respond, the door burst open. They all jumped up, prepared to face the enemy when Ginger waltzed in carrying several bags. Jacques trailed behind with more bags and a broad smile.

Ginger plopped the bags on the table, forcing Rom and Lucas to step back as they stared at her. Bella hadn't moved an inch, holding back a smile.

"I didn't mean to startle y'all." She gave everyone a saucy grin. "I know how you like surprises. Have you figured out our next steps?"

Chapter Nineteen

EMPTY FOOD CONTAINERS, coffee cups, and plastic utensils had been pushed aside to make room in the middle of the table. Four heads bent over a map and stared at the lines and circles Lucas had drawn around points of interest in the small town of Hazel Green.

I wasn't sure what the three vamps were seeing that I wasn't. They'd been staring at the map for fifteen minutes without a word while Bella had left to arrange for their rooms.

"This entire trip could be a fool's errand, you know." Rom scratched at the stubble on his jaw that gave him a rakish appearance.

"But you don't believe that." Lucas eyed his friend with an insight I didn't have.

They'd known each other for decades, and even after being apart for several, Lucas hadn't lost the touch to read his friend. I chalked it up to their continued communication through text and video calls. I wouldn't have been surprised if they finished each other's sentences.

"No. But I'm not sure how to flush them out without them running."

"Would it help if they saw you around town?" I wasn't sure why they hadn't considered it already. It seemed the simplest approach. If Philipe stayed in contact with Rom, even if it was longer than every six months, he must trust him.

Rom glanced at Lucas. "It might not hurt. But how often would I have to walk around town on the off chance they'd see me?"

I shook my head emphatically, if for nothing more than getting his attention. "It's a small town. People talk. Even if Fiona and Philipe kept to themselves, they would want to know what the locals were saying. They'd want to know if there were strangers in town. If they heard of someone new, would they run without checking it out, or would they investigate to see if someone was on their tail?"

"What did you have in mind?" Rom asked her directly, his eyes a warm honey brown.

"A simple boy's night out with Lucas and Jacques. Lucas mentioned you normally travel with two bodyguards. Make friends with the bartender where a local or two might listen in. Tell them you're Romero and make up some story about why you might be spending a couple days in town. I guarantee the news of three hot new guys in town will spread like wildfire with the women." I picked up the last grape that was looking forlorn in the detritus and popped it in my mouth. "With a name like Romero, Fiona should definitely hear about you."

"Small towns do like to spread gossip," Lucas said. "But would he need to stay in Hazel Green for that to work?"

"No." Jacques stretched his back and then neck before leaning over to start collecting the trash. "It's too small a town. The last thing we need is the local sheriff watching us. That might spook Fiona and Philipe."

Of all the vamps I'd met, Jacques seemed the closest to understanding human behavior. Or maybe he was attuned to shifter behavior. They seemed more human than vamps.

Either way, I agreed with him. "He's right. Besides, it wouldn't be odd for someone to go to different bars in the area. In fact, that would make the story easier to believe and harder to confirm. You're in Fayetteville to visit some old friends or maybe looking for a new business opportunity. You wanted to get out and see more of the countryside and decided to stop in. One night might not be enough, but you don't want to go back the next night, maybe the one after."

"Adding in Fayetteville is an excellent idea." Lucas tapped the map for no particular reason. "Word might get back to others in town here, which would make our job a little easier."

Jacques was nodding. "The name will certainly make the rounds, and knowing you were seen with two other males will resonate with Philipe if he knows you that well. During the day, Lucas and Ginger can continue to monitor the grocery store while Bella and I follow the delivery boy. But I expect, if they're close, they'll come to you."

"So, I stay in the motel all day and what? Channel surf?" Romero didn't seem sold on sitting around.

Lucas didn't like it, either. "No one stays on their own. Three of us will remain at the motel while the other two monitor the grocery store until the delivery boy heads out. Ginger and I will trade babysitting duty with Bella and Jacques." He grinned at Romero. "You're used to being pampered."

Romero laughed and took on an air of superiority well-known for the species. "I can't help the role I was born to play."

It was said in jest, and Jacques was about to respond when he was interrupted.

The door, which had been left ajar, opened, and Bella strode in, dropping two keys on the table. "I got us two rooms. Jacques and I will double up."

Rom picked up the key closest to him. "I'll need to change the registered name on my room."

Lucas briefly explained the plan to Bella. After it was all laid out, Bella patted my shoulder.

"Excellent idea. However, I don't agree that we change Romero's room to his name." She picked up a pen Lucas had been using and drew a quick L-shaped block. A map of the motel. "The room we're in now is here." She wrote an X on the block representing our room on the long side of the building, two rooms away from where it turned left to the shorter side. "The two rooms I just rented are here and here." She put Xs in two side-by-side rooms in the smaller wing.

She studied the map for a moment. "Let's see if we can get this room rented in Romero's name." She made the last X in a room on the far side of the two newly rented rooms, away from the staircase where the two buildings met. "You'll only be there during the day, maybe go in and out a few times, and make the room look lived in for the cleaning staff. We can keep an eye on it from this room and see if we pick up visitors—friend or foe."

They all turned to Rom, waiting for his thoughts or questions.

"I want at least one vampire in the room next to where I'll be spending my days. If I know Philipe, he's likely to send someone with a message."

"Agreed," Lucas said. "Let's work out the schedule and hit the bar tonight."

THE FOLLOWING MORNING, I peered through a gap between curtain and window. I'd spent a good twenty minutes building a perfect opening. From the outside, the drape of the curtain looked natural, but I'd focused on creating a slit that I could peer through at eye level while leaning back in the chair. It was an inch-and-a-half opening that provided a view of the front door to what we called the "box"—the room registered to Rom—as well as the two rooms next to it.

I was the shortest person in the room so the others would have to scoot down in the chair a bit. No one should be able to see them from the outside. At least not without spending a great length of time staring at the window. By then, the visitor would be close enough for them to shut the trap.

The only weak part of the plan was the open staircase between the two buildings. Their special guest could make it to the stairs, but the only place to park a car was in front of the motel, so they'd have to be fast. If they tried to make a break for it out the back, they wouldn't get far. Only a single-person cement path ran between the back of the building and a six-foot chain-link fence. A vamp could easily scale it—if they chose to run—but they still wouldn't have their car.

"No one's out there. If Philipe gets our message, or worse, the vampires who've been chasing you, it will take them a couple of hours to trace my credit card and even longer to get here." Rom set a cup of coffee in front of me. "I've tried different beans this time. Tell me what you think."

I snorted. "Are you the one to blame for Lucas's addiction to espresso?"

"Hmm. I think it was a passion we both shared from the beginning. Maybe that was why it was so easy to have him around. We share many of the same interests." His gaze was intense, but I'd lived with vamps long enough that it no longer bothered me—as long as they weren't touching me while doing it. Unless it was Lucas or Devon's Family. And even with them, it had taken time for the fear of being mesmerized to fade.

I sipped the coffee while returning his stare until he grinned. "Mmm. That is good. Did you do something different with the beans?"

He shrugged. "I might have had them ground finer, but I think it's just the quality of the roast."

"So, what other interests do the two of you share?" I could have let the topic drop since I'd steered the conversation away from

155

it, but I was curious. And I wanted him to know that while I respected him, I wasn't scared of him—much.

He leaned back and took a swallow of coffee, seeming to savor it like a wine connoisseur. "You already know his penchant for books. We spent hours in the library during the wee hours of the morning debating politics, Council law, and why some Houses lost battles while others won them. It's the one thing I miss about not having him around."

"And why the two of you spend hours on the phone."

He chuckled. "So you know most of it." He ran his fingers over the table as if playing a piano. Maybe he did. He'd had plenty of time to learn. "There is one thing." He glanced at me under hooded eyes. "I don't know if I should even mention it. It's a highly guarded secret."

I rolled my eyes. "If you're trying to sell it, don't bother." I leaned in. "I'm all about gossip."

"A human trait."

"More than you know. And I'm pretty good at it. But the vamp world has its own gossip mill."

"Oh?"

I nodded. "You call it the aristocracy."

He threw his head back and laughed. It had a pleasant ring to it. If Cressa and Devon weren't such a perfect couple, I'd consider playing matchmaker.

"You're spot on. Lucas said you had insights like no one else he knew. I didn't understand it at the time, but I've seen it several times now. You are an enigma."

"That's a first. I don't think I've ever been called anything quite so...I don't know, mysterious doesn't quite cover it."

"Don't change that part of you. Sometimes, when humans are around vampires for too long, they tend to lose their own aura. The thing that makes them special. I don't know why. Maybe because in most vampire households we don't give the humans the challenges they need to hold on to their humanity. Perhaps that's something we can learn from you."

"You're an insightful vampire yourself. I'd say there's hope."

"You are a tease, Ms. Morrison."

"And you're deflecting, House Leader Romero."

He grinned. "So I am. And I'm also serious that only a handful know what I'm about to tell you. This stays between you and me. It wouldn't seem dignified for a House Leader or a member of the cadre."

"Please tell me you're not overselling it." I giggled. His tone became guarded, as if state secrets were about to be shared.

He glanced around the room, and I followed his gaze, prepared to find a small crowd of onlookers. I grinned so widely my cheeks hurt. The more stoic he became the harder it was to hold in the laughter.

He leaned in, beckoning me with a crooked finger. State secrets indeed. He had me so wrapped up in the mystery, I almost missed the minute crinkle at the edge of his lips. I'd only known him a day, but I'd say that was the start of a grin.

"We're obsessed with bingo."

I fell back, not sure I'd heard him right and feeling somewhat deflated. I stared into those honeyed eyes, the sincerity so real. But there was a light behind them, the touch of the beast, but not in hunger or anger. He was playing me.

"You do know what bingo is in the human world, right?"

He nodded in all seriousness. "Little cards with numbers in rows and columns. A free space in the middle. Depending on the bingo hall, some use those dot markers, but we prefer the places that still use the little wooden chips or multi-colored plastic ones. I prefer the dark blue or the red ones."

I released something between a honk and a snort, which was unfortunate because I breathed in air while a laugh burst out. The two forces lodged in my throat, and I couldn't catch a breath.

Next thing I knew, I was on my back, and Rom was pressing

KIM ALLRED

on my chest with the palms of his hands, trying to force the air out, but it wasn't working. I wondered if I would actually turn blue before I met my maker. A vamp shoving a sword through my heart or slicing it across my neck would have been a more honorable way to die. Like a Klingon.

The giggles came on again like little bubbles of compressed air. I was turned onto my side, and Rom slapped my back. I'd be worried if I didn't find this entire episode idiotic. Did the vamp ever get first aid or trauma training, or was he just guessing on the best way to help me?

Suddenly, my breath rushed out, and I had no idea which of Rom's various techniques worked. He was still bending over me, his face flushed with concern, and my giggles erupted all over again. Then I started coughing when the door burst open.

We both turned to glance up at Lucas's surprised face, which darkened the longer we stared at him. He was back early from a store run, and even as I got my coughing under control, I could only imagine what the pair of us looked like from his vantage point.

But only one thing came to mind as I was caught in his sapphire glare.

"Bingo?"

Chapter Twenty

"I STILL CAN'T BELIEVE he told you." Lucas stared out the front windshield as he drove us back to the motel after the third day of a bored-out-of-my-mind stakeout. His hands gripped the steering wheel, and his knuckles might have been turning white.

I giggled. He wouldn't let it go, and every time he brought it up, I instantly pictured him and Rom hunched over a long table between two gray-haired ladies. The women would lean over, pointing as they double-checked the vamp's multiple boards, whispering words of advice and encouragement. Or maybe the women were the cranky sort, explaining how they were doing it all wrong. Lucas and Rom would nod along, but their gazes would be stuck on the tumbling balls, eagerly awaiting the next call. It was just too precious.

Somehow, I managed to spit out, "I promise I won't tell a soul."

"Including Cressa."

It wasn't a question. "I'll do my best."

"Swear. Right now, in this van, swear you won't say a word to Cressa."

The giggles stopped. He was serious. I must have missed something about masculinity in the vamp world. Did he really think other vamps would think less of him if they discovered his secret obsession with bingo?

Rom had seemed just as serious.

"What's this all about? It's been how many days, and you're still grumbling over this?" When he didn't answer me, I noted his tight jaw and rigid posture. "Would it be easier if I shared something I thought was embarrassing even though Cressa didn't give it a second thought when I mentioned it?"

His gaze flickered to me then back to the road. "Would it be true?"

I sighed. "No. But I'll confess that Cressa and I might have been seen in a bingo parlor once or twice."

This time he turned his whole head to determine my sincerity.

"If that's true, why do you find it so funny when it's me and Rom?"

"Aah. Now I see the problem. I'm not laughing about you and Rom playing bingo. I understand what draws you to the game." That got a flicker of surprise. "It's just the image of you surrounded by gray-haired women feeding you snacks."

"Not everyone is old."

Still sensitive. I glanced out my side window. It was better to let him stew on it for a bit.

"Why do you think we're drawn to it?"

Finally. We were getting somewhere. I shrugged my shoulder. "Rom is a House leader with lots of pressure. His side business of granting favors must come with its own stress. Like Devon, his mind is always churning, trying to stay ahead of the game.

"You might not be a House leader but, as cadre, you have many responsibilities. Even when you were a bodyguard for Rom, it was apparent he gave you more responsibilities than others."

"Why would you think that?"

I snorted. "Anyone can see he values your opinion. The point is, bingo is one of those games where you don't think about anything other than each little ball. You stare at dozens of cards, waiting for the call. It's not really about winning. And if I had to guess, I'd say you don't always call a winner, even when you have one, letting some of the regulars have a chance in the spotlight. It's all about clearing your head. Even with the mental task of searching the columns and rows, you're not thinking of anything but the cards in front of you."

We drove in silence, and I returned to stare out the window.

When we approached town, his hand touched mine, and I grabbed it. When he squeezed back, I knew he was alright.

"I don't know what I'd do without you." He kissed my hand.

"I don't know how you managed this long without me."

When he pulled into the motel's parking lot, we both glanced at the air mattress in the back and laughed. It had been days since we'd shared any real form of intimacy.

The van door opened, and Bella stuck her head inside. "I think we might have some activity. Let's go." She picked up the groceries we'd bought before leaving the stakeout.

I grabbed my purse, and we hustled to the room.

"Where are Rom and Jacques?" Lucas asked.

"Rom had returned to our room for a meal when I spotted a woman in the office who appeared to be asking questions. She looked like she might have been touching the clerk, so I made an assumption she might be mesmerizing him. Then she returned to a car with a single driver. It's the gray sedan on the other side of the lot."

"Have you been back to your room?"

"No. I was on the staircase, waiting for you. Jacques has a clear line of sight to the vehicle. He'll keep us updated when she moves."

I glanced out the peephole I'd made in the curtains. The doors to both rooms were visible. The trap was set if this woman was actually a vamp.

"Do you think the other person in the car is Philipe?" If it wasn't, Philipe had more vamps involved than we ever considered.

Lucas considered the question. "It wouldn't be wise."

"I agree." Bella tapped my shoulder, and I relinquished my seat. "If this is Fiona, she might have mesmerized a human to drive her here."

I grabbed my dagger and prepared for whatever was to come. Minutes ticked by. "What are they waiting for?" I hated that Lucas and Bella were so calm. My skin itched, my feet refused to settle in one spot, and my fingers ached from gripping the dagger so tightly.

Bella glanced at her cell then watched for movement beyond the gap in the drapes. "The woman is moving for the motel."

I took a deep breath and closed my eyes, searching for that zen moment Simone taught me—the calm before the storm.

"Go!" Bella yelled.

I trailed two steps behind Lucas with Bella on my heels. Rom and Jacques were already out their door. By her quick movements, it was obvious the woman was a vamp. No one moved like a vamp, but she didn't move fast enough to escape.

Rom pulled her back to the room where he'd been waiting with Jacques. When Jacques called out a warning, he shoved her through the door. More vamps were coming.

Rom grabbed my arm and pushed me in with the vamp. "Guard her." He slammed the door behind me.

I stood in an attack posture that Simone had taught for guarding a prisoner. My dagger was in one hand while I raised the other in an attempt to calm the vamp, who brandished her own weapon. "We're not here to harm you. We only have a few questions, but we need to take care of whoever followed you first."

"You're human?"

"Is that going to be a problem?" I said it with more bravado than I felt. And I had to admit I was a bit hurt when she lowered her weapon and cocked her head to one side.

"I've never known Romero to keep a human as a bodyguard."

"Maybe you should stay in touch more frequently."

I had no idea what was going on outside, but I could hear swords clashing. "How many vamps followed you?"

The woman laughed. "You have no idea what you've brought down upon yourselves."

I would have laughed in turn, but I was beginning to think she was right.

"Halt!"

The word was yelled from outside and didn't sound like anyone from our group. But it was enough to startle me.

The vamp rushed me.

My reaction was pure instinct. I immediately kicked out, clipping her arm with the dagger. When she stumbled by, I spun and kicked her in the back. The force smacked her into the wall. She turned around and wiped her nose, leaving streaks of crimson on her hand. After taking a long moment to stare at the blood, her face became a vengeful mask.

I was in trouble, but I didn't wait. I raced toward her then sidestepped at the last moment. The vamp fell for it. Not knowing if this was Fiona or not, I didn't want to stab her, so I tripped her as she went by.

She must have been expecting it because she regained her footing before falling. In a move I'd only seen Simone perform, she ran two more steps then jumped into the air, twirling and directing her momentum back to me.

I knew how to defend against it, but there wasn't enough space. My only other option was to attempt my own jump and kick.

She was ready for it. Her dagger cut across my arm.

Its sharp bite made me gasp, but I landed square on my feet, facing her. I hated it when they grinned like they knew something I didn't. We circled each other, each of us waiting for the other's next move.

Her grin grew wider.

I'm not sure how it would have ended had it been just the two of us. The door burst open, and before I could react, she called out, "Don't hurt her." Then someone kicked the back of my knees, and I dropped, hitting the deck hard.

My dagger was ripped from me as I was hauled up by an arm. Rough hands pulled my arms behind me, and I felt the plastic restraints zip tight around my wrists. I looked up at the male vamp gripping my arm—as if I had any place to run. He was rugged and muscled to the point his shirt could barely contain his mass.

The female vamp strode up to me and gave me a long, appraising look. The respect that shined in her eyes surprised me. "A human who fights like a vampire. I'll be interested in hearing this story." She nodded at the other vamp. "Take her to the others, then clean out this room."

I was dragged into the parking lot, where my heart sank. Our entire group stood with their hands behind their backs, most likely zip tied. They were blood-spattered but appeared to be in one piece. The fact their captors sported their fair share of blood gave me a small amount of pleasure.

I was pushed into the lineup as more than a dozen vamps circled us. They all looked to the female vamp I'd been tussling with. She nodded to one of the vamps. He took out a phone and walked along the line, taking a snapshot of each of us. Then he appeared to be sending them to someone. Or maybe more than one someone.

No one spoke as we waited. I'd expected Rom to say something, but he might be hoping no one recognized him as a House leader. If this was Venizi's group, I would expect us to be dead. Something else was going on. I glanced at Jacques, who stood next to me. He stared straight ahead—calm and stoic.

Lucas had caught my gaze before I was added to the line. The only thing I garnered from him was relief I was alive.

A ping announced an incoming text. The vamp glanced at his

phone then nodded to the female, who immediately shouted orders.

"Load them up. Get their belongings and bring their vehicles. I want this place scrubbed and secured."

A black van pulled up, and the back doors swung open. A long bench seat ran along both sides of the van. Once we were helped up and seated, another vamp jumped up holding black material in his hands.

The female vamp stepped to the back of the van and peered up at Rom. "I'm sorry for this, but you'll soon understand."

Another vamp jumped in and one by one took what turned out to be a hood from the other vamp and began covering our heads. I couldn't see Lucas, who was on the far side of the same bench, but I caught Bella's gaze. She nodded to me before the cover went over her head.

Then darkness descended. The fabric was light, and while breathing was easy, it didn't help my fledgling claustrophobia. No one spoke as the van started up and drove away.

I wasn't sure how far we drove, but it was an uncomfortable ride with my arms behind my back. After about ten minutes on the road, I felt the change in speed and heard the sound of a busy highway, which I assumed was the interstate. There was no telling what direction we were headed. It was a long time afterward before the van slowed as we left the interstate then made a sharp turn. I woke when the van stopped, unaware I'd nodded off. I heard voices, but they were too low to pick up any words.

Several minutes later, the van continued for a short drive before stopping again. The minute the doors opened, a cool breeze floated through, and I breathed easier.

"Take the hoods off." The male voice sounded irritated. "I doubt that was needed once they were in the van."

"I apologize, sir. We wanted to be careful." It sounded like the female vamp.

"Just get them off."

Bright light hit my eyes, and I squinted. The female vamp stood next to a male vamp. His expression held the same irritation as his voice had. I glanced around the van to find everyone else squinting as their eyes adjusted. Rom's hood was the last one removed.

He shook his head and slowly opened his eyes, then glared down at the man outside. His eyes widened in apparent recognition.

The male vamp reached out and touched Rom's leg. "I'm sorry, old friend. This was the only way I could secure your safety."

Rom stretched his legs. "You better have a deep wine cellar."

The vamp laughed. "And much more." He smiled at the rest of us. "I am Philipe Renaud. Welcome to The Retreat." He clapped his hands. "Untie our guests, bring their belongings, and see them to their suites."

Chapter Twenty-One

Lucas stared at his reflection in the mirror. Their suite came with an array of clothes in several sizes, and he selected a dark-blue pinstripe suit with a silver-blue tie. He hadn't worn anything so fine for the last two weeks, and he hadn't realized how much he missed it. Or perhaps his good mood came from the fresh blood he'd received from one of the many donors Philipe housed at The Retreat. Another word for a safe house, though this was the grandest one he'd ever seen.

They'd been directed to their rooms as soon as they entered the manor and given an hour to clean up before returning to the foyer. They met with Iris, the female vampire who played the role of Fiona at the motel and was Philipe's head of security, for a quick tour of the retreat. Besides the standard features of a grand estate, there was an outdoor swimming pool, two tennis courts, a nine-hole golf course, and a twenty-seat movie theater.

Quaint cottages that housed the staff dotted the landscape. There were two stables that housed horses for riding, cows for milk, goats for cheese, and dozens of chickens for eggs. Meat and fish were brought in by House staff every couple of months under extremely rigorous security measures.

The most surprising of all, but perhaps not, considering the Family's mission, wasn't the massive library that took up a good portion of the first floor of the manor, but the library building that was connected to the manor by a glass-enclosed breezeway. It was a quarter the size of the manor and was filled with books, most of them memoirs from hundreds of vampire families. Ancient books and artifacts also graced the two-story building. The Renaud Family built annexes around the globe to house an ever-growing inventory, and it made sense that the most valuable might be housed outside of the mainstream libraries. Once the tour ended, they were sent back to their rooms for much-needed rest.

Lucas considered their fight at the motel while he fastened his cufflinks. It hadn't been much of one. Neither he nor Rom wanted to hurt anyone when they assumed it was Fiona who'd come to their motel room. When they were swarmed by vampires wearing masks and black camo, they weren't sure what they'd stepped into. It hadn't taken long to deduce the vampires weren't fighting to kill.

Once Rom understood the attackers' hesitancy to draw blood, he dropped his sword, most likely suspecting Philipe had set his own trap. Who would have thought a bookworm was so savvy with battle techniques? Lucas chuckled. Who else but someone who'd had decades to study books on the topic? The Family's security forces had trained in special combat techniques. Several of which Lucas would share with Devon and the cadre.

When he was satisfied that he was properly attired, he sat next to Ginger, who was dead to the world amid the satin sheets. Neither of them had had proper sleep since New York, and she deserved every moment she got. He kissed her forehead. She'd find him once she was up and dressed—whenever that might be.

The halls on the second floor were quiet, and he didn't run into anyone until after he'd glanced inside several rooms on the first floor.

"You'll find Philipe and Romero on the south patio," Iris called from behind him after he'd peeked into an empty salon.

He turned and smiled. "I'm usually good at ferreting out my way in a new manor, but this one isn't built like others."

She returned his smile and led him down the long hall. "From what I've been told, Letitia Renaud, who came from the old country a couple hundred years ago, was the one who designed the estate. Of course, only a portion of it had been built back then, but she'd had architectural drawings rendered of her final dream. At the time, it wasn't considered a safe house. She was an extremely old ancient and had tired of the world. She wanted to build a community of her own making, and her brother found it easier to buy her land, give her money, and not ask questions.

"She developed a blood disease and had been gone several decades before Philipe required a safe house. After Letitia, the manor was meant as a retreat for the immediate Family, though most were uncomfortable with the confinement so far from civilization." She laughed. "Vampires are social animals. At least, the aristocrats seem to be."

"I can't argue your assessment. Even so, it must be difficult living in isolation for so long."

"I originally had the same thoughts and believed I'd been demoted when the old man asked me to take this assignment. Turns out he knew me better than I knew myself. I can't think of a better place to live. Every person here is allowed two weeks a year away from the estate as long as they're willing to go someplace outside the States. A portion of our security staff does nothing but schedule vacations, locations, and security for every vampire and human who lives here. Surprisingly, there are many who only leave every several years by their own choice."

"It's truly an amazing enterprise. I think I could probably spend months here just in the library alone."

"Is that all?" she teased.

He bent low as if sharing a secret. "I was only speaking to the library in the manor. I think the library building would require a couple of years to just scratch the surface of books."

She chuckled then walked through the solarium to a smaller sunroom where French doors led to a patio. "I'll leave you to it. I'll be sure the rest of your party finds their way once they're up and about." She nodded and sauntered off.

The patio looked out over the south end of the valley. Thousands of acres, all owned by the Renauds. Other than knowing they were still somewhere in the South, they were surrounded by mountains and thick forests. No doubt, a portion of that land was owned by the Renauds as well, to prevent development.

A long table that seated twenty was centered on the patio with two smaller tables on the far side and a comfortable lounge area on the right. The seating surrounded an outdoor fireplace where embers glowed, warding off the slight chill in the early-evening air.

Rom and Philipe were in deep conversation and only turned when Lucas stood next to them.

"Ah, Lucas Maynard. Welcome to my home." Philipe stood and shook Lucas's hand. "Sit, sit. I have many questions, but have a drink while we wait for the rest of your party. I see the clothing fits well."

"Yes, thank you for that. I feel like a dignified vampire again."

Philipe wrinkled his nose. "It's not easy being on the run. Fiona and I experienced a few weeks of it before we found our way here, though that was decades ago."

They spent the next hour laughing over tales of the old days. Rom and Lucas shared stories of when Lucas was part of the Rousseau Family. Philipe imparted his memories of a young, restless Rom, and his father's lost wits at what to do with the cocky vampire.

Surprisingly, Ginger was the first of their group to arrive. She was dressed in a modest mid-calf dress in a bright floral design that hugged her frame. Her hair was pulled back to flow down the nape of her neck. In one word—she was delectable. Her stylish ankle boots clicked on the stone patio floor, and her smile could have lit the place had it been dark.

Philipe stood, took both her hands, and gave her the full European greeting, kissing both cheeks, which she returned without a hiccup. She squeezed Lucas's hand when she took a seat next to him and winked at Rom.

"Iris was quite impressed with your fighting prowess." Philipe poured her a glass of wine. "It's not common to find a human, let alone female, with those skills."

"Devon's cadre taught me everything I know. Though I hadn't planned to be tested quite so soon."

"Yes, I heard about the trouble with Venizi." Philipe refilled the other glasses. "That vampire has been a sword in our side toward progress for way too long."

Minutes later, Bella joined them. She preferred a stately black suit, and her hair had been pulled back into a ponytail. For someone who was more comfortable in tactical gear, she knew how to dress for the occasion.

"Where's Jacques?" Lucas asked.

Bella snorted. "He couldn't stop talking about the golf course. One of the security detail invited him to play a round. Jacques said I could fill him in later, then he scurried off like a rat after cheese."

"I'd say we should wait for Fiona," Philipe said, "but last I saw of her earlier today, she was headed to the library next door. She's on the trail of a family history that had been thought lost some two hundred years ago. And similar to Jacques, it could be some time before she reappears. I'll be sure to have her gathered up in time for dinner."

He settled back in his seat with a drink in hand and a clouded expression. After a minute, it cleared, and he began his story.

"I'm not sure how you first heard of *De første dage*, but I'd been pleasantly unaware of it until that fateful call from Guildford Trelane. I'd been lost in the stacks and had to rush back to my office when a custodian told me he was on the line. We'd built a friendship some years before. He was an avid reader and always stopped by when he was in the city. This was San Francisco that I'm talking about, of course.

"I'd been at what was, at the time, the only library on the West Coast for about forty years. When Guildford called, the Los Angeles library was under construction, and because it would be larger, the plan was to make the San Francisco location an annex when the other opened."

He stopped when a server came in with a platter of appetizers and several plates to pass around. A tea and coffee service was placed next to the food. Philipe laughed when the servers exited. "While she might become lost to time while in the library, Fiona's hostess skills are always present. This is her attempt to keep us sober before dinner." He placed two appetizers on his plate and poured coffee for himself. "Please help yourself, and don't feel obligated to drink the tea or coffee. I can't tell you how many tipsy vampires we've fed over the years.

"Now, where was I? Ah, the coming move. Each of the libraries and annexes would be sending books to the Los Angeles branch, and I'd assigned Fiona to the task. She had books strewn about everywhere. Quite orderly, of course, but she was the only one besides me who understood her filing system. Perhaps that was one reason no one ever noticed the book. It hadn't been earmarked for Los Angeles, but she happened to find several books that were physically in the inventory without a reference to their location in our files. Strange enough even then.

"When Guildford asked about it, Fiona was the one who located it in her stack of books. I was honestly shocked when Guildford said he wanted to drive down to look at it. If he was that interested in it, I thought I should read it before he arrived in case he wanted to discuss its contents."

His hand shook, and he set the coffee cup on the table. "Even now, its mere existence scares me and the future of our race." He shook his head. "When Guildford arrived, and after meeting his family and assistant, I settled him into a quiet room to read. Afterwards, we had a long discussion about it. I'd hoped it was some vampire's foolish fiction or perhaps it had been written by an ancient who'd lost their senses. But Guildford considered it a true accounting. Something that had been hidden from the general populace in hopes it would never see the light of day."

He pulled out a handkerchief and dabbed at his eyes. "He told me dreamwalkers were real. At the time, I nodded as if I believed him, though I began to question his sanity at such a statement. Then he invited me to dinner, and I spent more time around his assistant, Hamilton. I'll never forget that young man. It wasn't unusual for a vampire, even a House leader, to have a human assistant, but I could tell there was something different about him from the very beginning.

"I was going to ask Guildford about the man the following day, but he'd been called home. Perhaps he felt an urgency to be with his security team. I have no idea why he traveled without them. I heard about the accident the following day. Everyone gone except for his daughter. What a tragedy. But the timing wasn't lost on me or Fiona, though we set our fear aside for a time.

"Shortly after, I was reassigned as curator for the Los Angeles branch, and I brought Fiona along. It was widely known, at least within the Family, that although we weren't married, I wouldn't go anywhere without her. I brought the book with me, but instead of putting it on the shelves, I showed it out for restoration. I didn't feel safe leaving it where others could find it.

"I traveled to New Orleans and showed it to the old man. He didn't question its validity or the danger it presented. He said vampire society wasn't ready to hear the truth and that it was too dangerous to be left within the inventory. He assigned me to a special project to audit all the libraries in the States."

"A cover story?" Lucas asked.

"Quite so. During the audit, Fiona placed the false book in the stacks and recorded it in the inventory as out for restoration. We wanted to create as much confusion as possible if anyone came looking." His gaze twinkled when he glanced at Lucas, but he continued his story. "Once we were back in Los Angeles, Fiona and I packed our essentials, left our apartment, told my assistant we were going on holiday, and fled here on the old man's orders. While we'd been performing the audits, he renovated the manor, vetted and relocated staff, and arranged for a special security team. It's been quiet ever since—with one exception.

"About forty years ago, or maybe it was longer than that, Venizi came snooping about. When he received continual resistance to his inquiries about the book, he seemed content to let his request go."

"He must have determined the book was safely underground." Lucas poured a cup of coffee. If what he suspected to be in the book was correct, Lorenzo would never want it to see the light of day.

"That's what Fiona said, and I couldn't argue the sentiment." He sat back and trained a curious gaze at Lucas. "So, tell me. What made House Trelane become so interested in the book after all this time?"

Lucas had expected the question but wasn't sure how much to reveal. Now that they'd found Philipe, this mission had become real. He glanced first at Bella, then Ginger.

"He already knows what's in the book," Ginger encouraged. "Rom knows now. If Devon is going to ask for allies, they have to understand the risk. This is what we've staked our lives on. Cressa would agree to this.

He sat back and gave Philipe a long look. He had to know what was coming. Or maybe he didn't. Either way, the only way forward was to lay it all out.

Lucas stood on a precipice. He knew what he had to do. This was what Devon and everyone had pinned their hopes on. He'd been adamant that he be given this assignment, but he never fully considered the full ramifications. Or maybe he just set them aside.

How many lives would be impacted by this one act? How many lives damaged, and how many more improved? Hamilton had been the one to plant the seed all those years ago. He just hadn't expected how long it would take to grow roots.

Hamilton was a dreamwalker. Their species had already lost so much, and Hamilton didn't want to hide anymore. But was revealing the truth of their past just the first step to repeating history?

Ginger trusted him to do the right thing. Devon had as well. This was the moment he walked off the ledge. He stared at Philipe for a long time before finally asking, "What do you know about dreamwalkers?"

Chapter Twenty-Two

I PULLED the emerald-green gown from the hanger. Philipe had requested a formal dinner, though from what Bella told me, Fiona had been hoping for a quiet dinner in the salon. Who would have thought it was the male that wanted the fancy meal? I hugged the dress against me and studied my reflection. Maybe. I tossed the dress on the bed next to the navy-blue one and wandered back into the closet. If it was a solo dinner with Lucas, I'd already be decked out in the red, one-shouldered silk number with the fitted bodice and layered skirt.

I sighed. Maybe I'd put it on after we got back to our room. It would be worth it just to have Lucas strip it from me. I tugged down the copper-colored gown. It was a simple A-line sleeveless dress, but the material shimmered, and the back dipped low. It was sophisticated. It was perfect.

I laid the dress over the back of a chair and drew a bath. Lucas wouldn't be back for at least an hour. He wanted to call Sergi and see if he could reach Devon. When he'd asked Philipe what he knew about dreamwalkers, I had no doubt Lucas would tell Philipe the truth. Then, maybe Philipe would show us the book.

But Philipe had ended the conversation, preferring Fiona to be in attendance before anything more was revealed. So, the topic was paused until the customary drinks before dinner. And that gave Lucas too much time to think.

"You don't have to ask approval," I'd told him once we got back to our room.

"It's not approval. I want them to be aware of the situation." His tone held an edge, and he punched the wall before leaning his forehead against it. "Ever since I heard of the *De første dage*, and Cressa asked about the Renaud libraries, I've thought of nothing else. Until now, it's been nothing but a rumor, just like the dreamwalkers. But once we learn the truth and hold the book in our hands, there won't be a question of civil war."

It was rare to see Lucas so upset, but he was passionate about the topic and seemed to think it all rested on him. I pressed my body against his back and wrapped my arms around his waist. "You're not the one making the decision on sharing the contents of the book to vampire society. Devon. Colantha. Hamilton. The Wolf. They're all ready for this next step. The book is just one piece." I stepped back and grabbed his hand, turning him toward me. "Even if they weren't involved, and you learned about the book and dreamwalkers on your own, you wouldn't be able to keep it to yourself for long. You always do the right thing. That's what I love about you most."

He hugged me for the longest time. Then he picked up his cell and walked out the door.

I slipped into the bath and breathed in the mixed floral scent, reveling in the warm, silky feel of the water. I let my mind wander as I considered the days we'd chased the book while vampires hunted us. Almost losing Lucas had shaken me to the core. But something good came out of it. I learned more about him, parts of himself he kept hidden. There was so much more for us to learn about the other.

Then I smiled as an idea began to form. Maybe Santiga Bay wouldn't be our next stop.

An hour and a half later, I completed the last touches of makeup and tugged at a few tendrils of hair that a housemaid was kind enough to put up for me. I was still in my bra and panties when I strolled out of the bathroom and jumped when Lucas walked out of the closet.

I plastered a hand against my chest. "You scared me."

He grinned. "Sorry. I didn't want to disturb your hair and makeup session. Besides, I wanted to see the end result. You look rather delectable." He stepped close and pulled me to him.

"Don't mess up my hair."

"I wouldn't think of it." He pressed a kiss to my neck and then my collarbone before pushing a knee against my upper thigh. He knew all my hot buttons.

"That's not fair." I pushed him away.

"Put on your dress. I want the full effect." He wore a deep-chocolate suit, and his blond hair and beachboy look made me gooey inside. It was going to be a long evening before we could be alone. He worked on his tie while I disappeared into the closet.

The housemaid had hung the dress on a nearby stand along with the matching shoes. She'd laid out gold dangling earrings on the dressing table next to a long slim black box. Curious, I opened the box and took a step back.

A small gold charm in the shape of a dagger lay in black satin. It was strung on a thin, gold, twist-chain necklace.

I finished dressing and put on the earrings. I rolled a finger over the charm. Interesting.

Lucas turned when he heard me behind him. His gaze glowed with the force of the beast—bright electric blue. My nether regions heated instantly. This would definitely be a long night.

I held out my hand with the necklace in it. "I found this in the dressing room."

He stepped toward me, reaching for the necklace. "Turn around." His voice was deep and lustful, and I did as he asked.

He fastened the necklace and turned me around. "The dress is a perfect color on you, and I can't imagine anyone filling it out like you. But this necklace…" He picked it up and rubbed a thumb over the dagger. "This was made with you in mind."

"I don't understand."

"This isn't part of Renaud's collection. I had this made in Fayetteville. Let's just say between an amazing jeweler, Rom, and a little persuasion, I was able to have this fashioned. I noticed you wear charms on a chain and thought I'd add a new one."

"But why now?"

He didn't answer and appeared to be weighing the correct answer. In the end, all he said was, "Can't a guy buy something nice for his girl?"

I threw my arms around his neck. "As often as he wants."

He kissed me, his lips soft and gentle and full of promise. "As beautiful as you look, I can't wait to strip that dress off you."

His words, so similar to my earlier thoughts, made me shiver.

"Why are you in such a good mood? Did Sergi and Devon give you the advice you were looking for?"

"I didn't call them."

I tilted my head, instantly curious at what could have made him change his mind so completely. "Why not?"

He leaned his forehead against mine. "You gave me all the advice I needed."

PHILIPE, Rom, Jacques, and Bella were already in the sitting room when Lucas and I arrived for drinks. It didn't seem unusual to see Philipe and Rom in such fine attire, but Jacques was like a new vamp, and it was apparent he wasn't overly comfortable in the suit and tie. Bella, on the other hand, fit into the burgundy gown as if it had been made for her. And I lifted a brow when Rom's gaze appeared to note it as well.

"Wine or something stronger?" Philipe asked.

"Wine for me." I glanced around the room that was filled with paintings and sculptures. If I were Cressa, I might channel my internal Pandora and determine what a fence would pay for each treasure. I held in a snicker as Philipe handed me a glass. And though I never heard Lucas answer one way or another, Philipe passed him a scotch, seeming to pick up on his growing tension.

We'd barely sat when the men stood as a young woman entered the room, her elegant gown of navy blue complementing her white-blonde hair that had been pulled back into a chignon. She looked my age, though her sharp gaze held centuries of wisdom, considering she had to have been at least a hundred years old to have been a custodian in the 1920s.

"I'm so sorry for my absence until now." Her voice was melodic, and her smile sincere. "I'm sure Philipe told you I tend to lose myself in the stacks. I would have been here sooner, but we rarely get visitors, and our cook was beside himself on what to prepare. Then he became flustered thinking the soufflé had been ruined. He's really too much of a perfectionist. I can't remember him ever serving a bad meal."

"Except that one time when Father came to visit and brought several pounds of crawdads," Philipe reminded her.

Her laugh was full-bodied. "Oh my, yes. But that wasn't the cook's fault. Somewhere along the way, the crawdads had thawed and then were frozen again. They were quite bad. I don't think any of us have been able to touch one since."

They both laughed at the memories as Philipe poured her a glass of wine. Introductions were made, and the couple sat together on a sofa and turned their gaze on Lucas.

"Sorry to put you on the spot, as they say, but Fiona and I haven't been able to talk about anything else since you mentioned dreamwalkers. They're a myth among vampires, you know."

I wasn't sure what direction Lucas would take the conversation, but he squeezed my wrist, and I knew he'd be fine. Rom shifted in his chair, and though he knew part of what Lucas had to share, it only skimmed the surface.

"Vampire society has been led to believe they are a myth, but I think you know better." When Philipe's stoic expression didn't change, Lucas wasn't deterred. He settled back and sipped his scotch. "It all started with a simple trade. The services of a human thief for a debt owed. You said you'd heard of the tragic Trelane accident and Lyra being the only survivor. She'd been horribly traumatized by the event with the loss of her parents and Hamilton, her first love. At some point during her recovery, she began hearing voices and spoke of horrible dreams. Everyone thought she was lost to insanity—all except Devon and Sergi. Instead of sending her to an asylum, Devon hid her within the manor, creating a livable environment where she could be safe."

Lucas spoke briefly of Devon's absence due to the Poppy and his eventual rise as House leader. Then he shared the rumors Devon had heard about dreamwalkers and his belief they might somehow help Lyra. But his decades of research came up empty until The Wolf brought him Cressa.

Then Lucas told them about Devon's and Cressa's shared dreams.

"You're telling me her dreams were prescient?" Philipe asked, his astonished gaze meeting Fiona's.

"From what I understand, not all of them are, but we know of one that came true and another that was close enough to a real occurrence." Lucas accepted a refill of scotch from Jacques, and he took a long moment to appreciate it.

I was so proud of him, I wanted to kiss him. But he was on a roll, and I didn't dare touch him in case it broke his concentration.

Once he had a moment to prepare for the next reveal, he continued. "Cressa eventually asked her mother about the dreams and learned of her father and the medallion he'd had made for her. It was Devon who convinced her mother to help, and she gave him a single name." He hesitated and took a large swallow. I wasn't sure if he'd done it for dramatic effect or to calm his nerves.

"Colantha Dupré." He shared Cressa's story of her travel to New Orleans to find the woman who claimed to be a dreamwalker. Then he jumped to Cressa's abduction by Venizi from an accident eerily similar to Guildford's.

"Devon believed the only way to find Cressa was by reaching her through her dreams. But he needed help, so he went to New Orleans to find Colantha Dupré. At first, he thought she might be using strong voodoo, but it didn't take long for Devon to realize she was the real deal.

"Colantha came to Santiga Bay to help with our search." Lucas shifted in his seat and set his glass down, holding the gaze of Philipe, Fiona, and Rom. "The others in this room will back me up. Colantha is, in fact, everything she says she is. She took us to what she calls a construct. A dreamworld where you believe everything is real." He scooted to the edge of the sofa, completely engaged with our hosts. "All your senses are alive—touch, smell, taste, hearing. Quite frankly, it's almost indescribable."

"And you've both been there?" Fiona turned to Bella and Jacques, and, looking extremely uncomfortable, they both nodded. "Why do I feel there's more to the story?"

"We learned two things during our rescue of Cressa from Shadow Island. First, we learned that Colantha can bring non-dreamwalkers into a construct and hold them there unless they have the mental training to break the connection."

Lucas was aware this would be the sticking point between the vamps and dreamwalkers, so he gave them time to digest the information. While Rom turned a shade paler, Philipe and Fiona didn't appear surprised.

"And the second item?" Philipe asked. He appeared to have moved beyond doubt of the existence of dreamwalkers and was merely confirming details.

"During Cressa's time on Shadow Island, she discovered Venizi was holding a prisoner in a guarded building. She became aware of the prisoner when he reached out to her in a dream."

Fiona edged closer, and Philipe reached for her arm as if to hold her back. "Who was this prisoner? Was she able to save him?"

Lucas nodded. "It required a team of vampires, shifters, and Colantha, but we managed to extract him." He took a deep breath before delivering the bombshell.

"The prisoner was Hamilton."

LUCAS FOLLOWED the group into the dining room, letting Bella and Jacques bear the brunt of the questions over what it was like to be in a construct and the brazen rescue from Shadow Island. Ginger tapped his arm several times before he realized he was gripping her hand too tightly.

"Take a deep breath," Ginger suggested. "It's going to be a long night, but you're doing great."

"I hope I've done the right thing."

"Of course, you did. It's important for Philipe to hear Bella's and Jacques's opinions."

The conversation at dinner shouldn't have been a surprise after everything Lucas had revealed. Philipe and Fiona were amazed that Hamilton was still alive and, after getting a shave and a long bath, didn't look much older than the last time Lyra had seen him. No one knew dreamwalkers lived that long, but everyone admitted they knew next to nothing about them other than secretly guarded myths.

"You said something about Lyra getting better once Cressa arrived at the manor?" Fiona swallowed a bite of salmon and washed it down with a sip of wine.

"She'd been having better days through the years, though she'd revert without warning." Lucas nudged Ginger to pass the potatoes, but a server was there in an instant. "From what Devon shared, she was more aware—and more precocious—after Cressa's arrival. But her recovery was most notable when Devon was framed for Boretsky's death and leadership of the House fell to her. It prevented a sanction on the House."

"I heard about that episode," Philipe said. He moved the mashed potatoes around his plate, mixing them with the glazed green beans. "The Council moved much too quickly in recommending sanctions. No doubt Venizi drove them into a frenzy."

"I'm still curious about one thing." Lucas chuckled. "I guess my list is longer than one item, but it was something Colantha mentioned when attempting to convince Hamilton to trust her." He gave Bella a brief glance and was surprised to see she'd stopped to savor the wine. She seemed as curious as the others about his question. He'd forgotten that much of what he'd learned about Colantha hadn't been completely shared with the cadre. Not because of mistrust, but because events in the House had been moving too rapidly, and their focus had been on information critical to the security of the Family.

"She mentioned she was an heiress to the Seven Tribes and the daughter of someone named Adelice."

Fiona, who had been buttering a roll, dropped her knife while Philipe's fork of mashed potatoes and beans stopped halfway to his mouth. They looked at each other.

"It couldn't be the same Adelice," Fiona said.

"It's just a coincidence. It has to be." Philipe set down his fork and glanced around the table. "You mentioned a medallion at the beginning of your story. Do you know what it looks like?"

Lucas had continued eating, expecting a lengthier discussion about Colantha's claim, and wasn't prepared for a question about the medallion. Fortunately, Ginger jumped in to answer for him.

"The medallion is embossed with three objects—the Blood Poppy, an ibis, and something called the Dagger of Omar. On one side, they're represented in that exact order. On the back side, they're in the opposite order. From what Cressa told me, or what

Colantha told her, the specific order of the items on the two sides represents the connection between vampire and dreamwalker. The medallion also acts as a conduit to provide more control in a construct."

Philipe stood, his chair almost toppling over before one of the servers grabbed it. "Please, finish your meal. I'll meet you all in the library for dessert and brandy." Then he rushed from the room.

Fiona finished the rest of her wine and held the glass up for the server to pour more. "This is all so much more than I'd expected. Please, as Philipe asked, finish your meal. Cook spent so much time preparing it."

Bella and Jacques tried to hold their grins, and Ginger was giddy. Lucas wasn't sure which part of their discussion—either Colantha's ancestry or the objects on the medallion—caused Philipe to race out of the room. But he could only wait and see if it had been enough for Philipe to share what he knew of dreamwalkers.

Rom kept the conversation flowing for another half hour, as it was clear Bella wasn't going to stop eating anytime soon. Not wanting his partner to feel alone, Jacques continued to clear the plate of his second helping. But Lucas pushed his plate away, his nerves playing havoc with his stomach.

When the group finally left the dining room and arrived in the library, Philipe stood next to a lectern. It had been turned to face the row of chairs that had been positioned in a half circle around it. On the lectern, easily visible from the chairs, a book lay open. The only thing missing was a spotlight to shine down on it.

Lucas didn't need to be told that the book was the *De første dage*.

Chapter Twenty-Three

WE TOOK THE OFFERED SEATS, each of us staring at the book on the lectern as if we'd been mesmerized. When we were all seated, Fiona picked up a tray with brandy snifters and cups of espresso. Rom, Lucas, and Jacques took a snifter while Bella and I took espressos.

"I realize how pretentious this looks." Philipe wiped his brow then stuck his hands in his pockets. "It's been quite some time since I've given a lecture, and I don't mean to this evening, but I tend to fall back to my days as a curator whenever I have more than just Fiona to impart information." He leaned an elbow on the lectern, seeming to fall more into his role. "First, this isn't the original *De første dage*. Fiona and I felt the book was too fragile, as well as dangerous, and decided to reduce the risk by keeping it hidden. Since we've had time over the decades, we made three copies by hand. These also pose a risk and are kept in their individual secret locations. This—" he waved to the book, "—is one of those three. We didn't add any notes or observations in the copies. Each book is in the exact words and languages as the original."

"Wait. It's written in more than one language?" Lucas asked.

"Two from what we can tell. One is old vampiric, which in

itself is difficult to decipher for most vampires. Though Philipe and I can read it easily enough, we developed a decent key in the hopes that one day others would have access to the book. The other language has proven to be more problematic. It's not something either of us is familiar with or remembers seeing before. However, Fiona has found various texts that appear similar, perhaps a dialect difference."

"You believe dreamwalkers have their own language?" Lucas's tone was one of wonderment. This had to be more than he'd ever hoped for when given this assignment.

Philipe pointed to Lucas. "Exactly." He turned to Fiona. "We were on the right track."

Fiona shook her head as she smiled at him. "Having a third person suggest the same hypothesis is a far cry from proof. If we had just one other source material we might be able to create a cipher, but if there's something in the Renaud inventory, then it must be in the old country."

"What if there was someone who could read it?" I asked. It seemed a simple solution. Everyone was up to speed that dreamwalkers existed. I shrugged. "Maybe Colantha can read it, or maybe she recognizes the language. If she's an heiress to the Seven Tribes, she must have seen an ancient text." I glanced at the others. "I mean, it makes sense, doesn't it?"

"That's an excellent idea." Philipe glanced at Fiona, who nodded approval. "I planned on giving you a copy of the book to take to Devon. Would he be able to contact this Colantha Dupré?"

"We've been gone for a couple of weeks," Lucas said. "I don't know if Colantha is still at the manor, but if she isn't, we can contact her."

"While there's a great deal I can't tell you, there are a few things we've learned." He began to pace like instructors do when they get on a roll. "Much of it describes societal customs, political hierarchies, and economic conditions. Quite ahead of the times compared to the other species of that day and age. The text also identifies another race that has some form of symbiotic relationship with vampires. They called the race dreamwalkers, and this connection to vampires stems from one thing—the Blood Poppy."

I broke away from the spell he'd cast and noticed everyone focused on Philipe, apparently enthralled with the information being shared.

"The problem is," Fiona continued for him, "the reason for this connection must be explained in the second language. This relationship between the two species didn't happen overnight. They'd been at war for years until one day the two sides decided they'd had enough of meaningless death. They reached some form of accord at a place called Omar. There's a picture of the dreamwalker medallion in the book. It looks just as Ginger described it."

"You know..." Philipe stared at the book and tapped his fingers along the edge of the lectern. "The more I recall of the meeting with Guildford, Hamilton speculated that the Vampire Council purposely hid the truth of our origins and our relationship with another species. It worried Guildford, even though there wasn't any proof to Hamilton's claims."

"Colantha said the Council became concerned about the dreamwalker's powers." Lucas had settled back in the chair, his brow furrowed in concentration. He was digging this. "There was trouble with some rogue dreamwalkers who took advantage of their abilities. Instead of waiting for the dreamwalkers to handle the situation in-house, the vampires took things into their own hands."

"But instead of simply taking care of the troublesome dreamwalkers, they decided genocide would be best." Although Rom had been silent since entering the library, he'd been paying attention.

"That's a stretch." Philipe stepped away from the lectern and stuck his hands in his pockets.

"I don't think so." I set my empty cup down. "Colantha used that word. Genocide."

The room quieted for several minutes. Genocide wasn't a pleasant story for anyone's history.

"The other part of the book has to be deciphered before any thought of taking this to the Council," Philipe said.

"But will they believe the translation if it came from a dreamwalker?" Rom set his snifter on a nearby table. "Just playing devil's advocate here. If today's Council is as suspicious or downright disbelieving of dreamwalkers as previous Councils, will they take the word of a single dreamwalker?"

Philipe picked up the book and handed it to Fiona. "Suddenly, I'm feeling very tired."

She took the book and his hand. "Perhaps if we had a cipher, we could confirm what's written."

I considered the possibility, and Lucas glanced over. I had no doubt we were thinking the same thing. "What if we asked Colantha whether a dreamwalker language exists? Or maybe one did a long time ago, but like Latin, is no longer spoken. Perhaps she could provide a cipher. Would that be enough for an unbiased review of the text?"

"It would be a start." Fiona answered the question, and Philipe nodded. "If we could locate one or more books where the cipher could be used, that would reduce any doubt."

"It's been a long day." Rom stood. "I suggest we get a good night's sleep and let the enormous amount of information that has been shared today settle in. We can finish the discussion at breakfast."

I woke the next morning when Lucas kissed my temple. I reached for him, my brain fuzzy from sleep, confused as to why he wasn't spooning me. An eye popped open. "You're dressed."

He grinned and tousled my hair. "Keep sleeping. Rom called about an early game of golf before breakfast. I'll meet you in the dining room afterward. Or, if you're still in bed when I finish, I'll pull you out myself."

"'Kay."

I vaguely heard a door close. Sometime later, my eye popped open again. I was still face down in my pillow, and I lifted my head to check the clock on the nightstand. Nine a.m. I turned to find an empty spot next to me. The sheets were cold. Then I remembered. Golf. Ugh.

A hot shower woke me enough to hear grumbling from my tummy, but I needed coffee. I slipped on the leggings I'd bought at a discount store while on the run and grabbed a sweater dress from the closet. I rubbed my eyes, still trying to focus. I needed that coffee in the worst way. The ballet flats would have to do.

I found my way to the dining room, but the table was still being set. One of the staff pointed me to the salon, where I found Fiona reading a book.

"Morning." I took the seat across from her where, thankfully, a coffee service waited.

She set down the book. "Did you sleep well?"

"Like the dead." I picked up one of the empty cups and filled it. The scent alone was enough to clear the remaining cobwebs.

She smiled. "The men are finishing up the last hole and should join us soon for breakfast. Do you need anything to tide you over until then?"

"The coffee will do for now. But if they take too long on that last hole, I can't make any guarantees I'll wait for them."

Fiona laughed. "We've gotten in the habit of eating late. We usually have coffee and a croissant or beignet and then get lost in the books until ten when Millie has to come find us for a decent breakfast."

"That's a schedule I could live with." I glanced around. "Where's Bella and Jacques?"

"Jacques made up the foursome for golf, and Bella is training with the security team."

"Of course, she is. I should have known."

"I understand from Iris that you have skill in that area."

"Cressa taught me defensive martial arts a few years ago as a way to defend myself. We shared an apartment before we got involved with vamps. Sorry, vampires."

Fiona smiled. "I'm not offended as the older vampires are. Go on."

"Cressa's career required her to stay nimble, and martial arts seemed to suit her." I didn't see a reason to share her career choices. "When she ended up working for Devon, we had some trouble with vampires from another House, and it seemed wise that I learn how to defend myself. One thing led to another with the threat of sanction, and next thing I knew Sergi and Simone thought it amusing to give me a dagger."

When Fiona laughed, I smiled. "That's really how it went down. I think Simone started it, teasing me, you know. Then Sergi handed me the dagger and said 'let's see what you got.'" I sipped my coffee. "I have to say, I'm pleased they aren't laughing anymore."

"Good for you. This issue between species has always been a problem. But then, not everyone has read as much as Philipe and me to understand how wars start. Even in this day of supposed enlightenment. But enough of that. What are your next plans?"

"Lucas needs to report back to Devon on what we've learned. He should be back soon from his trip to meet with Aramburu."

"Really? I haven't heard anything about that House for some time."

"Maybe I shouldn't have said anything."

Fiona waved a dismissive hand. "Nothing that's been shared during your visit will leave the Family. We understand the stakes. It's critical that House Trelane garner as many allies as possible."

"Well, during the raid on Shadow Island when we recovered

Hamilton, there were two vampires that Cressa had met several times before. They told her they worked for Aramburu and that the House gave Devon their regards. I guess that was an open invitation to visit."

Fiona nodded as she gazed out the window. "They would make formidable allies. They started out as a warrior House, as many did all those centuries ago. From what little I've heard about them since, they pulled back from vampire society and embraced technology. They have established strong ties in several industries yet remain private."

"From what Cressa said, they don't seem pleased with the current Council."

Fiona chuckled. "Who is?"

"This might sound like a strange question, but do you know where House Bertrand is located?"

She considered the question. "I believe Chicago."

Before I could press for more details, we were interrupted.

"There you are," Philipe hurried across the room. "We thought you might already be at breakfast."

"We preferred to wait for you. Where's everyone else?"

"Lucas and Rom went upstairs to change, and Jacques went to find Bella. Let's wait for them in the dining room, if you're finished here."

I rose with Fiona, and Philipe extended his elbows for each of us to take as he guided us out of the room.

"Ginger was asking about House Bertrand. They're in Chicago, I believe."

"Yes, one of the major Houses in the area and a strong ally to Renaud and Trelane."

"Who won the golf match?" I changed the topic, not wanting to labor the point on House Bertrand with Lucas nearby.

"It was just a practice play." Philipe tried to brush off the question.

"In the human world, a game of golf might start out as practice, but someone always ends up keeping score. Are you sure there was no betting going on?" I teased but knew I'd hit the mark when a bit of pink touched Philipe's cheeks.

Fiona laughed. "I think he's embarrassed to say he lost the wager. Were you betting individually or in pairs?"

He grumbled. "I thought for sure Rom and I would tromp them, but apparently, House Trelane has a wide array of skills."

I squeezed his arm as we arrived in the dining room where the others waited. I leaned over and whispered, "We call that beginners luck."

He seemed to appreciate the sentiment and was more cheerful when he addressed the rest of the room. "I'm surprised you were able to change faster than I was able to walk two beautiful women to breakfast."

The food could have fed an army, and I stuffed myself to the point that going back to bed to sleep it off seemed a great idea. The conversation was lighthearted and avoided any talk of the book, war, or Venizi.

As breakfast wound down, Lucas broke the news. "As much as the four of us would like to stay and enjoy a couple more days of your incredible hospitality, we have pressing business to return to."

"Of course," Philipe answered. "We have a security team ready to take you to a car rental. I'm afraid the airport is too far."

"A car rental is fine. Shall we say an hour?"

Philipe nodded. "Fiona has a few things she wants to send with you. We'll meet you in the foyer."

We didn't have much to pack, so we spent the extra time sitting by the window staring at the valley. Then we grasped hands and walked down to the foyer, where everyone waited except for Rom.

"Rom has decided to stay another few days. It's been decades since we've seen each other, and he'd like to read one of the copies of the book." Philipe nodded to the small package that lay on the table behind them. "I've provided a different dust jacket to disguise the book I'm sending with you. It won't bear up under close scrutiny, obviously, so I suggest you keep it wrapped in the small satchel. I ask that you never leave it out of your reach until you're behind the gates of the Trelane manor. I'm sorry to be so paranoid, but..."

Lucas waved his hand. "I agree with your precautions and wish I had a plane of my own to fly directly home. We'll remain low-key until we reach the safety of the manor."

Philipe seemed somewhat appeased. "You'll contact me the second you're home to let me know the book arrived safely. Oh, and I'm sure Sergi will think of this on his own, but I suggest a secure place where a very limited number of people have access, or quite frankly, even know about it."

Lucas smiled. "I can assure you all precautions will be put in motion to secure it."

Philipe chuckled. "Of course."

"You're like a mother hen," Fiona teased. "Based on what we've heard last night, and their harrowing story in searching for us, I don't know of anyone more aware of the book's importance."

"You know the real one will be required for the Council." Lucas wasn't telling them anything they didn't already know, but he wanted to cement the point.

Philipe nodded. "When it's time for the Council to review it, it will be made available. However, it will be done in the most secure of environments with the Council, Sentinels, and Eliminators present. I will also ask for specific House leaders to be present." He paused and seemed to be considering something. "With Devon working with The Wolf, I might also request Remus's presence. If there's a decision to sweep this under the rug again, it won't be just the Council making that decision."

"I agree." Lucas glanced at me before adding, "But I would also suggest that Colantha Dupré be present. It's only fair that at least one dreamwalker be included since this impacts them the most."

"Of course. That was a clear oversight. I can't wait to meet her myself."

The two shook hands, and Fiona kissed each on their cheeks.

"I assume Rom is already reading one of the copies," Lucas said.

"He said you'd understand." Philipe walked them through the doors and down the steps to the van where Bella and Jacques waited.

"We said our goodbyes earlier this morning."

"While the seats aren't the most comfortable, you won't be required to wear the restraints or head coverings. My security sometimes gets too heavy-handed."

"I appreciate everything you've done to make our stay pleasant." Lucas shook his hand and climbed in behind the others.

The drive to the nearest car rental agency was three hours away, though I thought they drove us that far to make it more difficult to pinpoint where the retreat was. None of us minded.

It took another couple of hours to get to the airport in Atlanta. After Jacques and Bella entered the airport, I pulled Lucas aside.

"I was wondering if we could make a stop before going home."

Chapter Twenty-Four

"I SHOULD HAVE CALLED FIRST." Lucas stared up at the mansion as the rental car crept up the long, winding drive. The grand manor sat in the middle of heavily landscaped acreage behind eight-foot-tall brick walls.

"You didn't want to." Ginger moved from watching him to marveling at the beauty of the place.

"Maybe this is a mistake."

She laid a hand on his arm, her head swiveling to take it all in. "This is long overdue, and you know it."

He gave her a side glance. "Maybe I should never have told you about her."

She barked out a laugh. "And how long would that have lasted?" She sighed. "Neither of us are very good about talking about our past. But I feel better after sharing mine with you. I guess what they say is true."

"What's that?"

"Talking helps."

He grunted. That sentiment wasn't always true, but she was right this time. He had felt better talking to her about Rosalynn. And as much as his gut wrenched at seeing his sister after all this time, he had to fix this chapter of his life. But as he pulled in front of the steps to the manor, he was second-guessing himself.

They'd left Bella and Jacques in downtown Chicago while they made the drive to Lake Forest for this surprise visit. The wait at the front gate had been surprisingly short considering he hadn't called ahead. At this point, he was on a fifty-fifty split on whether he wanted his sister to be available.

He would have remained a statue in the driveway if Ginger hadn't grabbed his hand to drag him up the steps where the doors immediately opened. A butler greeted them and directed them to a nearby room to wait.

He sat in one of the antique armchairs and watched Ginger flit about the room, investigating the artwork and the single bookcase.

They were there for five minutes before a tall vampire with broad shoulders, dark hair cut in a modern style, and a goatee strode in. He'd seen a picture of Mason Bertrand but wasn't expecting the broad smile of welcome.

"Lucas Maynard. Welcome to our home. It's been long overdue." He held out his hand, and if his statement had anything to do with the distance that had built between Lucas and his sister, it wasn't apparent.

The vampire had a powerful magnetism that made Lucas want to like him, but he continued to remain stubborn. He'd observe and hold his opinions until after he saw his sister.

"I'm sorry for the unexpected arrival." He shook Mason's hand and felt the power behind this House leader.

"Not at all. It's not unusual for us to get visitors living so close to the city. You were lucky to catch us between trips, though we've reduced those lately. It's nice to have the time to enjoy our home."

He turned when Ginger stepped up to them. "And who is your beautiful companion?"

Ginger held out her hand. "Ginger Morrison of House Trelane."

Mason kissed her hand, and his brow rose. "You're human?"

"Yes."

"Is that a problem?" Lucas wouldn't tolerate any disrespect.

"No. Of course, not." Mason didn't seem startled by his question. "My security mentioned you were returning from an assignment. I don't remember ever seeing a human deployed with cadre before."

Lucas's smile was tolerant. "She's resourceful."

"I see." He turned to Ginger. "I didn't mean to offend."

"That's alright. It still surprises me sometimes. Until I have to pull out my dagger."

Mason laughed in delight and winked at Lucas. "I see what you mean."

He waved for them to follow him as he led them through the light and airy manor. Flowers filled vases throughout the hallways and in some of the rooms Lucas glanced in. A definite feminine touch he attributed to Rosalynn.

"I thought this might be the best place to wait for Rosa. She spends a great deal of time in the solarium, and she sits by the window and stares at the garden." The English-styled garden was impressive, with a multitude of flower beds, shade trees, benches, and a fountain centered in a small lake. "It always makes me nervous thinking she might be planning yet another redesign of the gardens. Not that there's anything I can do about it.

"I believe our butler mentioned your sister was in a meeting. It's a conference call with Zurich and Okinawa for some charitable foundations she operates. Rosa's involved with so many it's difficult to keep up with them all. But she should be done soon. I've asked for a tea service to be brought." He snapped his fingers. "I'm afraid you caught me off my game. Will you be staying overnight? Perhaps a few days?"

"We didn't want to intrude." Lucas brushed imaginary lint from his pants. "We have urgent business and need to get back to House Trelane, but Chicago was on the way, and—" He didn't know how to finish the statement. Maybe something along the lines of he'd been an ass to not speak with Rosalynn after all this time. That his neglect was his unresolved anger with his father and brothers, and he'd been taking it out on her.

"You don't have to say anymore. In fact—" Mason turned to Ginger. "Would you mind if I stole Lucas away for a few minutes? You're free to walk around the gardens if you prefer or just relax with a glass of Pinot Gris. Or perhaps a merlot?"

"It's not a problem. But a Pinot Gris would be lovely. It would go better with the tea."

"Of course." Mason smiled at Lucas. "I've learned never to argue with a woman."

Lucas returned the smile and glanced over his shoulder as he followed Mason out of the room. Ginger smiled with crossed fingers on both hands. He would definitely blame her if this didn't go well. They walked down two short hallways before they stepped into a masculine office complete with dark burgundy walls, cherrywood bookcases, and a massive desk that took up one corner of the room. The wood floor was covered with dozens of Persian carpets. Tasteful art filled what spare wall space there was, and sculptures poked out from nooks and crannies in the bookshelves. Bertrand wasn't hurting for money.

Mason walked to a bar service station and held up a decanter of dark amber that Lucas assumed was scotch. He nodded—in need of the fortification.

"I know this room seems rather brutish after the lightness of the manor. I suggested Rosa change it. This was my father's study, and she knew how much I loved coming in here, mostly to catch a whiff of pipe smoke whenever Father was in deep concentration. She refused, of course, and said my study wasn't something for her to mess with. Except for the dark carpet, which she had pulled out in favor of the rugs. It was an excellent change."

He passed Lucas the glass of scotch and led him to the two chairs facing the unlit fireplace. They sat and sipped scotch, neither saying a word. Lucas thought he should start the conversation, but it was Mason who asked for the meeting, so he waited the vampire out.

"We should have done this decades ago." Mason tapped a finger against the arm of the chair. "I suppose it's my Family's fault as much as anyone's. I knew Rosa was in love with someone else, but try as I might, I couldn't get Father to change his mind about the marriage."

"I wasn't aware."

"Neither was Rosa until afterward. It was a precarious time for the House, and though, sorry to say, your father's House had nothing to offer other than name, that was what Father thought our House needed. Who's to say whether he was right?"

"I was always curious why the need to marry into a smaller House. But now that I'm older and not as headstrong, I can see it from Bertrand's standpoint. The Maynard name still holds a great deal of weight in many circles, and though my father is an ass, he's comfortable enough if he doesn't do anything stupid with his assets. Marcus would be upset if he was left with just a skeleton of a House."

"I don't know what Rosa will tell you. That's between brother and sister. I wanted you to know that I've come to love your sister. Very much. The only thing missing are children. I think that's why she spends so much time with her charities."

"It's the same everywhere. And from what I hear, the Council is no further along in determining why the fall in our fertility rates. I know there aren't many orphaned vampires, but have you considered adoption?"

"Yes, you're right. What children do come available are quickly adopted, though we're on a waitlist. One we no longer hold out much hope on."

"I'm truly sorry for that. And I'm sorry for not reaching out sooner. It's my own arrogance and obstinance that stopped me, and all I did was hurt Rosalynn in the process."

"If you know your sister, then you know she has a forgiving

heart." He finished his scotch and set the glass down before standing. "Now, let's see if she's off the phone yet. I don't want to leave your companion waiting alone."

When they returned to the solarium, Rosalynn was laughing at something Ginger said. She hadn't aged a day since he'd last seen her. Not to him. Except for the smile. He couldn't remember the last time he'd seen her laugh. When she noticed them walk in, she turned, and her gaze immediately caught his eye. Her smile grew wider, and her eyes sparkled.

His sweet, beautiful sister had become a stunning mistress of a major House. And instead of suffering under the brutish hand of someone like her father, she'd married a gentle vampire. No doubt a keen businessman, but an obvious pushover where his wife was concerned.

Rosalynn jumped up and almost ran to him. He simply held his arms open and caught her, hugging her tightly. He could barely see Ginger through his blurred vision, but she was grinning from ear to ear, and he couldn't love her more than he did at that moment.

"I'm so sorry, Rosalynn." He couldn't remember the last time he'd hugged her. Time he would never get back.

"Hush. None of that. Those horrible times with Father are long over." She pulled back and ran a hand under her nose. "I can't imagine what I'm doing to my makeup." She laughed and pulled out an embroidered handkerchief to dab her eyes.

"Dear," Mason stepped behind her and settled a hand on her shoulder. "Why don't you take Lucas for a stroll around the garden? It will give me time to get to know Ginger. I'll hold the food until you return."

She reached for his hand and squeezed it. "That's a marvelous idea." She tilted her face up and gave her husband a stunning smile. "We won't be long." Then she grabbed Lucas's hand and pulled him toward the French doors leading to the garden.

"Don't worry about Mason. He'll make Ginger feel at home."

Lucas chuckled. "Ginger makes friends easily. She'll be fine."

"She seems wonderful. A perfect match for you, I think."

"Together for less than five minutes after decades apart and you're already playing matchmaker?" he teased.

"I think it's too late for that. You're smitten with her, and I can see why. She sings your praises. I have a feeling she has some interesting stories to share, and Mason will get them out of her. The two of us will discuss your visit for days. Ginger says you can't stay long."

"We have an important artifact we need to get back to Santiga Bay. I wish we could stay for a few days, but the timing isn't right."

"Then we need to make the most of it. Let me take you to the pond, and we can talk."

They weaved through several garden paths, each area its own garden within a garden. "Do you give tours of the gardens?"

"We do." She laughed. "I can't tell you how many magazine shoots we've had here, and I host several parties here from spring through fall. Some of them for charities, some for the local garden clubs, and others for vampire gatherings. I know Mason doesn't look the type, but he loves spending time in the garden with me, planting new varieties or deadheading blooms. It's a peaceful respite from his business and my charities."

She led him to a wooden bench overlooking a lake similar to the one at Oasis. The trees were different but just as numerous. Wildflowers rather than a manicured garden grew within the tall grasses. Water lilies skimmed the surface of the lake where two swans and a small group of ducks paddled around.

"The swans were a present from Mason's father. There are days when Mason and I just sit out here and watch them. I hate to say anything good about our father, but this turned out to be the best thing for me. Oh, somewhere deep down, I still love Eric and probably always will. But it was a young love, a first love, and he's married now. From what I'm told, he's very happy."

"You know I only wanted the best for you. It was a choice you should have been able to make on your own."

"Father isn't a kind man. He's selfish and stuck in the old ways. Marcus isn't much better, but from what Mason tells me, he's beginning to have a change of heart now that Father is close to relinquishing leadership."

"I hadn't heard that, but to be honest, I don't keep up with them."

"And no reason you should. The only reason Mason does is because of our mutual business dealings, which he's slowly pulling out of. Our brother noticed it and seems to understand that unless House Maynard changes their growing alliance with Venizi, Mason will continue to dissolve their partnership. In the last few years, we've followed Trelane's dealings with the shifters. We now have several business partnerships with a couple of the local packs, and there are more on the horizon."

"It's one of the smartest decisions Devon ever made. Of course, he and The Wolf have a mutual score to settle with Venizi, and while it was a rocky road in the beginning, the two seem as tight as ever on the future of the races."

She nodded and pulled a bag of bird food out of her pocket. She tossed a handful into the lake, and the ducks swarmed to it before the swans noticed. "Mason followed Trelane's trouble with the Council after Boretsky's murder. He planned on reaching out but wanted to see how the House did with Devon under his beast's control." She tossed out another handful, then turned toward him.

"I can't tell you how proud the two of us are with your rise through the Houses. From what we hear, Father boasts that your accomplishments are his doing, but Mason and I know the truth. Your success is despite the brutality of our father." She tossed another handful to the swans, who finally noticed the excited ducks.

"In fact, we took a trip to New Orleans last year to visit the

Renaud Library. Of course, we had to meet with Lafitte and Romero. They had such wonderful things to say about you."

"They never said anything." He chuckled. "Although they wouldn't. They'd prefer I worked out the demons on my own."

She took his hand. "And now I think the last of Father has been put to rest. We no longer need to think of him. I have a wonderful life here with a strong-willed but kind and loyal vampire. I love him with an intensity I didn't think I'd find again. And I know he loves me."

"He loves you very much. It's obvious every time he says your name."

"We should get back to them before Mason bores Ginger with his tall tales or pulls too many secrets from her."

"I think he'll find it rather difficult to get anything out of Ginger she doesn't want to share. She's quite practiced at changing a conversation and steering it down so many paths, you can never remember what the original topic was."

"Now that we're speaking again, I expect constant communication and a longer visit."

He laughed as they took a different route back to the manor. "The communication won't be a problem. A longer visit might be problematic for a while." He pulled her into an alcove created by a collection of ornamental firs. "This isn't known information yet, so this is between me, you, and Mason. Devon will be calling on his strongest allies. We're uncovering startling information that will shake vampire society to its roots. I can't say more, but this isn't a ruse."

"You're talking about the possibility of a civil war." Her voice was low but surprisingly not overly alarmed.

"Have either of you heard something?"

She shook her head. "Not yet. But Mason is watching. He suspects something is brewing with the Council and Trelane's censure, and more specifically, with Trelane's private battle with Venizi. Word of Magic Poppy has spread among the Houses along with the rumor that a vampire is at the root of it—though it's only mentioned in tight circles."

"I'll keep you apprised when I can. For now, House Trelane is on lockdown. The only reason we're not at the manor is because our mission was critical to Devon's plans."

Her worried frown turned into a smile. "And you took the time to stop and see your sister. I can't tell you what that means to me."

"You have Ginger to thank for that."

"I know. But you're stubborn enough that you wouldn't have come unless you knew this was long overdue."

"And maybe I'm just as much a pushover for my woman as Mason is for his beautiful vampire."

She turned them toward the patio. "Does Ginger let you get away with such easy praise?"

"Only because she knows it makes me feel better."

They were still laughing when they entered the solarium where Mason and Ginger were already eating tea sandwiches.

"Sorry," Ginger said around a bite. "My stomach growled so loudly, Mason felt sorry for me."

They spent several hours reminiscing about childhoods, Rosalynn's charity work, and some business before it was time to depart. He didn't want to go and wished he had more time, but they were communicating, and a heaviness that felt like a boulder rolled off his chest. He never realized how much their distance bothered him.

When the four of them stood outside the front door of the manor, Rosalynn strung an arm through his. "Now, remember, I expect to hear from you the minute you arrive home so I know you both arrived safely." She kissed his cheek before turning to take Ginger's arm to say their goodbyes.

Mason walked with Lucas to the waiting car. "While you and Ginger took a last stroll around the garden, Rosa filled me in on your discussion regarding Trelane and the lockdown. News of the raid at Venizi's island traveled fast. As you can imagine, rumors are already growing about the rising conflict between the two Houses. Many don't expect anything to come of it, assuming the Council will eventually demand a cease-fire. But I think they're wrong."

"Why would you come to that conclusion?"

"Trelane has spent years building his business empire outside vampire society. Since he's constrained from doing business with the Houses due to his censure, most would argue what choice did he have. But no one believed he'd get cozy with the shifters. Although he wasn't the first to do business with them, he's been the most vocal in discussing similar opportunities with his closest allies. With the success he's been having, why trouble himself with Venizi or the censure? But he knows the Council is divided between the old ways and those who seek to change with the times.

"He wouldn't be pressuring Venizi unless he had a solid hand to play. I've met Trelane at various functions, and House Bertrand, under my father's leadership, has always held an allegiance to House Trelane. I'd like you to take a message to Devon that House Bertrand stands with House Trelane. If there's anything I can do to assist in whatever's coming, all he has to do is call."

Lucas held out his hand and gripped Mason's as he spoke. "Your words carry great value, and you can be assured I'll let Devon know he can count on House Bertrand. He'll reach out soon." He gave Mason's hand a final shake. "Take care of my sister."

"You have my word, brother."

Lucas grinned. "I like the sound of that."

"And take care of that human of yours. Your sister and I have already grown quite fond of her."

Lucas looked past Mason's shoulder to see Ginger chatting with Rosalynn a few feet away. "Easy enough to do. She's my salvation."

Chapter Twenty-Five

I WALTZED into the manor and hugged an unsuspecting Mateo, who was manning the door. "It's so good to be home. Did you miss us?"

Mateo had a quick wit, and with a pleasant smile, said, "Were you gone? We hardly noticed."

I gave him a good-natured punch in the arm. He didn't flinch or move. Vamps. I was still smiling as I ran up the steps, barely reaching the second floor before I was stopped cold by a chilling voice, almost tripping over my feet.

"You're expected in Devon's office. Now."

I turned and smiled down at the frosty vamp staring up at me. She was in her Wonder Woman stance, hands on hips, and if she had the superhero's Lasso of Truth, I would have been hogtied and dragged to Devon's office. Thank the stars magic wasn't a thing.

"No one told me."

"I'm telling you."

"Aah. Can I at least pee?"

It was fun to poke at Simone when I thought I could get away with it. When she scowled, one side of her lip lifting as her fangs dropped, I had to admit I might have gone a bit too far. But nature was calling. And since she didn't want to chance it, she nodded —stiffly.

"Five minutes." She didn't move, and I took that as a sign to skedaddle while I could.

I raced to my room, slammed the door, stripped off my sweater and pants then dropped onto the toilet. I wasn't lying about that. We hadn't stopped once since leaving San Francisco. We'd been greeted by a security lead car, two extra vamps in the limo with us, and a second security team close behind. With two cadre in the limo and a copy of the *De første dage*, there wasn't any chance of stopping before we reached the manor. I shouldn't have drunk so much coffee on the plane.

I was in such a good mood, even Simone couldn't dampen my spirits. Lucas hadn't stopped smiling since leaving Chicago. He was pleased to return from a successful mission with a copy of the book, but his visit with his sister trumped all of that.

All I could hope for now was that five minutes with Sergi and Simone wouldn't dampen his joy. Bella and Jacques had looked at him strangely when we met them at O'Hare and then proceeded to tease him all the way home, including the almost three-hour drive from San Francisco. The traffic had been horrid.

One thing about visiting one's family—whether a great trip or the worst ever—it sticks with you. And there was no doubt Lucas's visit with Rosalynn would erase all the bad memories.

I slipped on black leggings, a long-sleeved, oversized bright turquoise shirt, and my ballet flats and raced down the hall then stairs, skidding to a stop in front of Devon's office door. I took a couple deep breaths and finger-combed my hair before opening the door and stepping inside.

Simone sat at Devon's desk with the cadre around her. Jacques sat in a corner by the unlit fireplace, Lyra on a chair near him, and Decker on a barstool. I dropped onto the sofa near Lyra and turned to face Simone.

She glanced around the room and seemed satisfied everyone

was present. "Before we go over the results of Lucas's mission, I would like to extend a thank you to Ginger from Devon and the cadre for saving Lucas's life. He told me his wounds were severe enough that he most likely wouldn't have survived without your quick thinking. If not from his wounds, then certainly from the next wave of vampires."

I blinked. Her words were unexpected, and I wasn't sure what to say. I blinked a couple more times before saying the first thing I could put words to. "I know you think everything I did was because of the personal relationship we share. But I would have done the same for any of you." I didn't want to, but I gave Lucas a quick side-glance, and he nodded with a slight grin. I breathed a sigh that I hadn't said anything stupid.

"We believe you." Her smile should have been comforting. "As your reward, Sergi will be expecting a full report of the incident on his desk first thing in the morning. You should have a copy of the current report format on your phone."

"Great." I gave her an extra wide smile. "I appreciate it." Inside, I was dying. I'd never had to fill out a report before. So much for a fun evening alone with Lucas.

"Now, on to business." Simone turned to Lucas. "Give us the highlights, and please tell us you have good news."

Lucas spent the next hour reviewing our steps from the moment we left Santiga Bay to when we returned, including our visit to House Bertrand to visit his sister. I filled in the days he was wounded and unconscious. He ended his report by placing the book on Devon's desk.

Everyone stared at it. Lyra walked as if in a trance to stand next to Bella. It was a small book, no larger than a paperback you'd buy at the grocery store and about half as thick. Sergi opened the cover and gingerly turned each page, even though they'd been told it was a copy.

"Old vampiric." Sergi turned a few more pages, then looked at Lucas. "Will you be able to read this?"

"It will take a few pages to get comfortable with it, but it shouldn't be a problem. But I'd appreciate any assistance."

"I'd like to read it when you're done." Sergi jumped toward the back of the book, and his eyes squinted. "I don't recognize this language."

Lucas nodded. "We think it might be a language of the dreamwalkers. I was hoping Colantha could take a look."

"Colantha and Hamilton returned to New Orleans when Devon and Cressa left for Spain." Simone made notes on her tablet.

"Why did she leave?" Lucas asked.

"I'm afraid that was my doing." Lyra returned to her seat, seeming satisfied with the close-up look. "Colantha believed I was too much of a distraction for Hamilton. Everything was fine the first couple of days, but it was apparent he wasn't assimilating as well as he should. We think it was too much stimuli. She promised to return when Devon and Cressa are home." Lyra looked sad, and I reached for her hand. "I don't know if Hamilton will return. It depends on how much progress they make."

"That's a good thing," I said. "We were lucky he kept it together long enough to save himself. He was locked away for a long time. But he has Colantha, and he knows you're waiting for him. It won't be too long. But I know how difficult this must be."

"Can we get back to business?" Simone asked.

Lyra snorted. I wasn't sure if she meant to, but everyone laughed. I glanced at Simone, who was doing her best to hold back her grin.

Simone cleared her throat. "Decker. I imagine Remus will want to see the book. How's his old vampiric?"

Decker scratched his head. "I'm not sure. He can probably read it, but wouldn't it be best to have it translated so everyone can read it."

"That's my objective." Lucas picked up the book and laid it in his lap. "I'll read through it once, then I'll go back and translate it."

"I can help with that," I offered. Simone and Sergi looked skeptical. "One of my many short-lived jobs was converting speech to text for a finance company." When the only response was silent stares, I rolled my eyes for effect. "This was before there was technology to do it. I'm a fairly fast typer. If Lucas is comfortable with it, he just speaks the words out loud as he translates, and I'll type it. He can review the pages as we go to make sure they're accurate. Even with his review, it should save a lot of time. Or you can buy software to do it."

Simone considered it. "Lucas?"

"I should have thought of it myself. Whether Ginger or someone else, I agree it would greatly reduce my effort to complete the work. I'd rather not use the software for this."

"Good. Once you're done, we can copy the translation." Simone closed her tablet.

"No." Lucas's jaw stiffened. This was something he wouldn't back down from. He'd made a promise to Philipe.

"What do you mean?" Simone's tone came with an edge.

"I made a commitment. Even without it, I would still insist. This book has been hidden for centuries. Vampires are willing to kill to keep it that way. We need to know what the book says—in both languages—before we can share it with anyone. Until then, or until Devon says otherwise, the copy of the book, the translation, and a saved backup should be stored together in a single location only known to Devon and the cadre. We'll destroy the hard drive on the computer to ensure the files are deleted."

"That seems obsessive," Simone said.

"I agree with Lucas." Sergi laid down his tablet and strode to the window. He stared out at who knew what, but it was more than a minute before he spoke. "I have to admit, I was beginning to believe the book was a myth after all. That the whispers of reunification were nothing more than a ruse to keep the myth alive. But now we have the building blocks of truth."

He turned back to the room. "Lucas is right. We should have

sent backup with them. You had vampires follow you in Los Angeles when you and Cressa searched for the book. Based on what Philipe confirmed, the book has something to do with dreamwalkers. We need to tread carefully. The cadre—" He turned and glanced at everyone. "Actually, everyone in this room should read the translated copy. As mentioned earlier, Devon will want Remus to read it. But only one copy, one reader at a time. And I think Remus should read it here. Nothing related to the book leaves the manor."

Simone considered his words. She seemed to struggle with the whole dreamwalker thing, but in the end, she nodded. "Let's get the translation completed. That will be Lucas's and Ginger's primary task. The rest of us will continue with security details and training. Devon should be back in the next few days. We're adjourned for now. Decker, can you stay? I'd like to update you on the rogues at Oasis."

The room began to clear, but before I escaped, Simone called out. "And Ginger, don't forget your report."

She always had to have the last word.

ONCE I ESCAPED Devon's office with my homework assignment, I walked up the stairs with Lyra, and we stopped on the second-floor landing.

"Anytime you need to talk, just text me, and I'm there." Not that I could do much for her, but these times called for a shoulder, not a lecture or empty words. "And I don't mean just about Hamilton. Although I don't mind reminding you how much that man loves you. He just needs to reconcile his second chance at life. But this has to be incredibly tough on you. I don't have much experience in this area, but I can make a mean margarita."

She laughed and pulled me in for a hug. "You always know the right thing to say. How about lunch tomorrow? Lucas will be reading the book, so you'll have time before the translation starts."

"Perfect. Just let me know when and where."

"I wish we could go to a tea house."

"Or a club."

"I'll think of something. Will we see you at dinner?"

"I don't know. I thought I got enough sleep on the plane, but I'm pretty beat. Dinner in my room sounds pretty good right now."

"I understand. I'll let Cook know."

"Thanks." I wandered down to my room as Lyra climbed to the third floor. I stripped off my clothes, turned on the tub, and added bath salts. I bounced on my toes as I waited for the tub to get half-filled then stepped in, wincing at the heat of the water until my skin sensitized to it.

I'd barely relaxed against the tub when Lucas strolled in, whistling a tune I didn't recognize.

"Why are you in such a good mood?"

"That was a perfect meeting, and you're amazing."

"Well, I'll agree with one of those statements." I ran a hand over my knee, slick from the salted water that filled the room with a lavender and rosemary scent. His gaze followed the motion, and I smiled. Maybe we'd get that night together after all.

"So, what detail did you get assigned this evening?" I picked up a large sponge and soaked it in the water before running it over an arm.

"Um. Detail? Oh. No detail. Simone wants the healer to look me over, so I'm off duty until tomorrow." He took off his jacket and hung it from a hook. His shirt was next as he dropped it on the floor. He always looked so hot in a tank, showing off his lean, muscled physique.

I rested a foot on the edge of the tub while I squeezed water out of the sponge before running it over my leg in a slow back-and-forth motion. "I'm too tired to go to dinner with the Family. Lyra is having Cook send something up."

He'd unbuckled his belt and was sliding his pants down. "We must have had the same idea because I stopped by the kitchen on my way here." He knelt next to the tub in nothing but his tank and jockeys and took the sponge from me.

"Oh."

He sponged my back in slow, sensuous strokes that made me shiver in the steaming water. "Cook heard we were arriving home today, so he made lasagna."

"Did you tell him what a wonderful vampire he is?" Cook's homemade lasagna included freshly made pasta. The thought of it made my stomach grumble.

"Of course. Can you hold this for a moment?" He handed me the sponge and stripped off his tank, his stomach muscles rippling with the movement. His jockeys went next, and I scooted back for him to sink into the tub facing me. He ran his hand over mine as he took the sponge back.

"The others won't be happy with the heavy pasta dish." Cook made lasagna on rare occasions since Cressa, Anna, and I were the only ones who consumed large servings. The vamps considered it too heavy and ate little of it.

"He's also cooking a fresh halibut dish. I think the lasagna was meant for you." He took my hand and ran the sponge over my arm and then under it before moving to the next.

"I feel like we're in this weird space. It was like what Sergi said. All that time wondering if the book really existed. Now that we have a copy of it, all we have are more questions."

The sponge moved across my breasts, and I leaned my head back and closed my eyes, reveling in each warm stroke.

"We have to take each step as it comes." He straightened his legs and pulled me up to sit on his lap. His cock was hard and rubbed me in all the right places as I straddled him. "First the translations, then we wait for Colantha."

I took the sponge from him and ran it across his chest. "Maybe you can send her a short paragraph or two, just to see if she recognizes it. Who knows, maybe she's aware of a dreamwalker alphabet."

I moved the sponge over his shoulders when he lifted my ass until I was over him, wiggling my hips to find the right spot for him to slip inside.

"Let's table the discussion for dinner." He gripped my hips and gently rocked me.

I dropped the sponge. "How long do we have?"

"Little less than an hour." He kissed me as his hands moved to my ass. Water splashed over the side.

I gripped his shoulders and leaned back, giving him room to dip his head to my breasts. His fangs released and scraped against my heated skin.

All thoughts disappeared except for one. I loved this vamp with my heart and soul. When I thought he might die, a hollowness had enveloped me. A stark terror of a world without Lucas. I tugged him closer, and he lifted his head to run his fangs up my neck. He paused, his tongue flickering over a spot. A vein.

"Bite me, Lucas. Take my blood."

He'd refused when he was weak and needed it. When he understood we needed his strength to complete our mission, he stopped fussing. I thought he'd ignore me this time. Without warning, his fangs bit into my flesh, and when my hips slowed, he gripped them to keep our rhythm going as the sting from the first sharp bite dissolved into an incredible tingling sensation with each gentle pull at my neck.

Lucas swore my room was nearly soundproof. If not, the entire second floor would hear my scream of pleasure as my body shook from the release. My head fell back, and I might have temporarily blacked out as stars exploded in my head. Colorful flashes of light burst like fireworks as he continued our fast-paced rocking, his fingers digging into my flesh, and all I could think of was—more. I wanted more. Needed more. And several minutes later, maybe less, maybe more, I heard his groan as he reached his own climax.

I fell against him, and he wrapped his arms around me as the cold air on my back sent shivers through me.

"Hold onto me." He managed to get his legs underneath him and stood with me in his arms.

We dripped onto a floor covered in bath water, and I giggled. "Grab a couple of towels." He turned so I could reach the towel rack and then carried me past the doorway. I slid down his body until my feet touched the cushy carpet.

He took a towel and ran it over my body, rubbing vigorously, which made my skin pinken. New sensations started all over again. He brusquely dried my hair until I squealed. I tried to dry him off with the second towel, but he was too quick and did it himself. The entire process lasted mere minutes as he lifted me again and tossed me onto the bed.

I scrambled underneath the covers, and he was there in a heartbeat. He pushed my legs up and entered me again. I was surprised he was up for another round so soon, but I wasn't complaining, thrilled as he released a bit of the beast.

We finished with only five minutes to bask in our afterglow before a knock sounded.

"Stay where you are." I jumped out of bed and tossed clothes around, searching for my robe. I'd only been back a few hours, and clothes were already strewn around the room. I really was a mess. I found my robe, tied it quickly, then slowly opened the door to peek down the hall. No one in sight. I picked up the tray, managing to not knock over the bottle of wine, and thought I'd come again just from the aromas sneaking out from under the silver-domed lids.

We ate on the bed, me in my robe, and Lucas in his jockeys. I could stare at his chest for hours and licked my lips after each bite of the succulent lasagna.

"You keep doing that, I won't wait until you finish your meal."

I grinned and took another bite. "Making up for lost time?"

"It's difficult to properly make love to you when someone might knock down the door at any moment."

"Hmm. I don't remember it being that much of a problem."

He snickered. "I suppose you never worry with your dagger on the nightstand."

"It's more that I have a big, strong, and amazingly skilled vamp in my bed. What's there to worry about?"

"Skilled?"

"Mmm." I swallowed a gulp of wine and winked. "In every possible way."

He laughed and picked up my hand, giving it a gentle kiss. I helped get everything back on the tray, and he moved it to the table. We settled under the covers, our bodies touching. He wrapped his fingers through mine, rubbing his thumb along my skin.

When his eyes met mine, they glowed the warm sapphire of his inner beast for too brief a moment. "This mission made me realize something. Something I've known for some time but wasn't sure the best way to express it. Being near death and then seeing my sister. I don't want to waste moments, especially with a war looming. A war that I have no clear idea what shape it will take."

He ran his hand over my hair then slid a finger down my cheek and along my jaw. "I'm desperately in love with you. And I'm not sure what that means for us, or how you feel. I don't want to scare you away, but I can't consider my future without knowing you'll have a place in it."

I blinked away the tears that came out of nowhere. And he wiped one away that had escaped down my cheek. I gripped his hand. "We live in uncertain times. And if I didn't know it before, over the last few weeks, I've gotten a first-hand look at what that future might hold. The reality is that it might be ten times worse. I don't want to walk it alone, and neither should the vampire I love."

He stared at me, the glow in his gaze intensifying. I didn't know if it was him searching for the truth of my statement or his beast. But when his gaze warmed and the glow faded, he seemed to have found synchrony with his other half.

He grinned, and he was that beachboy vamp I first glimpsed when Cressa found me in the closet after Christopher's goons had terrorized me. I couldn't take my eyes off him then, and for however long this lasted, I'd never tire of looking at him.

He kissed me. It was slow and sweet. "You're sure about this?"

"You mean, am I sure I'll stick with you through this coming war or that I'm insanely in love with you?"

"When you put it that way, both."

I ran a hand over his cheek then gripped the back of his neck. "We're in this together. Two hearts, two minds."

He laid his head against my shoulder, and I wrapped an arm over his chest. His breathing slowed as he drifted off to sleep. I was likely jinxing myself, but we only lived once. So, I allowed the joy to spread through me as I nestled against him.

At that moment, I was the happiest I'd ever been. And whatever came, I wouldn't waste a moment loving Lucas.

∾

Thank You For Reading!

BUT DON'T GO! Keep reading for more of House Trelane.

Betrayed in Blood

DEVON TRELANE, leader of House Trelane, is preparing for war —a battle of winner-take-all. He's aligning his allies and fortifying his defenses. But new secrets are uncovered that raise the stakes higher than he thought possible—secrets that could tear vampire society apart.

But first, he has a personal decision to make. He'd made a deal with Cressa Langtry, aka Pandora. Work for him to complete his mission in exchange for clearing her debt. It was time to release her from that debt. Would she stay and face battle with him? Or find safety among the dreamwalkers?

Cressa never felt like she had a true home until she came to House Trelane, where she was cherished, accepted, and had something to give back. When given the opportunity to walk away from it all, was this the time for her and her best friend, Ginger, to escape the coming war? Or was it time for her to double down on her feelings for Devon?

When news about her biological father reaches her, she makes a decision to track him down. Until she understands where she came from, she'll never be able to commit to her future.

And now a glimpse...

Betrayed in Blood

MADRID, Spain - Present Day

BEADS OF SWEAT dampened my brow and the edges of my cream-colored sundress. The sangria worked its magic in cooling me down and contributed to my not giving a damn how wilted I looked. I glanced across the table of the sidewalk cafe where Devon Trelane lounged. He wore a long-sleeved shirt, rolled up to mid-forearm and unbuttoned enough for me to get a decent look at his chest, and crisp linen pants. A new fact I'd learned was that vamp's body temperature self-regulated in most climates. It had something to do with the magic of their blood. They would suffer the same as humans in extreme temps, but in this earlier-than-usual heat wave, he looked as fresh as a GQ model, his hair pristine and not one ounce of visible sweat.

"We could go back to the hotel and enjoy the refreshing view of the city from inside our air-conditioned suite." He wouldn't go for it without some encouragement, so I batted my eyes in the universal gesture that suggested a high likelihood of sexual horseplay, but he just stared off into the distance, his mirrored sunglasses masking his thoughts.

"I'd like to visit the National Archaeological Museum."

"Really? After all that time at the Renaud Library?"

"It has an impressive collection of ancient artifacts from the human royal families dating back centuries." When I didn't look persuaded, he added, "It's air-conditioned."

He knew me too well. I sucked down the rest of the sangria and stood. Perhaps a bit too fast, and I swayed. "Let's go." I ignored the temporary double vision.

Devon was beside me in a nano-second, wrapping an arm around my waist. He felt my forehead. "You might have heat exhaustion."

"Maybe I just drank the sangria too fast."

"Your second sangria in extreme temperatures. You're used to life on the coast. I should have been more thoughtful."

I pulled him closer, my head falling back to stare up at him. "I might have miscalculated my ability to combine the two. But they were really tasty."

He grinned. "Maybe returning to the hotel isn't such a bad idea."

"Oh, no. You passed on that invitation, mister. Besides, the museum is closer." I ran a hand through his hair and pulled him down for a long, sensuous kiss, tongues colliding, promises made. "But, if you swear we'll only walk around the exhibits once, there might be a solid chance of spending the rest of the day in bed."

After setting a floppy hat back on my head, he led me down the street, holding hands. Who thought a vamp did that? Well, maybe Lucas. Ginger had that vamp wrapped around her little finger.

"The first walk around the Renaud library was to rule out suspicious vampires. But you've been a good sport. How about dinner with exquisite cuisine and a rooftop view? Candlelight, good wine—"

"Master Trelane."

Devon tensed, and all talk of a romantic dinner evaporated. We turned around, splitting apart for a more defensible position.

I smiled when I spotted the blond-haired vamp, who stood a few feet away, his hands held out to show he didn't have a weapon. Devon, on the other hand, was expressionless at the unexpected intrusion.

The vamp had an easy smile that could charm the pants off anyone—male or female. He glanced at the building behind us. "The Museo Arqueológico Nacional." Erik, who always seemed to take the lead over his brother in striking up a conversation, pointed at the building. "A fine selection for an afternoon of leisure. And to see La Dama de Elche is worth the trip to Madrid alone."

Devon didn't respond, and when he bent to the right to look beyond the Oslo twin, I followed his line of sight. If there was one, the other had to be close.

And there he was. Ulrik leaned against a midnight blue Rolls Royce limo. His smile was broad, and he wasn't looking at Devon or his brother. His smile was for me, and I waved.

Devon glanced at me, and though this face was expressionless with those damn sunglasses still concealing his eyes, I could only assume that he was mentally shaking his head. I put my arm down, but it was difficult to hold back the grin.

These were friends. Weren't they?

Devon turned his attention back to Erik. "I have a feeling I won't be seeing La Dama de Elche today."

"Sad but true. It's unfortunate. Perhaps on your way out of town. But Aramburu is a busy man, which is why we were late in collecting you." He held an arm out toward the car. "If you would be so kind, we have a long drive to El Recinto."

"Will we be remaining there as his guest?" Devon asked.

I stepped closer to Devon. The fog from the sangria had cleared, and I no longer cared about the oppressive heat. The Oslo twins wouldn't harm us, but there were cryptic vamp nonverbals at play. Maybe they were just sizing each other up and not testing boundaries. I had to remember Devon hadn't met them before.

"For a day or two. Schedules have been rearranged, and a room prepared."

When they reached the car, Ulrik had the rear passenger door open and waved them inside.

"We'll need to stop at the hotel." Devon looked at the twins. He was firm on that point.

"Not necessary," Ulrik said. "We took the liberty of having the maid collect your things. Your bags are in the trunk."

When Devon's jaw clenched and his posture turned rigid, I expected the twins to take a step back. I was surprised when they held their ground.

"Don't worry. Your weapons are safely stored and will be returned to you once your visit is over."

When Devon stood at the open door but didn't get in, Erik shrugged and entered first. I glanced at Devon, and he nodded. This was apparently not the welcome reception he'd been expecting. And I had to admit, checking us out of the hotel seemed like they didn't trust us.

On the other hand, House Aramburu had survived for centuries outside vampire society. Perhaps Aramburu was itchy, even with allies. Though he tried to hide it from me, Devon had been a bundle of nerves since we landed in Madrid.

I climbed in, and Devon followed. We sat on the plush bench seat while the twins took seats across from us. The driver wasted no time in pulling away from the curb.

"I know these aren't standard procedures among allies, but Aramburu is an extremely cautious vampire who wants his visitors safe. There has been a recent increase in interlopers." Erik continued his warm smile as if this were just another day at the office.

"Venizi?"

Ulrik shrugged. "Who's to say? They don't get much of a chance to speak."

Yikes. A take-no-prisoner defense.

Erik poured drinks as they settled into the drive. It would be more peaceful if Devon relaxed, but his tension was a palpable presence. Ulrik ignored us and focused on the rear window or, if I had to guess, searched for anyone who might be following us.

Thirty minutes rolled by as Erik provided a running commentary on the city and the local customs as we traveled into the countryside.

"Tell me, Erik." Devon lifted his empty glass, and the vamp refilled it. "What are the Oslo twins doing in Spain working for Aramburu?"

"Look outside. It's warm many months of the year. It might get cold during the evenings, but El Recinto is below snow levels most of the winter."

Ulrik glanced over. "And we travel a great deal."

"I'm dying to know. How did you get off Venizi's island?" I asked. If they were offended by my not-so-subtle question about whether they escaped on their own or if Lorenzo let them go, they didn't show it.

Erik laughed, and even Ulrik, still focused on the traffic behind us, grinned. "Fortunately, Venizi was more interested in the two of you than us. We were able to leave with the other passengers. Then we thought it might be the best time to leave the country."

"But you were fighting his security teams," I pressed.

"In the mansion, yes. But so were others who felt the need to defend themselves in the confusion. Once we were outside, our weapons unseen, it was easy to blend into the crowd. We were delayed leaving the ship once we reached the mainland, but it wasn't our faces they were searching for."

Devon squeezed my hand, signaling he was satisfied with the response. For now.

An hour passed before the car slowed and turned into a small hamlet. The place appeared deserted.

"Are you armed?" Erik asked.

Devon nodded while Ulrik opened a concealed panel by his armrest and removed a sword, handing it to Erik before pulling out another.

"And the lovely Cressa?"

"I have my dagger." I glanced around but didn't see the threat Erik must have seen.

The car turned behind an old mission-style church and slowed to a stop.

"We have unwanted visitors following us," Erik said. "We had to wait to reach guarded territory before allowing them to get any closer to El Recinto. Normally, I wouldn't ask our guests to participate, but there are two cars, so this might be more than Ulrik and I can care for before our chase car arrives. They typically remain a mile behind us." He opened the door and got out.

Devon followed, and I scurried out of the limo after him. Once Ulrik joined us, we turned to face the two cars that pulled into the dirt lot.

A sundress wasn't my choice to wear to a fight, but at least the flared skirt wasn't restrictive. The sandals might be cumbersome, and while not offering much protection for my feet, they fit comfortably enough.

There were four vamps in each car. Eight vamps to our five after the driver shut off the Rolls and stepped in line next to us. I'd seen Ulrik and Erik in action on several occasions, and they had impressive skills. But I had no idea of the opposing vamps' abilities and breathed a bit easier knowing a backup car wasn't far behind.

After a few minutes of staring at us, one of the vamps stepped in front of the others. "We can make this easy. We have no wish to anger Aramburu, but we need you to relinquish Trelane and his human whore to us. They have much to answer for back in the States."

The anger boiled off Devon. I guessed it might have been the whore comment. It irritated me, considering Lorenzo's plans for me while on his island, but I doubted these vamps would understand. And rather than me having to hold Devon back, he grabbed my wrist, keeping me at his side.

I slowly relaxed my grip on the dagger.

Erik took a step closer to me. "Aramburu will not allow interference with his business meetings. He has no care about House issues in the States. If your Master has business with House Trelane, he can wait until Trelane returns home. Your interference in Spain is neither wanted nor acceptable. I suggest you turn around and return to the airport."

The other vamp grinned and made a demonstration of counting how many vamps were on each side. "I think you're outnumbered."

I'd been so comfortable in the air-conditioned Rolls, and though it was a touch cooler at the higher elevation, it was still miserably warm. And I was irritated by Venizi's gall. The twins might not be certain who sent these vamps, but no one else had a large enough beef with Devon to chase us to Spain. Add in the realization that my first meeting with Aramburu would be in a blood-streaked sundress, escalated my emotions to highly pissed off.

I pulled away from Devon and took a step forward. They want to mess with the human whore, then let's see if they had game.

"I've had enough of this bullshit. You want a piece of Trelane's whore—come and get me. It's a hell of a lot better than being Venizi's mesmerized slut."

The vamps' eyes bulged. I gave them my best demonic smile. I doubted it compared to Simone's fang-filled grin or Sergi's scary-as-hell leer, but the lead vamp glanced at the others standing next to me.

"What? Scared of a little human female?"

That did it. The vamp launched himself, and I didn't wait. I ran to meet him. Devon would be pissed, but he'd only be a step behind.

I couldn't use my favored surfboard maneuver where I leaped, kicked them in the chest, and followed them to the ground, standing on them as I slashed them with my dagger. Not in sandals. But I had other maneuvers to choose from, and as much as this was going to hurt, this vamp was going down.

When he was almost on me, I dropped and rolled, hitting him in the legs and taking him down like a bowling pin. I grimaced at the road rash on my arms and legs as I leaped up. The vamp was shaking his head, coming up on a knee, and I stabbed him in the back of the neck. When he remained on his knee, I stabbed a kidney, this time twisting the knife. He dropped.

The first ones were always easy. It didn't matter whether any of them had been told not to mess around with Trelane's female—they never listened. One mark in my favor. But once they saw me in action, their doubts fled, and the next one wouldn't be as effortless.

I didn't waste time after I pulled my dagger, ready for the next one. When Devon yelled, "Duck," I wasn't sure he meant me, but I dropped like a stone. I felt a slice along my back as a vamp stumbled by. I leaped into a crouch. The sting on my back confirmed I'd been cut, but it must have only been skin deep because my legs and arms still worked.

The vamp who nicked me ran a few more steps before a sword took his head.

Erik gave me a quick salute before engaging another vamp.

I searched for Devon. He fought two vamps, both of them bloody. Crimson soaked one of his sleeves. The Oslo twins and the driver were still engaged with a dwindling number of Venizi vamps, so I ran for Devon.

One vamp fell after a dicey stab to his middle before Devon twisted to block the second one who came at him. Rather than get in his way, I went after the first vamp. His wounds were sufficient to keep him immobile. When he saw me coming, he managed to get to his feet, if a bit wobbly.

I didn't slow down, and this time, I used my jumping round-house kick, twisting and leaping to clip his jaw. I landed on my feet and ducked as he swung his sword. The air whistled by. That was close. But I ignored it and came up with my blade, driving it into his chest.

Before I could twist the blade, arms pulled me back, and I struggled until a sword took the vamp's head.

I glanced up to see Ulrik smiling, his sword and shirt drenched in blood.

"It's over." Devon's words calmed me, and I leaned into him, breathing hard.

Erik strolled over and glared at the head. Then he grinned at me. "Your skills have improved."

I turned to take in the scene. Bodies and heads were strewn everywhere, and Aramburu's second car had arrived. Venizi never sent the right number of vamps when he went after his enemy. It wouldn't take long before he stopped making that mistake.

"Did we lose anyone?" I asked.

"No," Erik said.

"You didn't save anyone for questioning?" Devon asked.

"Aramburu doesn't take prisoners. He doesn't ask questions. If you come at him, he responds with deadly force."

"Will you return them?"

Erik spat on the dead vamp at his feet. "Whether it was Venizi or not, vamps not returning home are a strong enough message. The bodies will be burned in the pit." He took a moment to study Devon and then me. "You have no major injuries?"

When we both shook our heads, he nodded toward the church. "We typically use this spot for clearing away anyone foolish enough to follow us. The church appears abandoned, but it has running water and private rooms to clean up. We try to keep blood out of the Rolls. You have thirty minutes. Aramburu will be most angered by this." Then his smile returned. "But it will be tempered by stories of our fair Cressa and her battle cry as she engaged the enemy."

I stared at him, then at Devon. "I don't have a battle cry."

Devon just smiled.

Thank You Again!

Betrayed in Blood
Of Blood and Dreams - Book 6
Coming Summer 2024

~

MAKE sure you never miss a new release!

Join my FB Readers Group - **Kim Allred's Heart Racing Romance**
Join my **newsletter**...I'm pretty much unobtrusive.
Follow me at **Amazon**, **Goodreads**, or **Bookbub**

If you can't wait and want to check out my other series, visit my **website**.

As a special treat, if you haven't already downloaded it, consider reading the free prequel to the Of Blood and Dreams series - *Lyra*. This novella is set one hundred years before the start of the series.

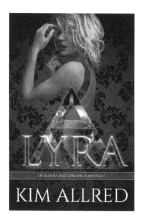

The catalyst. The victim. The bridge.

The Roaring Twenties. The time of flappers and Prohibition.

For Lyra, a young vampire and aspiring painter, the world is her canvas.

When she meets Hamilton, a sculptor and her family's gardener, time stops. He understands her like no one else.

But he's a human. And he's not the only one drawn to her. An ancient and powerful vampire has declared his desire to seduce her.

A perfect storm that sets the stage for all that is to come.

About the Author

Kim Allred lives in an old timber town in the Pacific Northwest where she raises alpacas, llamas and an undetermined number of free-range chickens. Just like most of her characters, she loves sharing stories while sipping a glass of fine wine or slurping a strong cup of brew.

Her spirit of adventure has taken her on many journeys including a ten-day dogsledding trip in northern Alaska and sleeping under the stars on the savannas of eastern Africa.

Kim is currently working on a follow-on series in the world of Mórdha Stone Chronicles series and the next books in her paranormal romance series — Of Blood and Dreams. Her new time travel series, Time Renegades, is on the horizon.

facebook.com/kimallredwriter

instagram.com/kimallredauthor

pinterest.com/kimallredauthor

Made in the USA
Middletown, DE
06 April 2024

52683224R00142